OUT
OF THE
SHADOWS

SIGMUND BROUWER

Thorndike Press • Waterville, Maine

Published in 2003 by arrangement with Tyndale House Publishers, Inc.

Thorndike Press® Large Print Christian Mystery Series.

The tree indicium is a trademark of Thorndike Press.

The text of this Large Print edition is unabridged. Other aspects of the book may vary from the original edition.

Set in 16 pt. Plantin by Minnie B. Raven.

Printed in the United States on permanent paper.

Library of Congress Cataloging-in-Publication Data

Brouwer, Sigmund, 1959–
    Out of the shadows / Sigmund Brouwer.
        p. cm.
    ISBN 0-7862-4879-3 (lg. print : hc : alk. paper)
    1. Charleston (S.C.) — Fiction.   2. Maternal deprivation — Fiction.   3. Mothers and sons — Fiction.   4. Large type books.   I. Title.
PS3552.R6825 O97 2003
813'.54—dc21   2002032447

with love to Morgan Olivia

PSALM 23

The Lord is my shepherd;
I shall not want.
He maketh me lie down
in green pastures:
he leadeth me
beside the still waters.
He restoreth my soul:
he leadeth me
in the paths of righteousness
for his name's sake.
Yea, though I walk
through the valley
of the shadow of death,
I will fear no evil:
for thou art with me;
thy rod and thy staff
they comfort me.
Thou preparest a table before me
in the presence of mine enemies:
thou anointest my head with oil;
my cup runneth over.
Surely goodness and mercy
shall follow me
all the days of my life:
and I will dwell
in the house of the Lord
for ever.

PROLOGUE

When I opened my eyes into the searing pain of consciousness, white-hot knives of agony drew my total focus to the leg I could not see, folded somewhere beneath me. My left arm was jammed into the spoke of the steering wheel, and my other arm lay neatly in my lap.

I lifted my head from my chest. Confused and lost in the black of the night, I found it difficult to orient myself. Gradually, I understood that the car was tilted sideways, tipping me slightly toward the driver's side door, which was ajar and hanging down into tall, thick grass. The menacing, eerie shadows that frightened me further, I realized, were caused by the dying dome light, triggered by the open door. My focus improved, and I saw a tiny pale light shining at me from the ground outside the car, the reflection of the moon. It took me a few more seconds to realize the reflection came not from soggy ground but from the slowly rising tide, weaving into the grasses of the marsh, now almost up to the car's floorboard.

I was trapped. My first reaction was to push away from the steering wheel. I screamed at a new burst of torment and fell back against the seat.

Slowly, I pieced more of it together, the fragments of memory that I could find. I looked for the others. We'd been traveling to Charleston, coming into town from Highway 17.

I was not alone in the front of the car. On the opposite side, against the passenger door, was my cousin Pendleton, motionless, unmarked.

Claire? Claire!

With all the strength and resolve that I could muster, I strained to turn my head to look over my right shoulder. Even that slight movement took its toll, and shards of pain detonated along my leg, roiling over me in waves.

I sucked for air, fighting unconsciousness. In the dim light, I saw too much. The passenger on the opposite side of the backseat — Claire's younger stepbrother Philip — was slumped on his side, hair matted with blood, his face shattered beyond recognition, the window beside him mashed against rough concrete. As Philip fought to breathe, bubbles of blood snapped from his nostrils.

I yelled again for Claire.

Still no answer.

I twisted to look behind me to the left side of the backseat, disregarding the new dimensions of agony. Was she there?

With a wrench of desperation, I finally saw it was empty.

I yelled one more time. Only the night noises of frogs and insects answered.

Blinded by a car's headlights that swept the corner, showing the serrated edges of the marsh grass waving in the night breeze, I was unaware of the passage of time as I faded in and out of my torture. I fought for clarity, and as the beacon showed me the crumpled mass of the front end of the car that trapped me, I was able to take it all in, seeing the hood sprung, bent and twisted where it had slammed into the base of a bridge.

How long have we been here? Where is Claire?

When a second set of headlights flashed over the car through the open door, I briefly saw my leg and realized that my foot was twisted at the wrong angle, almost straight backward. Just below my knee, jagged bone protruded from the fabric of my pants.

I retched dryly.

The cars pulled to a stop close to the wreck that held me. One door opened, then another. A man from each car stopped in front of the headlights nearest me.

"You did right, calling me," one voice said softly. "I'll remember that."

"Thought you wouldn't mind getting woke out of bed, Chief. Her being a deMarionne and all."

"Sergeant, I already told you I'd remember. Now get a flare a hundred yards north and another a hundred yards south. Last thing we need is another idiot driving into a bridge abutment like this. Miracle this car didn't flip and drown them all."

"Yes, sir."

The sergeant immediately moved to the trunk of his patrol car, using his flashlight to locate the flares.

Both cars were parked on the slightly higher ground. I wanted to call up to them, to plead for help to get me to the safety of dry ground. But my voice would not obey me.

I heard the man speak to the woman in the backseat of his own car. "Miss deMarionne, it would be best if you waited inside."

Claire was safe. She'd gone for help.

My relief lasted only until my next thought. *And she's left me behind the steering wheel. In the marsh. With the water rising.*

Claire did not answer the man's voice. She had begun to sob. I tried to call for her again but could not direct any sound from my throat. My mouth moved in silence, my head tilted back as if I were a fish gasping in air.

"You sit pretty," the voice continued to her.

I knew this man and his voice. Police Chief Edgar Layton. We had first met when I was ten, shortly after my mother had abandoned me. He'd interviewed me, unkindly, standing tall above me, asking terrible questions about my mother and making notes in a pad dwarfed by his large hand.

He once watched as my uncle beat me at the police station. And, in my teens, I'd heard the rumors about him, simply because his power depended so thoroughly on the parents of the other teenagers around me. It was commonly known that when the individual involved required the special diplomacy granted to a certain type of citizen, Police Chief Layton took personal charge of the crime or accident to rearrange the details.

Like now. Out here in the dark, out here in the low country. Armed with a flashlight of his own. And with a camera.

I continued to try to call out Claire's name. Why hadn't she come for me? Why was she in the car, ignoring me? I needed her.

As I heard the siren of an approaching ambulance, Layton's large strides brought him to the side of the wreck. He moved to the driver's side of the car and slid his flashlight beam over the windshield. In front of me it was clear; on the opposite side, shattered and opaque.

Layton took one step to stand even with the driver's door. This side of the car was undamaged; the other side had taken the brunt of the impact against the bridge. The driver's door opened farther only with difficulty. Layton grunted as it scraped back along the mud and torn grass. He flicked his flashlight beam over the interior. Over me.

Once again, I started to shout Claire's name, but still I had no voice. Shock had reduced me to a catatonic state. I was aware of my surroundings but helpless to react. It felt like I was in one of those dreams where you fight to walk or speak. I doubt I even blinked. To him, perhaps, with the light bouncing off my eyes, I was a corpse, with my hands still on the steering wheel. A gleam of gold showed from my new wedding band. My marriage to Claire was still a secret.

The flashlight beam moved through the interior like a searchlight in a prison yard. Layton took in every peculiarity.

I heard Layton take another step, his feet squishing through the mud and rising water.

He opened the rear door. He did not spend much time assessing Claire's brother. Layton moved inside the car, resting his knee on the empty space of the seat directly behind me. I felt his weight as he rested his elbow on the top of the front seat, touching my neck lightly, as if checking to see if I was warm or cold. To me, there was a curious intimacy about that.

His hand left me, and the flashlight beam played over Pendleton on the opposite side of the front seat.

Layton grunted. In spite of the smothering odor of salt-water marsh mixed with spilled antifreeze, the repulsive smell of alcohol and blood in the close quarters of the car was obvious. Light bounced back at Layton — the reflection off the glass of a bottle of bourbon in the lap of Pendleton, who was neatly cradled by the imploded

15

door on the front passenger side.

The sirens were closer, maybe a mile away.

Layton lifted his camera. Popped a shot of the interior of the backseat. Without waiting for the bulb to cool, he pulled it from the camera attachment. If it burned his fingertips, Layton didn't flinch. He had a job to do. More photos to take.

In the darkness, each new snap of the shutter was a white flash that outlined the interior of the broken car, showing in my waking nightmare the large form of Police Chief Edgar Layton hunched over like a gargoyle.

Five more shutter snaps. Five more flashbulbs — glass milky from searing heat — hastily torn from the camera. By the time the ambulance arrived, Layton had returned to the patrol car.

He stood in the headlights of the patrol car, waiting for the ambulance driver. I saw him delicately lick the tips of his fingers.

"What's the call?" the ambulance driver asked.

"Kid on the passenger front is fine," Layton answered.

He blew on his fingertips, his breath cooling the moisture on his skin. "Driver needs help. Kid in the backseat probably beyond help. Do what you can."

"Sure, Chief."

Layton slipped inside his patrol car again.

The ambulance attendants had returned to the ambulance to get a stretcher. It was silent. Silent enough that I could hear Claire still crying in the backseat.

I desperately did not want to die. A desire not based on fear. But because of the love Claire and I had. As I began to fade, sadness overwhelmed me. Would I die, this close to Claire but utterly alone, without her touch to comfort me?

Claire, I tried to say. *Claire.*

But it was another voice that spoke to her as I approached the abyss of unconsciousness. "Start from the beginning," Layton said in a soothing voice.

"I was asleep . . . the crash must have knocked me out . . . I was able to crawl out the back door and —"

"You ran for help. I know that. What I want to know, was it like this when you left the car?"

"Like this?" Claire asked between sobs. "With Nick dead?"

Tell her, my mind shouted uselessly at Layton. *Tell her I'm not dead.*

"Was Nick at the steering wheel?"

17

Layton said. "That's what I want to know."

She sobbed.

"Tell me," he said. "I need to know everything."

That, as I would come to understand, was Edgar Layton's way. To know everything.

"When you woke," he said, his voice getting colder, "was Nick at the steering wheel?"

"Yes," she answered, so softly that I thought I had imagined her answer. "Yes, he was."

I thought I was dying. I thought the blackness closing on the edges of my awareness was the blackness of death. I hated the final thoughts I believed were now about to escort me into death.

Why had she lied?

Claire's betrayal, as I slipped away, hurt far more than my shredded leg.

Abandoned.

Again.

CHAPTER 1

As I walked up the sidewalk to the piazza of the deMarionne mansion on the evening of my return to Charleston, I knew that I neared a moment where, on each side, everything in my past and future would hang in perfect balance.

Unlike many of the events of the four days that followed, this was a moment of crystalline significance that required no further thought or consideration. I understood its fullness and finality at that moment. With each halting step toward the gloom of the piazza, I was keenly aware that I also approached the edge of my own Rubicon, with its dark, swirling waters between me and the uncertainty that waited beyond the boundaries of the far shore.

Shadows swallowed me as I stopped in front of the mansion's massive door. Wicker chairs, which had been barely visible from the street through the white railing, filled much of the length of the gray-painted boards of the piazza. Above, moths frantically struck at the glow of a lightbulb. Dusk had settled to deep purple, sending the caress of saltwater breezes past these waterfront mansions and on through the dark, twisting cobblestone alleys of the old quarters of Charleston.

On the door, an arm's length away, was the thick, ornate handle of an iron knocker, molded into the circle of a snake eating its own tail — a shape I had always found appropriate for this mansion.

I had spent fifteen years approaching this moment. Yet I still had the choice to turn back, to remain safe, with my advance silent and my presence unknown and my retreat unseen.

Countless other times on this piazza, I had raised the ancient iron of the door knocker. Countless other times I had let it drop to announce my call here at the deMarionne mansion.

But those days belonged to my life two decades earlier — before I'd become a black sheep, long assumed to have run away or been taken by wolves. I doubted, though, that anyone had cared to wonder about my fate. I had never truly been considered one of them, for I had been tainted early on by my mother's reputation. To the world — which in Charleston simply means to those who matter in Charleston — my mother was remembered as a tramp and runaway thief who had abandoned her only son.

That she had left me before my tenth birthday was one of the central truths in my life, something I had buried so deeply during my years away from Charleston that I had never expected to begin any search for her, let alone at the deMarionne mansion, bolstered by icy resolve that masked my long-held fury.

Here, on the piazza, I hesitated in the interval before the final moment that so clearly marked a division between my past and the future I had decided to claim. Outwardly, this hesitation might have appeared as uncertainty.

Not so. This brief hitch in time on the piazza came as I savored my fury and anticipated its release.

Unable to escape my southern past, however, I could not unleash this wrath without some semblance of civility. I took satisfaction, then, that my hand did not tremble as I reached for the door knocker to irrevocably set everything in motion.

This was the moment.

Once, then twice, I lifted the heavy weight of the black iron snake eating its tail. And let it fall.

The echoing deep clank of iron against

iron faded, leaving behind nothing but the fluttering of moths' wings against the lightbulb. I stared straight at the spy hole set in the door and waited. A familiar pain seeped into my awareness, an uninvited guest I had learned to expect at the end of a long day of travel, from the unyielding yoke of a plastic limb cutting into the long-healed stump of my right leg. This pain brought me fleeting, ironic amusement; I had no need, at this moment, of its reminder.

The door opened slowly and completed my sense of irony. I should have expected this person at the door, and her manner of opening it.

The black woman holding the interior handle peered around the edge of the door as suspiciously as she had almost a decade and a half earlier. Except for short curly hair gone from ebony to white, except for glasses set in a heavy frame, except for wrinkles around her mouth further deepened to reflect the perpetual frown that had shaped her face, Ella was still Ella, crisp maid's apron over the functional black blouse and long skirt.

I had never known her last name. Decades earlier, Martin Luther King, Jr. and a Memphis garbage strike might have begun to change the nation's perception of racial status, but here in Charleston, many of the old families proudly retained a paternal attitude toward their servants.

"I am here to call upon Helen deMarionne," I said to Ella.

"I am afraid Mizz deMarionne is not taking visitors."

"I believe she will overlook the inconvenience."

"You, sir, are mistaken." Among the older Charlestonian servants, a pecking order was established by the quality of family in which they were employed. As part of the deMarionne household, and as one who had ladled her acid over me for years, Ella was as fully capable of snobbery and disdain as any blue blood.

"Inform her, then, that if she does not receive this visitor, he shall begin to serenade her forcefully enough to disrupt the neighbors."

Ella glared at me, the same fierce, intimidating stare I remembered from all those years before. But I was no longer a lanky, longhaired teenager, tiptoeing in Ella's presence among the other antiques of the deMarionne mansion.

"Something from *Showboat*," I said. "That would suit this neighborhood, wouldn't you agree?"

"I agree I should call the police. Which I shall if you do not leave immediately."

"What a lovely disturbance that would make. And highly entertaining for the neighbors."

As she pondered her options and the resolution on my face, Ella blinked slowly behind her thick glasses, finally swallowing her defeat with the appearance of a lizard closing its eyes to choke down a large insect.

"I shall see if Mizz deMarionne will permit an appointment."

The massive door closed on silent hinges.

Ella had not asked me my name. Which meant, although all these years had passed, she had recognized me in return.

Which also explained why I had not been invited inside to wait.

My taxi journey from the airport on this evening had taken me into the heart of old Charleston, that collection of ancient buildings on a flat peninsula barely eight feet above sea level. I'd sat in silence in the backseat of the taxi, reading the familiar street names as I traveled closer and closer to my childhood haunts. King. Tradd.

Then the crossing of Broad Street, which was the invisible boundary that separated the aristocracy on the south side from all those in the rest of Charleston to the north.

The taxi driver had taken me past the familiar outlines of the mansions turned sideways to the street — in Charleston's peculiar manner of protection from the eyes of tourists and commoners — until finally he had reached the tip of the city, at a bed-and-breakfast, where I had checked in and rid myself of my single piece of luggage.

From there, I had walked only a couple of blocks, passing an impressive array of Charleston's storied East Battery antebellum mansions — ornamental ironwork, raised entrance, massive three-story columns, carriage house in the back, hidden gardens.

The deMarionne mansion, like the others, faced the seawall on the other side of the street, giving a daytime view of Fort Sumter smudged on the water's horizon, where — as newcomers were told only half jokingly — Charleston's Ashley and Cooper Rivers converged to form the Atlantic Ocean just beyond. From behind the oleanders that lined the promenade of East

Battery, passersby would point at Sumter as they imagined its role at the start of the War between the States. It was at this seawall that a battery of guns had been placed to protect the city during the War of 1812; if Charleston worships anything, it is its own history, and the ensuing East Battery street name endured with pride. As did the name of the family that had owned this East Battery mansion for four generations.

The deMarionnes.

Their family history appeared in every Charleston guidebook, along with the predictable exterior and interior photos of the mansion. More than a century earlier, Jonathan deMarionne had been a blockade runner, dodging Union forces as he brought rum and gunpowder to the besieged city, trading his goods for gold and silver. His good fortune ended a week before the war itself did, when a Yankee cannonball took off his arm at the shoulder and he died instantly of shock. Since he was a difficult man, subject to drunkenness and violence, his widow found little to grieve, and in the economic chaos that followed the Confederate surrender, she took whatever solace she needed by shrewdly tripling the already massive fortune he had accumulated, avoiding the many marriage offers that followed, leaving her money to her two sons, who — in a Charleston tradition not mentioned in the guidebooks — stayed in banking and law and did little more than hoard the family fortune. Nor did the guidebooks add that this money had provided for the private schools and debutante balls for the indolent generations to come.

This I knew without a guidebook, knew without photos of the interior of the mansion that no tourist was ever invited inside to see.

For I had returned. Out of exile.

The door opened twenty minutes after I first knocked. It was not Helen deMarionne.

Ella frowned at me, her square black face crinkled with distaste. "Tomorrow evening," Ella said. "Seven o'clock. Mizz deMarionne will expect you then."

"Tonight," I said.

"Tomorrow evening," she said. "Gentlemen make appointments."

She swung the door shut in my face.

Denied. Again.

I had early determined to take my triumph with full control, not as a madman.

Instead of kicking futilely against a locked door, I departed from the mansion. Again.

I walked down the sidewalk toward the inn at the southern tip of Meeting Street, where I had checked in for the duration of my stay, a stone's throw from where I'd grown up in one of the antebellum mansions on South Battery.

As the uneven rhythm of my steps took me along the streets of my childhood and teen years, I was conscious that every good memory of Charleston was stained with darker memories of disappointment and betrayal, as if every wonderful thing I had been granted then had only been provided to taunt me with its future absence.

I did not need to look far to find disappointment.

To my right, looming over the old buildings like a dark sword stabbing at the bank of clouds that glowed above the streetlights of Charleston, was the steeple of St. Michael's Church, mocking me, mocking my long disillusioned faith, mocking the memories of my mother. And in mocking all of that, mocking my return to search for her after all these years away.

I should make it clear that upon my return to Charleston, I was a man without a sense of God, unless one counts denial as a begrudging form of relationship.

Much of that denial had to do with my mother, who I now see was one of the few examples of real faith in my childhood.

Church puzzled me then. It was pleasant enough when all that was required of my faith was to follow the instructions of Sunday school teachers who encouraged me to use crayons to color drawings of men in fishing boats. They did not like my questions, however, and learned to ignore my waving hand.

Christmas, for example, was confusing to me. I was expected early to stop believing in the legends of a bearded Santa Claus and flying reindeer, yet I was instructed to maintain faith in flying angels who sang above the manger and in bearded wise men who followed a moving star. I found Easter equally confusing; I was told that the Sunday morning egg hunts across the lawns of Charleston mansions were the result of a mythical bunny. These gaily attended events provided surreal contrast to the blood-drenched story preached in church an hour earlier about a man who was whipped, beaten, nailed by his hands and feet to a cross, then, I was told to believe, rose from the dead.

When I was old enough to join my mother with the adults in the church service, I endured long and boring sermons among the highbrow Charlestonian women, who wore wide-brimmed hats and white gloves and pastel dresses and smiled sweetly at each other across the pews, then turned and whispered vicious gossip during the passing of the collection plate.

Where is God in this? I wondered as a child.

Again and again my mother answered my questions as wisely as she could, telling me repeatedly that there was a difference between faith and religion, and in so doing, gently led me to trust in a God of love invisible beyond the man-made boundaries of the church. She promised me that God's love was forever, just as a mother's love was forever.

Then she abandoned me.

If my mother's unexplained departure was not enough to drive me from God, there were the formative years of my adulthood. I spent those years away from Charleston and the United States, yet I saw enough of the whirlpool that is American culture to scorn the little religion that

30

managed to surface among the other flotsam. I glimpsed the television shows where slick con artists promised healing in exchange for money sent to support their ministry. Newspapers gave me details about protesters hatefully and self-righteously shouting the name of Jesus as they condemned people who didn't share their beliefs; occasionally on AM radio I heard the arguments of those who insisted the world was only six thousand years old and fossils were planted by the devil to fool us; I heard the rantings of white supremacists and the claims of their fanatical religions.

Because of self-imposed isolation during my exile, books were my companions at all opportunities. Through the smoked glass of history accounts that let readers peer into the past, I learned the religious evils that had been hidden from me by the Sunday school teachers so determined to entertain us with crayons and paper: the popes who fathered illegitimate children, who built the golden glories of the Vatican through the sweat and blood of terrified, indulgence-seeking peasants; the history of Crusaders who raped and pillaged and killed tens of thousands in the name of a man of love; cultural eradication doled out by harsh, unyielding missionaries who followed the slave traders to the depths of Africa.

Lastly, in defense of the stubbornness of my soul's early flight from God, there were all the events before I left Charleston — events that seemed totally bereft of the touch of a God of love.

God, however, as I was about to discover, is a patient hunter.

I can now examine my years of exile and see earmarked on the pages of my personal history the times he beckoned, times that I resolutely turned aside to my own path. I imagine that in a way, I was like Jonah, determined to head in the opposite direction of God's calling.

For Jonah, the city he desperately wanted to avoid was Nineveh. For me, it was Charleston.

Unlike Jonah, however, it did not take the belly of a great fish to convince me to return.

But a letter.

So it was that I had returned to the place of birth — and death — of my childhood.

My mission was simple.

I wanted to find the truth about my mother. I wanted revenge. I wanted justice. I wanted the love I had abandoned.

I certainly did not expect to find God. Or the forgiveness I desperately needed.

❋ ❋ ❋

Along that street, I briefly closed my eyes against the outline of the steeple against the sky, as if the feeble barrier of the darkness behind pressed eyelids might stop the memories I had vowed to discard in the same way I had once promised never to return to this city.

Although some southerners place honor above all, I felt no remorse at breaking that promise. No, the letter that drew me home had granted me a total and unexpected absolution.

With that absolution, I intended to take my vengeance, pound by pound, no matter how closely I gouged near the hearts of those who had driven me away.

CHAPTER 2

"Good morning to our mystery guest. We've all been excited to meet you."

I had hoped to escape the bed-and-breakfast unobserved. My hand, in fact, was on the doorknob at the main entrance of the two-story Victorian mansion. Behind me were the gleaming hardwood floors and frayed Oriental rugs and the fresh smell of lemon furniture polish, for early as I had woken, the maids had arrived before.

I prepared my face with a smile before I turned. "Good morning, ma'am."

"It's a beautiful day to step outside. Did you sleep well?"

My questioner was in her midforties, bobbed blonde hair perfect, spring dress perfect, trim figure perfect, her southern vowels perfect. Although she was trying to distract me with idle conversation, I saw that her curious eyes sharply surveyed me from top to bottom. I wondered how she would catalog me. I wore tan slacks and a black golf shirt. I was in my early thirties. I had not shaved in a week, and the color of my new beard matched the dark hair cropped closely on my head.

"I did sleep well," I answered this morning's hostess. It was a lie. In attempting to fall asleep after returning from the deMarionne mansion, my thoughts had swung back and forth from the tortures of old memories to planning my search and vengeance.

"Wonderful," she beamed, tilting her head. "And your room?"

"Wonderful." Which was not a lie.

I'd been given the deluxe room with a twelve-foot ceiling, a lazy ceiling fan, a four-poster bed, and an entrance to the wide second-floor balcony that overlooked Charleston's White Point Gardens and the harbor beyond. The room had dried flower arrangements, faded wallpaper patterned with roses, an antique writing desk, early nineteenth-century sofa and chair, and a wide turret that overlooked a sprawling oak covered with Spanish moss. It was serene and comfortable and cozy, the opposite of everything I had felt since receiving the letter and enclosed plane tickets that had summoned me to Charleston from New Mexico.

"Louis Comfort Tiffany," the hostess said, glancing back up the curved stairs that led to the room above us.

"I beg your pardon?" I said.

"Louis Comfort. That's his full name." She pointed up the stairs. "Mr. Tiffany himself installed those stained-glass windows."

"Beautiful, ma'am." As were the pieces of mahogany furniture, the dozens of knickknacks filling every nook and ledge, the ancient gilded frames that held dark and murky oil paintings of people long dead. I would not have been surprised if my hostess could have identified each one by name. The difference between New York and Charleston, it has been said, is that Yankees put new Oriental rugs on their floors and paintings of other people's ancestors on their walls. In Charleston, as I could testify, our own ancestors stared down upon us, and the worn Oriental rugs had belonged to families since before the Revolution.

"Is this a vacation?" she asked. I guessed she was stalling me, hoping to see if anyone else would come from my room upstairs.

I caught her glancing at my left hand, bare of a wedding band. Checking in the night before, a different but nearly identical smiling, southern hostess had glanced at the same hand and informed me that Two Meeting Street Inn, the bed-and-breakfast I was now trying to escape, had been rated by all the premiere travel magazines as one of the South's most romantic getaways. Given the circumstances of my arrival, I also guessed that my lack of a wedding band would lead to gossip as soon as I managed to step outside and escape.

"Yes," I said. I maintained my polite smile, disguising my contempt for her syrupy southern gentility, which in its ostensibly innocent guise masked a unique and oblique style of probing and cutting. "A vacation."

I refused to yield any more information.

The evening before, as I had checked in, the first hostess had been equally inquisitive. Five nights in the mansion's premiere room had anonymously been prepaid for me, she'd commented, adding how romantic it was that someone was willing to spend so much to send for me in such a mysterious manner. Yes, I had agreed with that hostess, how romantic. She, just like this morning's hostess, could not stand not knowing who had provided this for me.

Neither could guess how badly I wanted to know that answer for myself.

In fact, I'd checked for messages upon first rising, hoping that this mystery person would contact me. Nothing. But I wasn't going to wait here to find out who had sent for me. I had my own agenda, well rehearsed during my sleepless night.

"You won't stay for breakfast? Fresh-baked cranberry muffins." My southern hostess glanced up the stairs again.

"No, ma'am. Much as it sounds enticing, I'm afraid I shall have to refuse that pleasure." Although I hated it, I'd learned early the southern conversation games and could play as well as anyone.

"What a shame you will be walking this beautiful city alone . . . ," she said with a final glance up the stairs.

To a Yankee, this might have seemed like a harmless observation. I knew better. For a southerner, especially a Charlestonian steeped in the antebellum traditions, her implication was less subtle than the working end of a baseball bat.

"Yes, ma'am," I said. I pushed the door open, letting sunlight flood the antiquities behind me. "It is a shame."

CHAPTER 3

For the most part, I was fond of lower King Street. Not the section south of Broad, where the ancient houses lined King Street in regal indifference to passersby. But north of Broad, where I now walked.

Here, the business of King was doing business. Not in the brash American, twentieth-century style of neon signage, sprawling parking lots, and franchise locations determined by demographic statistics. In contrast to the commercial zones of the suburbs, King was elegant, European — a quiet gentleman in a discreetly custom-tailored navy suit above the fray of lesser beings who fought for status by flaunting overpriced, off-the-rack designer labels.

King had been built long before the first black Model T came off assembly. Once amply wide for carriage traffic, it was now too narrow to allow much space for parking. Shoppers arrived by foot, leisurely studying the antiques and old books clustered in storefront windows, squinting in the odd pools of sunshine that gathered in stray gaps between the tightly squeezed old stone buildings, or stepping over occasional streams of water where proprietors had hosed down the sidewalk. Then stopping in narrow, elongated coffee shops where specials were written on chalkboards in pastel chalk and where waitresses knew many of the customers by name.

I kept myself on the sunny side of the street, walking at a pace that suited the charm of King, pausing often to stare into the different antique shop windows at the array of furniture, statues, and paintings, all from an era made famous by *Gone With the Wind.*

When I arrived at my first planned destination of the day, a bell sounded as I opened the door.

Antique shops on King tend to specialize. Jewelry. Art. Civil War prints and old magazines. Proprietors have extensive knowledge in limited areas and tend to prefer concentrating their potential for profits accordingly.

The interior of this store was crammed with furniture lined in ragged rows. Full-length mirrors hung from the walls. Chandeliers were so low they almost brushed my head as I passed beneath them. It felt more like a crammed discount warehouse than an upscale antique store. Yet I knew there were no discounts ever offered here, and the white price tags, written by hand and attached with knotted thread, would rarely show prices under four digits.

I stepped farther inside.

A fine chair caught my eye. It wasn't ornate, but true beauty in furniture resonates, projecting an aura of timeless quality that even the uninitiated in antiques understand. The chair was probably a century old, high backed, with thin arms and thin legs of exquisitely carved mahogany. What struck me most were the legs. Each ended in the shape of talons clutching a smooth ball. I'd seen this chair before, but I could not place it in my memory.

As I studied it, a tiny man, dark hair slicked back, stepped out from a row of armoires. He held a handkerchief and paused to sneeze before greeting me.

"May I be of assistance?" he asked between sniffles.

"I'm wondering if Elaine and Glennifer are still proprietors here?" I asked, knowing only death would have had the power to remove them.

The tiny man rolled his eyeballs upward. "Although I am certain they'll outlive me, it's my dream that someday they'll be gone, giving me a chance to make sense of all of this."

"Willy," a voice called out, "we can plainly hear you."

He rolled his eyeballs again and pointed me toward the back and the source of the voice.

"Make sense of this? It would take another lifetime to accomplish that," I said.

"We heard that too," another voice said, similar to the first.

I smiled and headed to the voices.

❋ ❋ ❋

At the back of the store, two old women sat at a large desk, facing each other over piles of paper and magazines. Each wore black, heel to collar. Each held her piled, gray hair in place with a fine white netting. They both turned to face me, their dark shiny eyes sunk deep in wrinkles.

"Good morning," I said.

Elaine and Glennifer were spinster twins, institutions of Charleston, notorious for their love of gossip. Making discreet offers to purchase furniture from Charleston blue bloods desperate to pay taxes or bank loans, they'd made a fortune on the knowledge gained by this gossip. While I hoped to exploit their delight in that gossip, I was genuinely glad to see them again. My mother had often brought me here, not to shop, but to educate me on the styles of furniture, as if we were touring a museum. Because she could not afford to, not once had my mother purchased anything in this shop, but the sisters, like all who met my mother, had delighted in her presence and encouraged her visits, despite the fact that she had not been born into Charleston's elite. I remembered, too, how kindly they had treated me.

"I wonder if you might recognize me," I said. "Try to picture me much younger. No beard."

The two old women stared closely at me, then, in the same moment, swiveled their heads toward each other.

"It's —," Elaine began.

"Nicholas Barrett," Glennifer finished.

"Exactly," Elaine said. "Oh, my."

"Oh, my is right," Glennifer said. "Nick Barrett. Back in Charleston."

"Curiosity aroused, ladies?" I asked.

"Of course, of course," Elaine said. "Find a chair and set. Tell us all. Where have you been since that horrible accident? It was such a terrible thing."

"Oh yes," Glennifer agreed. "Ghastly. Absolutely ghastly. We heard rumors . . ."

They hoped I would fill in the silence; I

hoped they could fill in some blanks.

I had not gone far to get my chair. Instead of sitting as requested, I whistled at the amount on the price tag, knowing it would get another rise from them.

"Louis XIV, young man," Glennifer sniffed. "I believe your mother would have taught you its worth. Surely your absence from Charleston did not rob you of southern refinement."

"There are those who would argue that refinement was not part of my breeding," I said. "Something I intend to disprove over the next few days."

Glennifer clapped her hands with glee. "Tell all. Do tell all!"

I decided, having offered the bait, that enough had been taken and that the hook could be securely set. "Not another word. Yet. I'm here to bargain."

"Bargain?" Elaine said, wrinkling her nose. "In this shop, we do not bargain. Do we, Glenny?"

"Certainly not." Glennifer giggled. "We negotiate."

"Let me begin, then," I said. "I can confirm or deny any multitude of rumors. But not until you give me some information that surely you two must know."

"He's flattering us, Glenny. Beware."

"Hush. We haven't had this kind of excitement in weeks. Absolute weeks."

"Helen deMarionne," I said. The letter that had brought me to Charleston contained an enigmatic phrase.

Ask Helen deMarionne the truth. She knew your mother best.

Since I had the day ahead of me before returning to the deMarionne mansion, I would take this opportunity to learn what I could. "Surely you must remember when she first arrived in Charleston. I'd like to know about her."

Whatever gossip had been spoken about Helen deMarionne would never have reached me when I was a boy. Children are too far removed from the adult world to have enough perspective to understand them, except in the way that a child looks upward, in affection or fear, love or distrust. I knew nothing about Helen, and here was the best place to start.

Again, their heads swiveled in the same direction toward me at the same time.

"Helen deMarionne! Oh, my. It's true then? You did marry Claire, didn't you? We have wondered all these years and never truly confirmed it."

Despite all the pain held in that statement, I laughed at their girlish eagerness. "Ladies. You tell all. When I am able, I tell all. That's my trade."

"*When* you are able?" Glennifer glared. "And when might that be?"

"A couple days." I didn't expect to be in Charleston much longer. Whoever had sent for me had paid for five nights at the inn.

"That doesn't seem like much of a trade to me." This from Glennifer.

"Oh, Glenny, what does it matter? As you said, we haven't had this kind of excitement in weeks. To imagine that Nick Barrett has returned. Don't you remember the rumors . . . ?"

"Ladies," I said, "Helen deMarionne."

I wanted their memories of her. And would not, at this point, share mine. Especially of the last time that Helen deMarionne and I had had a conversation.

It had happened in the hospital, as I recovered from the emergency surgery following the car accident. A bright young intern had sawed off my right leg just below the knee.

My first visitor that day had been Police Chief Edgar Layton, who interrogated me about the accident. An hour had passed after his departure, an hour in which I merely stared at the ceiling.

My leg pained me greatly; if I wished, I could ring the bell and a nurse would bring me morphine. My thirst tormented me; I had not reached for the pitcher near my bed to refill the empty glass on the bedside table. I had not even shifted in that hour. Because of what Layton had said to me, the emptiness of my future had drained my soul so totally that I was frozen in apathy to the needs of my body.

I was staring at the ceiling when the squeal of door hinges signaled another visitor. I did not care enough to look. *If it is Claire,* I told myself, *it is too late. If it is Claire, I still have no choice but to leave.*

As the swish of nylons and a brace of perfume reached me, I discovered I had lied to my heart. I did care. A sudden hope surged through me. Together, Claire and I would find a solution. Perhaps she would leave Charleston with me.

I struggled to my elbows as quickly as possible, my apathy and despair banished instantly.

Claire!

Only it was not Claire.

It was Helen deMarionne, Claire's stepmother. Helen dressed youthfully and had dyed her hair to match Claire's. Ash blonde swept up in a short beehive. Lips dark red, high cheekbones accented with blush.

She was elegant in a full-length summer dress, diamonds sparkling at her ears, from her neck, from her fingers. But her scorn was less than elegant.

"I can hardly bring myself to speak to you," Helen said.

"At least that hasn't changed," I said, bitter in my disappointment that it was Helen, not Claire, in the hospital room.

Helen stepped closer and slapped me hard across my face. "Because of you, my only son lies in a coma," she said, trembling. It was the first time I had seen any emotion in her. "And you make jokes."

"I'm sorry," I said. I truly meant it. "I should not have said that."

Helen went to the window and stared outside at grass and trees and flowers until she regained her icy composure. When she returned to the bed, she remained standing. To pull up a chair and sit at my bedside would have been more intimacy than she could bear.

"You knew I would oppose your marriage. You knew from the beginning that Claire was to marry Pendleton. That is our way."

I replied in a flat voice, "Not someone who comes from white trash instead of a sixth-generation Charleston family."

"If you want to put it in those words, yes. I have never disguised my feelings toward your interest in Claire."

"No, you haven't," I said. "Perhaps there is something admirable in that kind of honesty."

"Then let us continue in that admirable honesty. I have just spoken with the chief of police. He tells me you came to an agreement during his visit."

I moved my eyes away and stared at the ceiling. Emptiness began to fill me again. I was mildly surprised to discover this — that emptiness can fill a person.

Helen's voice grew sharp. "I understand you came to an agreement with Edgar Layton."

"Yes."

"The proposed monthly stipend was satisfactory?"

"Yes," I said.

"I want you to understand that. You cannot come back later and ask for more. In fact, you cannot come back. You do understand that."

"Yes."

"I have the legal agreement with me. Sign it, then." She put a pen in my clenched fist. "Sign it, then."

Helen held a piece of paper. She pulled a Bible out of the drawer next to the bed and placed it on top of my chest. "Sign it."

I would not betray my anguish to her. Somehow, I forced the small muscles of my fingers and hand to obey my will. I signed the paper, annulling my marriage to Claire.

"Geoffrey Alexander Gillon represents our family in legal matters. He will take care of the financial arrangements. Tomorrow you will be moved to a hospital in Asheville. Do not return to Charleston. Do not ever communicate with my daughter." She took the paper and put it in her purse.

I did not answer.

Helen walked away without a good-bye.

At the doorway, she stopped and stepped halfway back inside. "It was not easy to tell Claire that you were in a hospital somewhere in Atlanta," Helen said. "It was not easy forcing her to remain in Charleston to watch over her brother instead of driving to Atlanta to find you. She is crazy with grief and worry about you. It hurts me to see her in that state. I want her happy."

Helen shook her head. "There was a

time, long ago, when I was young and believed in love. Enough of who I was then remains that I half wanted to hear that you would not accept this agreement. I might have believed what you two had together was much stronger than any barriers I could have put in place. In time, I could have learned to live with it, if Claire truly was happy with you."

Helen's face was filled with disdain. "I'm glad I found out the truth now. It is worth the money I'm spending to keep you away from her."

She left. The Bible was still on my chest. Now I had abandoned Claire and signed the paper on top of the Bible. I picked it up and threw it at the wall.

A spasm of pain gripped the stump of my leg. My clenched jaws could not contain a gurgle of agony. Tears streamed freely down my face. It was not my leg that brought me these tears.

❊ ❊ ❊

"Helen deMarionne," Elaine said, taking me away from the memory. "Such a scandal when she married Maurice deMarionne. He was in his seventies. One foot in the grave. And then she appears from nowhere, absolutely nowhere, and helps him place his other foot in the grave."

51

"Laney," Glennifer said, "you make it sound like she murdered him. Maurice died from pneumonia."

Glennifer made a face for my benefit. "Believe me, if there had been anything at all suspicious about Maurice's passing, someone would have investigated. She was so much younger than he; all of us knew she was only interested in his money."

"I simply meant she was a young woman," Elaine said. "If Maurice got his money's worth, I'm sure it exhausted the poor man, and most surely it affected his health, leaving him susceptible to pneumonia."

Glennifer giggled. "Put that way, Laney, I'd have to agree with you."

"Helen came from out of nowhere?" I asked.

"Not exactly nowhere. She claimed to have come from the plantation areas of northern Georgia, but she simply had no family connections whatsoever."

"Oh yes," Elaine added. "In our debutante days, she would not have passed muster. Not at all. But times do change. It seems that —"

Elaine gasped. Her eyes widened. She reached across the desk and grabbed one of Glennifer's arms. "Glenny! Remember who invited Helen to the Christmas party and introduced her to Maurice deMarionne? Remember where . . ."

Glennifer gasped. She looked from Elaine to me and back to Elaine again. "At the Barrett mansion on South Battery!" Glennifer said.

"Yes, yes, yes," Elaine said with glee. "And you know who invited Helen, don't you!"

"Yes, yes, yes. I remember that evening. And the dreadful dress that Helen wore. So low cut that she didn't dare lean forward. Except occasionally for Maurice's benefit. People talked about that dress for months."

"Only because Maurice made such a fool of himself. How is it that men can have so much money and so little brains?"

Elaine turned her eyes to me. "Certainly you know that his daughter Claire resulted from his third marriage. Claire was only two years old at the time, his third wife divorced and gone only a month, and there he was, ready for marriage number four as soon as he saw Helen."

"I knew Helen was Claire's stepmother," I said, forcing another onslaught of memories to remain at bay.

"You are certainly right, Laney," Glennifer

said. "Maurice *was* an old goat. I wonder how long it would have taken for him to tire of Helen if he hadn't died first?"

"Helen deMarionne," I reminded them. "You were saying how she met him."

"Oh yes," Elaine said. "It is so peculiar that you would ask about her."

"So peculiar," Glennifer said. "After all, no one had heard of Helen or knew her background. Yet there she was, on the guest list. It certainly raised eyebrows when we discovered who had placed her there."

"Not only that," Elaine said, nodding firm agreement, "she had reserved a seat for Helen right beside poor old Maurice. He didn't have a chance after that."

"Who invited Helen?" I said, leaning forward. "Who placed her beside Maurice? Tell all. Tell all."

Elaine and Glennifer exchanged glances. Each nodded at the same time.

Elaine spoke for both of them. "Why, Nicholas, it was your mother."

CHAPTER 4

ROOM 2553. EDGAR LAYTON.

The letters were typed neatly on a square of ivory paper, held in place at eye level by a small rectangular sheet of clear acrylic. The ivory paper was tabbed so that it could be easily lifted from the protective plastic, which was designed to be lifted and discarded and replaced with another square of ivory paper with another patient's typewritten name when Edgar Layton no longer needed room 2553. Invisible behind the official neatness and implied transitory status of the neatly typed tab of paper was a three-word death sentence: ADVANCED COLON CANCER.

I knocked on the half-open door. No answer. I pushed it open, uncaring if the man inside wanted solitude as he neared death.

The private room seemed to say that Edgar Layton lived large, even in dying. No white antiseptic walls. No unpleasant odors of vomit or urine. No additional narrow beds crowded by visitors with nervous laughter. But a large bed centered in front of a massive color television. A phone sat on the bedside table; Picasso prints adorned the walls. Half-drawn curtains allowed the softness of morning sunshine to caress the patient where he lay sleeping.

At the nurses' station, they'd warned me that Edgar Layton might be drowsy from painkillers; they had been right. I moved a chair beside the bed and studied him in his morphine-induced sleep.

I found myself still fascinated by his massive skull. His dominant features — the heavy nose, stubborn jaw, large forehead — remained unchanged from my memories of him on the occasions our lives had intersected.

Here in the hospital, all those decades later, not much other than his massive skull remained to remind me of how I had once feared him.

Where once thick hair had given him pride, the top of his skull was now covered with age spots and thinning baby-soft hair. The skin around his cheekbones was deeply creased into the hollows of his cheeks, giving him a gauntness that almost allowed me to feel pity.

I was fascinated, too, in a morbid way, at how much his body had retreated into its frail shell. The blankets seemed to press him down, as if he were the husk of an insect wrapped in a cocoon of spider's webbing, long sucked dry of its juices and movement. His breathing was not a rasping snore, but a pinched struggle through an oxygen tube clipped to his nose. A man once so powerful, now so weak. The giant oak named Edgar Layton, immovable in any wind, impervious to every storm, had rotted quietly from within and was ready to topple.

This was a reminder that a man can defy God for only the brief instant that his life flickers across the expanse of eternity.

Watching Layton, I found no compassion.

I should have taken the reminder as a need to return to God myself. I should have allowed my heart to hear some echo of the compassion of the Son he had sent to walk this earth. But I had my own god of hatred and revenge, a god which thirsted for the sacrifice of my soul upon its altar. This assumed, of course, that I believed I had a soul. And that God was the creator behind it.

My clearest and earliest memory of wondering about God resulted because of a telescope.

I was five.

I do not recall the gentleman's name nor the exact whereabouts of his sea island retreat in the low country just south of Charleston. I suspect he was courting my mother, for I have a dim memory of enduring a long, boring meal on a screened veranda, with the echoes of owls and the grunts of bull gators punctuating our conversations.

This man had probably given up on his chances with her long before the meal finished, for instead of attempting to take my mother for a walk along the beach or indeed tempting her with his expensive telescope, he left her alone on a rocking chair on the veranda and escorted me to a viewing deck on the second story of the house.

I cannot picture the features of his face. But I do recall with clarity the scent of talc on his skin and his full, thick gray beard. The sensation of his fine hairs against my cheek as he leaned to help me look through the eyepiece is an integral part of my memory as is that moment of exhilaration as the view of the moon's valleys and mountains brought from me a gasp.

He laughed as I reached out — my eye still pressed into the eyepiece — with my fingers to grasp this magnificent apparition.

Because my memory of that first view

had such an impact on me, I also re-member the few words that we spoke.

"What is it that you see?" he asked.

"The moon," I said, unwilling to lift my head from the telescope.

"No," he replied. "The face of God. If you cannot see him in the moon and planets and stars, you will always be blind."

"Yes," I said immediately. "I see him."

In that moment, I lied, afraid that I would lose my eyesight and be robbed of what my optic nerves delivered, so des-perate was I to be allowed to continue to marvel at the sight of the moon in a way I did not know possible until then.

What more he spoke, I cannot say, for the next half hour of marvels dominate my memories of that evening.

That night, I saw for the first time the rings of Saturn and the moons of Jupiter. Although I didn't understand the terms or concepts, I saw a speck of distant light be-come pinpricks of light swirled in the shape of a galaxy.

I was hooked.

By the age of eight, I had my own inex-pensive telescope. I could point out all of the major constellations and most of the minor ones. I knew which part of the sky to scan for Mars, and when. The same for Venus.

By the age of ten, I understood the difference between *perigee* — the point in the orbit that is closest to Earth — and *apogee,* the point farthest from Earth. It fascinated me to think that the moon, some 250,000 miles away, regularly drifted between Earth and the sun, casting a shadow on us that was only sixty miles across — the *umbra* — and that the *penumbra* was a partial shadow four thousand miles wide. I understood occultation observations and gravitational lenses and astronomical units.

Each year I learned more, but with everything I learned reading as much as I could, I never once saw or considered evidence of God.

In fact, through the years into adulthood, what I learned brought me closer and closer to thinking that I had not lied to the old man with the gray whiskers but that he had lied to me on that enchanted evening when I was five. I believed there was nothing to see of God in the moon and the planets and the stars.

But then, there was a lot I did not know.

I sat in place in the hospital room, waiting for the moment until Edgar Layton finally blinked his eyes open.

It did not happen.

At least, not while I sat beside his bed.

The door opened.

I looked up.

A woman walked inside the room. She had long, wavy dark hair. She wore loose clothing, browns and blacks. She was perhaps a couple of years younger than I.

She stared at me for a few moments. A strange look of recognition seemed to cross her face. "What are you doing here?" she asked. "What is it you want with my father?"

What I want with your father is to watch his pain as he dies, I resisted the urge to say. *What I want is some sort of retribution for all that he took from me.*

Instead, I spoke quietly and gave another truth. "I want to ask him about my mother. She ran away from me on the night of July 12, a date I will never forget. I was not quite ten. I believe your father might be able to help me."

Again, she gave me a strange look. She opened her mouth to say something. She shut it. I guessed she changed her mind.

"My father is near death," she finally said. "I don't want him disturbed."

"I understand that," I said. "It's just that —"

"What you want is more important than

61

what he might want? Or what I might want?"

I had nothing to say to that.

"Please go," she said.

"Is there a place I can contact you if you change your mind?"

"I won't change my mind."

"My name is Nick Barrett," I said. "I'm staying at the inn at Two Meeting Street. If —"

"Good-bye," she said.

As I departed, I wondered why she was so angry with me. Most people waited until they got to know me better.

Perhaps, I thought, *she is a good judge of character.*

CHAPTER 5

The cousin I had last seen passed out drunk against the passenger side of the wrecked Plymouth Valiant worked in a second-floor office suite perched above one of the many third- and fourth-generation law firms that afflicted Broad Street.

This was my third planned destination of the day. I had saved the most enjoyable for last.

I stepped through the main door onto plush carpet to be greeted by the silence of hushed air-conditioning and the questioning stare of, naturally, an attractive secretary. When I walked past her desk to step unannounced into his office, her eyes flared with surprise.

I shut the door behind me and locked it. From outside, she knocked on the door as Pendleton looked up from his desk.

To his credit, his face showed no surprise. But then, he always had been able to put on an impressive front.

Pendleton Barrett sat behind a desk bare of papers and picked up his phone. He hit a button and spoke into the speaker. "Denise, it's fine. I know him."

The knocking on the outside of the door ceased.

His office was decorated to an interior designer's concept of postmodern New York hip. Minimalist furniture, stark and black. Abstract paintings. Flat-screen monitor. Black leather couch in the form of a semicircle.

I studied my cousin.

Pendleton had changed little — his handsome sallowness hardly gone further to seed, his dark suit and red silk tie fitted perfectly to a body that probably indulged in three hours of exercise a day.

I didn't sit. This wasn't going to take long.

"Unexpected," Pendleton said. "I'd say a pleasure, but why bother with the pretense."

"So that it matches the rest of your life."

"Oh, my," Pendleton said, clutching his heart. "You've just devastated me."

He meant that sarcastically; he had no idea it was my intent to accomplish it literally. But, like the night before on the piazza of the deMarionne mansion, I savored the anticipation of my vengeance.

One Friday during the summer of my tenth birthday, I had been swimming in the ocean with Pendleton.

"There's Claire," Pendleton said. "See, she's waving at us."

Both Pendleton and I were dog-paddling in the gray Atlantic, rising and falling with the gentle waves a hundred yards offshore. Only our heads, hair slicked back like seal pups, showed above the water. Pendleton with soft features, aristocratic and verging on effeminate, but rescued by eyes that seemed to know much. Me, square faced and freckled.

Pendleton waved back at Claire, kicking hard with his legs so that his shoulders and upper chest lifted him from the water; I was too shy to respond to her wave of greeting and unsure what to do with the feelings that hit me anytime I saw Claire, who now stood just past the dunes, where the waves compacted the sand into a wet, smooth base. She wore a navy blue one-piece bathing suit with a frilled skirt, and my heart flared with the crush I had on her. Behind her, rising into view above the dunes, was the Barrett beach house, a rambling two-story wooden structure on stilts to protect it from hurricane waves.

"Race you back," Pendleton said. "Ready . . . set . . . go!"

Pendleton was eleven, a year older than

I, both of us at the ages where a year's growth makes a tremendous difference in the strength of developing muscle and bone. I was the same height as Pendleton but easily fifteen pounds lighter and had yet to win a race against him — on foot across the beach, on bicycle to the ice cream parlor from the beach house, in the water.

This time, however, the gap between us did not widen. In the past few days since arriving for my annual two-week vacation with his family on Folly Island, I had been experimenting with a way to slip through the water by keeping my arms tighter to my body with each stroke, not losing as much energy to splashing. Now I felt a thrill of efficiency and power as I cut through the waves.

This time, unlike our other races, Claire was watching.

I swam hard, driven with a heroic determination that burned in a wonderful way, my heart ignited by her presence on the beach.

I didn't even realize I was winning. Not until we reached the final few yards, where the shallowness of the water forced me to my feet for an ungainly run with knees high. I was just ahead when Pendleton reached and yanked at the back of my swimming trunks.

As the trunks slid down, I twisted sideways to escape the mortification of being exposed to Claire. I fell as my legs caught in my trunks. I landed headfirst in the water, scraping my chin against the sand beneath as my head snapped backward on impact. I didn't lift my head to breathe; my first priority was the swim trunks that were down to my knees. I pulled hard, hoping my bare bottom remained below the surface of the shallow water. Only when my trunks were in place did I roll over and come up gasping.

Pendleton was already on shore, bent over, hands on knees, laughing hard.

It wasn't the laughter that infuriated me, but the unfairness of Pendleton's tactics. I dashed out of the water and rammed my shoulder into Pendleton's stomach. The momentum of my tackle took both of us down. We rolled twice, the points of our shoulders and knees leaving imprints in the wet sand. Pendleton used his superior weight to pin me. Both of us forgot about Claire.

"Stupid jerk!" Pendleton shouted, his face inches above mine. Sand was stuck to Pendleton's forehead. His eyes were wide with rage. "Say uncle!"

I pushed back. Uselessly. Pendleton straddled my chest, his knees on my upper arms.

"Say uncle!" Pendleton grabbed a handful of sand and rubbed it into my face. "Say uncle!"

I squirmed. Silent. Spitting out sand when Pendleton finally took his hand away.

"Uncle! Uncle! Uncle!" Pendleton screamed. "Say it!"

"Let him go," Claire said. She was only nine, but even then she had a presence. The striking blue eyes, the cameo symmetry, the blonde hair. "Don't fight."

"Not until I hear *uncle*," Pendleton said.

"Uncle," Claire said for me. "Now let him go or I'll never visit you again."

Her threat showed that even then, she must have known her power over both of us.

Pendleton rubbed a final handful of sand in my face. "Loser," Pendleton said. He stood. "Don't even know who was your own daddy."

I remained sitting on the sand. Angry. Humiliated. Confused. *Didn't know who was my own daddy?*

"You heard me," Pendleton said, reading my confusion correctly and enjoying it.

"They all laugh at you and your mama. 'Cause you're illegitimate. Your daddy could be anybody in Charleston. Probably some drunk or gambler your mama found in a bar one night. That's what my mother believes. That's what my mother tells other people about your mama."

I got to my feet. I wiped my face with the back of my arm. "My daddy was a war hero."

"No," Pendleton said, playing to Claire as audience, showing the single-minded focus on winning that would serve him well as he grew older. "*My* uncle David was a war hero. And *my* uncle David married your mother. But *my* uncle David Barrett wasn't your daddy."

I looked at Claire, helpless. "He married my mama . . . ," I said to her. "I've got a photograph of him in unifo—"

"Oh, they were married," Pendleton said. "But he went to Vietnam. And never came back. You were born a year and a half after he left. Don't you know anything about the birds and the bees?"

"Pendleton . . . ," Claire said, warning in her voice.

"Someone's got to tell him." Pendleton leered with victory. "Everyone else knows, so he should find out too."

Claire put a hand on my arm. "Just don't listen to him."

That I received Claire's sympathy infuriated Pendleton more.

"Babies only take nine months," he said. "*My* uncle David and *your* mother were gone from each other too long for *my* uncle David to be *your* father."

News of this magnitude, if true, is enough to destroy a boy's world. Because David Barrett had died in the Vietnam War, I had grown up with a photograph instead of a father, worshiping his clean, good looks in a naval uniform. Instead of listening to stories from him, I'd begged to hear stories of him and his exploits at the Citadel. At baseball games where other boys had their fathers to cheer them on, I'd consoled myself with the understanding that at least my own father had died a hero's death.

"Don't you get it?" Pendleton taunted. "Your mother's a tramp. A sleazebag. She cheated on my uncle. And you're her little illegitimate problem."

"Tramp?" I repeated with hesitation. "Sleazebag?" I did not know what the words meant.

"A sleazebag," Pendleton repeated with glee. "A tramp. Does bad things with other men. That's why you don't know who your daddy —"

My feet were planted. The sand was firm enough to give me a base. I'd never thrown a punch in my life, but from second base I could snap the ball into the catcher's glove with an audible pop. I uncoiled my shoulder and right arm and right fist into Pendleton's face like a throw to outgun a runner sneaking home from third.

The bone of my knuckles exploded into Pendleton's nose.

Pendleton fell back, blood spurting instantly across his face and onto his chest. He clasped both hands to his face, yowling through his fingers and the stream of blood.

"Get up!" I screamed. I'd never lost my temper before, not to the extent of actually hitting someone. Pendleton, with his extra advantage in weight, had always been the one to bully me. I expected Pendleton to rise and fight. I needed him to rise and fight. Angry as I was, I could not attack a fallen opponent. "Get up!"

Crablike, Pendleton tried pushing away instead — a revelation of cowardice that, as we grew older, he would hate me for as thoroughly as I would learn to hate him.

"It's not true," I said. Fallen or not, if

Pendleton spoke another word against my mother, I would drop on him, fists flying. "It's not true. Take it back!"

Claire knelt at Pendleton's side. She looked at the growing stream of blood running down Pendleton's wrists and onto the sand. She then looked up at me.

"You'd better go get some help," she said. Pendleton's yowling grew in disbelief at the pain and shock of his broken nose. "This isn't good."

❀ ❀ ❀

Pendleton broke the silence in the office first. "Helen called me. She told me you were back. So what are you looking for? The mama who walked out on you as a boy?"

Pendleton leaned back in his chair, smirking. "Face it. She abandoned you. Never came back for you. Never called. Never wrote. What do you think is going to happen if you ever find her? Some big tearful reunion?"

That was another one of Pendleton's strengths. He had an instinct for a person's weak point and would not hesitate to use it. Throwing a punch in his face — for the second time in my life — would probably have pleased him, for he would have then known about the hurt that I would not allow my expression to show.

"I'm here in this office because of the car accident," I said. I felt as if I were pulling a saber loose, ready to slash and cut as part of an ancient duel.

Pendleton shrugged.

To me, that said it all. His shrug. I contained my anger only because he would have no defense as I began to thrust my imaginary death sword.

"I now know the truth behind it," I said. "I know who was driving. I have a copy of the police report. The real one."

I watched him closely. Since getting the letter that had summoned me to Charleston, I had dreamed constantly of this moment, imagined the way his handsomeness would crack like the oil paint on Dorian Gray's portrait, imagined the way he would quail at the sight of my sword.

His answer surprised me. "Of course you know," he said. "You always have."

His assumption was wrong. If I had known then that he had been driving and moved me behind the steering wheel to place the blame on me, nothing could have kept me from Claire.

"Layton had photos of you behind the wheel," he continued. "What were you going to do, fight it in court? Make accusations you couldn't prove?"

Anger thickened my voice like bitter phlegm. "You owe me more than a decade of my life. And I'm here to settle that debt. I'm taking this public. The media will love it. You can deal with manslaughter charges and —"

"How dramatic," Pendleton said. "And in your pitiful way of honor, you decided to let me know first before announcing it to everyone else?"

Not only was I disappointed at the calm way he took it, the accuracy of his statement left me with little to say.

"Did you hope I would beg forgiveness?" he said, letting that smirk play on his face. "Grovel? Plead that you hide the hideous truth from all of Charleston?"

Again, his accuracy kept me silent, kept my imaginary blade in check.

"Think I moved you behind the steering wheel just so that I wouldn't get the blame for that accident? It was much more than that, Nick. More importantly, it let me put the blame on you. So Claire would think you'd killed her brother. A man takes his opportunities when he can. And while I didn't think you'd run like you did, the payoff was worth it."

Pendleton rose, a graceful movement

that I would never be able to achieve with my plastic limb. He moved to a shelf, took a framed photograph, and handed it to me.

I glanced at it. A wedding photo. Pendleton and Claire. I had not known.

I handed the photo back to him. I hoped he didn't notice the tremble in my hand. A tremble which, if I truly did hold a saber, would have loosened my grip and let it clatter on the floor.

"Go ahead and tell the world," Pendleton said. "You may think you can destroy everything I have with your announcement, but you are wrong."

He went back to his desk and sat on the edge of it. "Since the day you left town, Edgar Layton has bled me by using that same information. Sure, he had photos of you behind the steering wheel. He also had photos that showed blood on the passenger side, where I had no injuries that would have caused blood. Photos that showed the driver's side wasn't damaged enough to do what the accident did to your leg. He's a smart man. He pieced it together and reeled me in slowly, never demanding enough to really hurt me. But through the years, he's probably taken a million or two. From me. And, indirectly, from my wife's family. That and a couple of disastrous investments left me in a position where I tried something stupid and desperate and cut some corners on my taxes. Even now, with that bloodsucking leech on his deathbed and his blackmail about to end, it's too late for me. That accident has hurt me as much as it hurt you."

"I doubt it," I said.

A rueful smile crossed his face. "Every cloud has a silver lining," he said. "Until today, I never thought that my troubles with the IRS would provide me with any kind of joy. But you, my long-lost cousin, have just proved the merit of that saying."

The only thing I'd really heard him say was one phrase. *My wife's family. Claire's family.* I desperately wanted a place to sit now. I doubted I would be able to stand motionless for much longer.

"You might be happy to know that all my assets have been frozen," he continued. "By the IRS. Until the final court judgment is rendered. I doubt it will be resolved in my favor."

Another of his shrugs. "Fortunately, I am able to live off proceeds from my wife's trust fund. You did recognize her from that photo?"

I didn't trust my voice to answer. He studied my face with a cruel smile and came to his own conclusion.

"Ah yes," he said, "you did recognize her. It has been greatly convenient, you know, the income from her protected trust fund. And while we are separated, my finances are so poor she doesn't dare divorce me, afraid that I'll try to take too much of it as a settlement."

He allowed his smile to widen. "Tell the whole world about that car accident," Pendleton said. "You can't hurt me financially. I'm already at rock bottom. But you can hurt her. A scandal like this will play well, don't you think? Especially given the mayor's race she intends to enter next month. She's spent ten years building her base for this and has a good chance, really. Or had, until you arrived with this monumental news."

There my dream was. Not the red-hot coals of revenge. But ashes.

Pendleton chuckled. "I take it, then, you will not destroy her by going public?"

I had no answer.

"How about telling it to her privately?" he asked. "Have you done that?"

No answer. He knew I had not, or he would have heard it already from her.

Pendleton smoothed back his hair. "Let's turn this around, shall we? You see,

I really must remain married. I need her family money to live the Charleston life. If she and Helen discover that I killed Philip, my marriage will be over. No more family money. No more comfortable living. At that point, I won't care if the entire world knows the truth about that accident, for I will have nothing left to lose. A man with nothing to lose is a dangerous man, wouldn't you agree?"

He smiled, a carnivore. "Which means I believe I shall threaten you with the truth behind the car accident. If you tell her about it or tell anyone in private about the accident so that it reaches her, I'll do the rest of the damage myself. I'll be the one to take it to the media. It'll end her run for mayor before it gets started. In other words, by telling anyone this nasty little secret, you'll hurt her far more than you will me."

In defeat, I struggled for the illusion of disdain, as if with a shaking hand, I reached for that imaginary sword from the floor at my feet.

"I remember," I said, "how often you reminded me that you represent nothing but the finest in Charlestonian aristocracy. This civil resolution only proves it."

"It's an instinct," he said, thrusting aside my feeble parry. "I can understand your admiration of it. Your family's from the plantation side of the river. Civility is not expected of you or bred into you."

My smile and sense of control had long faded, but I managed to keep my voice even. "Bad form, Pendleton, insulting parentage. Have a half hour? I'll start on yours."

"At least I know my parentage."

There was silence as Pendleton let that hang. It took both of us back to the time on the beach when we were boys. He'd won then, and he'd won now.

I should have surrendered in this conversation long before. He knew it and I knew it.

"Good-bye," I said. It was a poor defense.

Pendleton waited until my back was turned and my hand was on the doorknob. "By the way," he asked, "how did it feel to find out that she and I had married?"

He assumed I'd long known. I had not. I fought the urge to turn around and make a stumbling, awkward tackle into his midsection. But if I turned, Pendleton would see on my face how it had felt.

"Good-bye, Pendleton," I repeated.

"Stay away from her, Nick," Pendleton called to my back. "She's mine. Always will be."

CHAPTER 6

I was in no mood to blithely walk among the tourists, not with defeat filling my belly like sour milk.

From Pendleton's office, I wandered to the bustle of the market area. I simply wanted to be among noise and people, with nothing to remind me of my past and of my failures and of my failures to deal with my past.

In that, too, I failed.

For in walking the few blocks to the market, like the night before, I could not avoid seeing church steeples rise above the centuries-old stone buildings gathered at their bases like chicks around a comforting hen.

And I remembered my mother once pointing at a particular steeple for me.

It was a day like this one, when the sun had brought out songbirds and tourists in droves.

"See how it reaches for the sky," she'd said. "Beautiful. White against a cloudless blue sky. Hard to miss, isn't it?"

I had obliged, craning my head upward. "I guess."

To me, at that age, pirate stories and war stories and escaped slave stories were exciting. Not church steeples.

"Now picture a full moon," Mama said on that beautiful day of my memories. She dropped her voice to a dramatic hush. "With the city below dark and still. Silver light shining down on that great white steeple above all the shadowed buildings. Picture the silver moonlight on that steeple. Picture the steeple rising into the sky like a white angel, wings folded at its side."

She whispered, "And then listen for a loud whistle, like ghosts screaming in the night."

Screams were good in stories.

"Ghosts in the night?" I whispered back.

Mama squatted so that she was speaking into my ear. She spoke slowly, getting into the rhythm of another story. "Hear the long, high whistle. And fear for your life. You are living in this city more than a hundred years ago. That screaming whistle is the sound of Yankee cannonballs coming in through the night, fired from ships so far away that the thunder of cannon fire reaches you long after those deadly balls of iron have ripped away the roof of your house, smashed into your bedroom, scattered the flames of your fireplace. Around you, houses erupt into flame, the wails of frightened babies fill the night. Again and again comes that screaming whistle of the next cannonball as you lie there, eyes wide, wondering if this is the cannonball that will snuff out your own life when it lands. And all because that great white steeple rising into the darkness gives the Yankees a target directly in the center of the sleeping city."

"Here?" I asked. "Cannons?"

Cannons were good too. Very good.

"Here," she said. "Cannons. Great guns of war. Pounding the city day after day after day."

"Tell me why." I was in the spell of Charleston's tragic enchantment.

"Because of the war between the North and the South. Because Charleston was a proud city and believed it had nothing to fear. Because politicians on both sides of the war had put themselves into a situation where the only way out was to allow hundreds of thousands of soldiers to die first."

She paused to search her memory.

" 'A city of ruins, of desolation,' " she quoted quietly, " 'of vacant houses, of widowed women, of rotting wharves, of deserted warehouses, of weed wild gardens, of miles of grass-grown streets, of acres of pitiful and voiceful barrenness — that is Charleston, wherein rebellion loftily reared its head five years ago.' "

She opened her eyes and gave me a crooked smile. "So wrote a journalist named Sidney Andrews in the year 1865."

She gestured at the buildings around them. "Another woman wrote to a friend outside the city at the end of the war. She didn't see what you see now. Instead . . ."

She closed her eyes again, drawing out another quote. " 'The houses were indescribable; the gable was out of one, the chimneys fallen from the next. Here a roof was shattered, there a piazza half gone, not a window remained. The streets looked as if piled with diamonds; the glass lay shivered so thick on the ground.' "

My mama had succeeded, as always, in taking me out of the present. I gazed around as if seeing the smoldering city, the crouched women in long dresses lifting the rubble to search for survivors.

We began walking again. She pointed at a block on the curb. "Carriage step. Where a horse-drawn carriage would stop so that women could step on that block to make it easier to get into the carriage. Later, I can show you a boot scrape, where people would scrape horse droppings from their shoes before entering a house because the streets were so dirty, they could not avoid stepping into manure. How the cobblestone streets were made with stones hauled across the ocean in ships that needed them for weight to keep them steady in storms. I could tell you about abandoned wine cellars beneath the sidewalks, now filled with rats. About earthquake bolts that hold a house together. About love stories and sword fights and pirates. This is your city, Nick. You can learn the stories and they will become yours, like they became mine."

I took my mama's hand and walked with her in silence until we were far enough away from St. Michael's Church that when we stopped, we had the same view of the steeple again, but from the opposite direction.

I asked the question that had been bothering me. "If the steeple was white and it gave soldiers something to aim at with their cannons at night, why didn't people do something about it?"

She had been waiting for that question, and she bent down and kissed me with a teacher's thrill of accomplishment.

"They painted it black for the rest of the

war," she said. "They painted it black because it was better to get rid of its glory than face the harm that came with drawing attention to it."

"I get it," I said in my innocence. "Like running away."

❋ ❋ ❋

Now, all these years later, St. Michael's steeple was still bright against the sky to remind me that it had survived because it had been better to be rid of its glory than draw attention to it.

I thought about Claire.

Once I had hoped that all that had been beautiful and glorious about our love for each other would survive if I ran away. If I rid myself of its glory.

But I'd been wrong.

Again, Pendleton had defeated me.

CHAPTER 7

Twenty-five hours earlier, I'd last stood on the piazza of the deMarionne mansion, angry and confident.

Now, robbed by Pendleton of my chance for vindication, I had returned this evening only out of stubbornness and curiosity.

The stubbornness came from the determination not to give Helen deMarionne the satisfaction of thinking I had run from her again, for if I failed to arrive at my appointed time she would most surely think I had lost my nerve.

The curiosity came from that one phrase in the letter that had drawn me to Charleston.

Ask Helen deMarionne the truth. She knew your mother best.

Even so, I did not expect to add much to my knowledge. The old quarter of Charleston is a quirky, reclusive cloister, with rules of living among the high society far closer to the aristocratic inbred circles of ancient European royalty than to the crass openness of the rest of the Americas. Helen deMarionne had probably agreed to see me out of her own curiosity, and I expected she would indulge in her customary arrogance, take satisfaction in divulging little, then send me on my way.

Which I would not take personally.

I had long since learned I would never be part of Charleston. It was half the reason I had guided tourists during my fourteenth summer. The money I made was money I did not have to accept like crumbs from the Barrett table.

By my fifteenth summer, however, the independence granted by that money mattered little compared to time I could spend with Helen's stepdaughter, Claire Eveleigh deMarionne. Against the alternative of money from slow walks with elderly nodding tourists, I gladly chose poverty and endless summer days on the beach with Claire.

I was always conscious that my presence in the household of the Charleston Barretts was an affair of charity because of my mother's departure, so I had learned disdain for the Charleston heritage and money of which I would always remain an outsider.

It was not the deMarionne name, then, which drew me to Claire Eveleigh, but first and foremost, her soul. We each confided in the other, hiding nothing of fears and hopes and questions about the mysteries of life and adulthood, shy only about our increasing awareness of the other as more than a friend. Claire was truly beautiful — tall, lithe, athletic, having the form of a goddess in her sleek swimsuit — with short blonde hair that turned white against tanned skin as the summer progressed. There was no danger, however, that we might stray beyond the occasional kiss stolen in the ocean as high waves hid us from the beach. Our extreme chasteness was ensured by the excessive chaperoning of Helen deMarionne, who had no intention of seeing her stepdaughter stray into an unsuitable marriage.

Despite the barriers put in place by this chaperoning — or by the separation of each successive winter while Claire attended a private school in Boston — despite the growing disapproval of Helen deMarionne, and despite obvious shortcomings of my financial future, four summers later — when I was nineteen and Claire was eighteen — we managed to escape long enough for a successful elopement and a brief honeymoon before returning to face the collective wrath of the deMarionnes and the Barretts.

It was a marriage that lasted only four days. Until the automobile accident. My exile from Charleston began upon leaving the hospital; I had not seen Claire nor spoken to her since.

❋ ❋ ❋

The first love — discovered then lost — is an incredible potion of youth and unfulfilled desire and noble idealism never given the chance to tarnish or decay. For every person, the heart absorbs so thoroughly the perfume of this love that no matter how many layers of new memories are added, at times wisps of this perfume, as subtle and unpredictable as a dancing breeze, will escape the fabric around the heart to renew the old longings for something forever gone.

While time and events and exile from Charleston had blunted my loss, I had never fully escaped that perfume. Each slow measured step tonight to the deMarionne mansion had filled me again with the perfume of this lost love as surely as if I were sixteen or seventeen again, sneaking home late at night with Claire's scent on my clothes adding giddiness to my steps.

Now, waiting on the piazza of the mansion as the echoes of my knocking against the door faded, I fought the bewildered pangs of sorrow that had taken me years to set aside.

Helen deMarionne had shown me no mercy decades earlier. I had no reason to expect it from her tonight.

Ella opened the door for me. With a curt nod, she invited me inside to the entrance hall.

She remained sullenly silent as she led me farther inside, where the entrance hall opened to fifteen-foot ceilings and to lights set hardly above a glow, lights that cast pinprick stars onto the dark glass of the tall, arched windows on all sides. In contrast to the heavy, warm air outside, the house carried the chill of air-conditioning, something I had always associated with the chill of Helen deMarionne.

The hall opened to the great central room of the house, with a suspended spiral staircase leading upward to the ballroom on the second floor and bedrooms on the third floor, the top of the spiral lost to sight in the depths of the shadows of a domed skylight.

The house was filled with the antique trappings of stolen nobility — marble Fu lions, one on top of each side of the fireplace mantle, taken from the Imperial Palace during the Boxer Rebellion; a coat of arms of a Russian czar; a jade Fabergé box on a Chippendale end table; mirrors framed with gilded gold; the dozens of other items accumulated and hoarded by the family over the generations.

As I followed Ella to the rear of the house, I had a glimpse of the dining room on the far side of the central room. It had not changed from my memory of it; the huge mahogany table was set for twenty with the porcelain dishes from Queen Victoria, matching silverware, and needlework linen napkins carefully arranged as if guests were expected any moment.

We reached the French doors that opened onto a large veranda that overlooked the garden. Ella swung the doors outward and motioned for me to step onto the balcony, then departed. With the returned warmth of the night air came the scent of azaleas and jasmine, a reminder of the garden below. I knew how the garden would look in daylight from this balcony with its iron-wrought railings.

Three oak trees, draped in Spanish moss, would dominate the view at first, until the visitor's eyes dropped to a wild profusion of subtropical flowers and foliage plants which, upon study, became a garden pattern of exquisite subtlety — rosemary, plumbago, crape myrtle, loquat, hibiscus, ruellia, ginger lilies.

This evening, the garden was lit by old-fashioned lamps, flames fed behind glass cages by natural gas. And beyond was the murky shape of the carriage house, once used to hold horses beneath the slave quarters above, then as the last century progressed, turned into a second residence.

I only glanced at the garden, however.

A round table with four chairs filled most of the balcony. I saw the outline of a woman seated at the table. Her face and shoulders were turned away from the house. From that outline came the voice that had sent me from Charleston.

"Please, sit, Nicholas Barrett," Helen deMarionne said. Her face was lost in darkness. She was framed by the shadows from the garden lights on one side, the house lights on the other. Her voice still held velvet-wrapped steel, the vowels as soft as her will was strong.

"Thank you," I said with equal, careful formality.

"Do you believe in a God of love?" she asked.

It was such an abrupt question, and so out of character for the Helen deMarionne I remembered, that I wasn't sure I'd heard correctly. "I beg your pardon?"

She heard the astonishment in my voice. "Never mind," she said, her voice tinged by embarrassment. Personal matters were not to be discussed among casual acquaintances; she had broken this unspoken rule of her society.

Helen motioned to the bone china serving dishes on the table. "I trust, despite your prolonged absence, that you haven't lost your taste for our low-country finest."

"I am not hungry," I said. My mouth watered at the aromas from the table. All my walking earlier had given my stomach an edge that was difficult to deny. I did not, however, want to be obligated to any pretended kindness from her.

"Surely you cannot refuse this southern hospitality. You well know that Ella makes a bouillabaisse rivaled by none — shrimp, scallops, clams, and crawfish tails. And, as I recall, you were particularly fond of her crab cakes with sweet pepper cream sauce, so I had them prepared as well."

"I am not hungry," I said.

"Well, then," Helen said, "I can see your

manners have not improved. How I had hoped otherwise."

She shifted in her chair to study me. "When Ella announced your arrival last night, I was undecided on where to visit with you. It was a matter of lighting. You see, I was curious as to how the years have treated you. But any light that shows you clearly is a double-edged sword, for it would allow you to judge my face in return, something that does not appeal to me. Nature is cruel to women, for it grants age a far more vigorous attack on us than on men."

Helen was capable of using her southern drawl as a seductive musical instrument, and coming from the shadows of her face, it was still a powerful spell maker, unaffected by whatever other changes of age she had disguised with her carefully chosen lighting. Her face was now sideways to me, and the softness of the shadows showed only the clean lines of the features of a beautiful face, hiding any sag of skin or puffed eyes or yellowed teeth. To me, it could have been twenty years earlier, in the presence of her intimidating charm and confident loveliness.

"I have observed over the years," she continued, "that some men start with the promise of young gods, but soft living covers them with a sludge of fat and, even before they reach forty they prove to be a visual disappointment. As they grow into men, they fall far short of their potential. Others — most often overlooked by women in their early years — are tempered and chiseled by difficult decisions made well, and their reward is a handsomeness that grows with time, changing their gawky awkwardness into a dignity which, frankly, is a tremendous attraction."

Helen lifted a glass of wine from the table and sipped it carefully before setting it down. "There is irony in that hard-earned knowledge, especially as a widow. By the time I was able to recognize in young men their value or lack, it was too late to be able to pursue them — for me or for Claire — with any effectiveness or hope of success. My gift of discernment is no gift, for now, near such men, I feel like a penniless child pressed against the window, staring at sweets inside the chocolate shop."

Helen stared out over the garden again and spoke without looking at me. "Tell me," she said, "since I chose the light that would hide you as it protects me, what kind of man does your face reveal you to be? Did I fail to recognize your potential? Did I make a mistake in separating you from Claire? And I am sad to say — you knew it was my desire all along — that her marriage to Pendleton was much of my doing."

"Perhaps," I said, "I'll try some of Ella's bouillabaisse."

I had thought that the hours since learning of the marriage from Pendleton would have provided a buffer. I was wrong. It still stabbed deeply, and I was afraid of saying anything that would show my weakness.

"Please understand," Helen said, "I am not asking your forgiveness. What was done, was done. I do not expect that you came here tonight in an effort to begin a reconciliation with me when we never had anything between us but hatred and suspicion."

"Perhaps," I said, "I'll try some of Ella's bouillabaisse."

Mechanically, wondering if I could trust the woodenness in my hands and arms, I ladled a bowl.

"Please inform Ella that her bouillabaisse is indeed unrivaled," I said. My hunger was gone, and the broth caked my suddenly dry mouth and throat like white glue. "I enjoy it very much."

"Why, after so long, have you returned to Charleston?" Helen asked. "And of all the people to visit, why me?"

"My mother," I said. I pushed aside thoughts of Claire, and I pushed aside the bouillabaisse, barely touched. "You knew her best."

"I beg your pardon?"

"I want to know why my mother ran away. I believe you can help me."

The creaking of crickets and katydids filled the night air until Helen spoke again. "You knew as a boy what everyone else knew. Why she ran away. Who she ran away with. Undoubtedly, you knew about the detective reports. Where she was sighted in the months and years that followed. Where the money was spent. As for me helping you, my acquaintance with your mother was half a lifetime ago. And it was only an acquaintance. You overstate considerably to say that I knew her best."

Helen knew my mother well enough to get an introduction to Maurice deMarionne from her. Why was she hiding that?

I did not ask. Knowledge is power, and what she might know vastly outweighed what I could know at this point. Playing dumb to the single fact I knew seemed the best tactic.

"One month ago," I said, "I received an envelope postmarked from Charleston. It held a note and an old police report signed by Edgar Layton."

"Yes," Helen said, "he supervised the search for your mother in the weeks that followed her sudden escape from Charleston."

"The police report in the envelope had nothing to do with that."

"Oh?"

"It covered another investigation. A simpler, shorter one. The car accident with me at the steering wheel. The one that killed your only son. My new brother-in-law at the time."

Helen had begun to sip her wine. Her hand froze halfway to her mouth.

"If there is something I should know about the accident . . ."

I shook my head. "Until tonight, I thought I was going to enjoy giving this report to you. That is no longer the situation."

"Why not?"

"I have reasons. My reasons."

"What is in that report?"

"No," I said.

"My son died because of that accident. I deserve to know."

I considered that. "First help me learn about my mother."

"Why me?" Helen set her wineglass down without taking a drink.

"Because of the note. Written in block letters. Near the end of this note were ten words that sent me here tonight. 'Ask Helen deMarionne the truth. She knew your mother best.' "

"What did the rest of the note say? Who sent you this envelope?"

"The envelope contained the note and the police report. Along with an airline ticket and prepaid hotel accommodations. The rest of the note is my business. As to who sent it to me, I don't know. But that is beside the point. Tell me what you know, and perhaps I'll tell you about the police report."

"I am a mother asking about her only son, and you offer me a trade." Her tone had the disdainful chill that I remembered well. "One truth for another. In these circumstances, rather vulgar, don't you think?"

"And I am a son asking about his only mother." I gestured with both hands, taking in the house, the garden, the balcony. "The original deMarionne fortune was built on trading that involved slaves and bootleg whiskey and black-market goods sold to desperate people who faced Yankee cannonballs and the devaluation of Confederate money. I am not the authority on which aspect of trade is vulgar."

"Touché."

"You will help me then." I did not present it as a question.

"That was decades ago," Helen said sharply. "Surely you've left it behind."

"Even for you," I said, "that is a callous remark. Much as you dislike me, think about a ten-year-old boy essentially orphaned in the way I was. How could anyone ever let that go?"

"Do not lecture me in my own household." She allowed her voice to soften slightly. "Much as I might deserve it."

"I would like it," I said softly in acknowledgment of her grudging apology, "if you could tell me about my mother."

Helen bowed her head. Formed a steeple with her fingertips. Leaned her chin and nose against the steeple. She did not lift her head until she was ready.

"All right then. I do know the attorney she visited on her final afternoon in Charleston. He was, perhaps, the last person in Charleston she spoke to. He's the one who gave her your trust fund money."

"I don't understand. I thought she'd stolen my trust fund money. Now you're saying it was given to her? But how could she force him . . . ?"

"You'll have to ask Gillon yourself."

"But if you knew it wasn't stolen, why didn't others?"

"Charleston keeps its secrets," Helen answered. "In our circles, there *is* a difference between public knowledge and private knowledge. Certainly many, like I, did know the circumstances. But that was not for consumption by the common people."

Common people like me, was the implication I understood. I ignored it. A small portion of my earlier anger began to return inside me, and it felt good. "I want everything you know," I said.

She sighed. "In our circles, we knew the investigation had been done badly."

"You're saying someone could have found her?"

"And then what? Even if she didn't go to prison, it was clear she had made a choice to leave you. How could we force her to become your mother again? We — and I mean our circle — did not allow you to be sent to a state institution where any other parentless child might have gone. We kept you among us."

"Collective guilt?" Anger truly was a much better emotion than defeat.

"In retrospect, perhaps. At the time, it seemed easier than —" Helen hesitated — "disturbing the surface of the scandal and facing what might lay beneath. Your mother . . ."

More hesitation.

"Nick," Helen said slowly, "I do know your mother had leverage over the Barrett family. And used it. But I don't know the details. You should be warned that this may lead you to knowing more about your mother than you care to understand."

"Give me the truth."

"Very well. As I said, you should speak to Geoffrey Alexander Gillon. Despite his political career, he still serves as the Barrett family attorney, at least on an informal advising level. I'm sure his name is familiar to you. I will call him tomorrow and tell him I sent you. That should be a fair trade for what I want to hear from you about the accident."

"Call him tonight. At home. Tell him I will be at his office at 7:30 tomorrow morning."

"Why the hurry?"

"Once again, my business." I will not lie. I enjoyed talking to her in this manner. "Make the call."

"I will make the call."

She leaned forward, as if she were about to say more. She was interrupted by a noise from the other side of the garden. The door to the carriage house had opened, leaking light into the garden.

"Mother!" The voice came from the figure in the doorway. A figure that carried a wineglass and stepped unsteadily out of the doorway and into the garden. "Mother, you assured me that tonight we would have our privacy."

"Nicholas Barrett arrived to pay a visit," Helen called back down into the garden. "Considering the length of his absence from Charleston, it would have been rude to turn him away."

"Nick?" The voice below was incredulous. "Nick Barrett?"

"Yes, dear. Nicholas."

"Nick." Now the woman's voice held anger. There was movement in the darkness. The figure came closer. Not until a wineglass shattered against the balcony railing did I realize the figure below had made a throwing motion in my direction.

"Forgive her," Helen said. "She stays in the carriage house and normally is an excellent guest. When she drinks, however, she loses both her sensibilities and her manners. The only consolation is that she does so privately, for fear of hurting her political dreams."

I closed my eyes. The voice below had ripped through me like grenade shards bursting a balloon.

Claire Eveleigh deMarionne.

CHAPTER 8

When I stepped out of the front door of the mansion, Ella shut the door firmly behind me, almost hitting my heels in her haste to ensure my departure. The dead bolt immediately clicked into position, another clear signal for my benefit.

Neither gesture registered on me with the effect Ella had intended. Not with my eyes drawn to the shape of a person sitting on a rocking chair halfway down the piazza.

I had half expected to see Claire after she disappeared from the garden and had certainly hoped for it, despite the intensity of longing and sorrow that had arrived with the sound of her voice reaching up to the balcony.

For years after my departure from Charleston, I had run scenes of a reunion through my head, trying to imagine her reaction to me, what I might say to her, where we might accidentally encounter each other, picturing places in Charleston or along the beach where circumstances might place her in my path. Those dreams had finally quit haunting me when I was able to bury them as adolescent speculations that had no place in my life; I had long ceased rehearsing the imagined dialog of my first words to her.

"Hello, Claire," I said now, lost for the words I had once dreamed.

"I have waited a long time for this chance," she answered. "I want you to hear me and watch me as I tell you what I have wanted to tell you for so long now."

She rose from the rocking chair. It wobbled. As did she. She moved forward, concentrating on following her feet, reaching me beneath the porch light and its fluttering moths. She stood, unsteady, less than three feet from me, tilting her head upward to stare at my face.

Dizzied by her presence, I felt a need to steady myself too.

Claire wore jeans and a loose gray sweatshirt that hung below her hips. The jeans were tight and her hips were narrow. With no makeup, the milk-soft complexion of cameo features, and hair as short as it had been when she and I floated in the ocean waves and held each other against the chill of the water, she could have still been sixteen. She had a small triangular scar just above her chin from when she had tripped into the edge of a coffee table as a five-year-old, a scar that I had always liked to gently trace with my fingertips. I nearly did so again as I returned her stare; the flood of emotions battered at the control I had learned to impose on my sorrow.

"I hate you," she said, speaking slowly in the manner that drunks use when they believe they can disguise their drunkenness. "That is what I have wanted to tell you for so long. Look in my eyes and see that hatred as I say it again. I hate you. Not because of what you did to my brother or even for what you did to me by running away. But because you never returned to give me the chance to forgive you for it."

I saw the shift of her shoulders. I had ample warning as she clumsily swung her hand. I braced myself instead of catching her wrist in my own hand, braced myself instead of swaying backward to easily miss the blow. Her hand hit me flush across the cheek.

"Coward," she said. "After he finally died, I stood at his funeral. Without you. Knowing my brother's killer had used me and discarded me."

"Claire," I said, "nothing could be further from the truth."

"Not one phone call. Not one letter." She slapped me again, an ineffectual swing that bounced off my nose in slow motion.

"I was ready to fight the entire world to keep you. I was insane with grief. Heartbroken."

"So heartbroken that you married Pendleton within months of the accident?"

She drew herself up with dignity. "Pendleton was here. You were not."

"Claire," I said, "I'm back because I wanted to tell you the truth."

"Which is?"

"Of no matter anymore. I discovered you married Pendleton."

Beyond the porch, on the street were the waters of the harbor, light from the moon gleaming off them. And beyond that, the ocean. I looked past Claire at all of it, trying to keep my mind blank. I had returned to tell her the truth, and now I was not able to do so. My first long silence over the years had been a burden I could barely endure; this new silence crushed my spirit.

"That's all you're going to say?" she asked.

"It's all I can say."

"Then you're right," she said. "Nothing between us matters. Now leave me alone."

"Claire . . ."

"Go," she said. She shifted her position and leaned against the wall, as if the conversation had exhausted her. "My life's dream has been accomplished. I told you what I wanted to tell you. I hate you. Now go away. I have no need to see you again."

"Claire . . ."

The dead bolt clicked. Ella swung open the door. As if she had been listening and waiting. "Mizz Claire," Ella said, "please come in now."

Ella put her shoulder beneath Claire's right arm and helped Claire to the doorway. Halfway inside, Ella turned and looked over Claire's shoulder.

"Good night, sir," Ella said to me. "You have outworn your welcome."

CHAPTER 9

Back in my room at the bed-and-breakfast for the second night of my return to Charleston, again I could not sleep.

It had taken hardly more than the first day for Charleston to defeat me.

I had learned I had no chance for revenge against Pendleton, also that I had no chance of finding my way back to Claire. All that remained was a search for my mother, with a fear for the answers I might find: She might be dead. Or she might be alive and that would mean she truly never wanted to be a part of my life. Ever.

In my mind echoed the anonymously sent letter that had brought me here.

Find enclosed an airline ticket and the police report that will let you return to Charleston. Five nights have been booked and paid for you at Two Meeting Street Inn. Go to the hospital and speak with Edgar Layton. You must do this soon, for Edgar has advanced colon cancer and is about to die. He has answers about your mother. He is not the only one. Ask Helen deMarionne the truth. She knew your mother best.

There was more to discover, however, than the truth about my mother.

I also wanted to know who had sent me this letter.

* * *

Of all that had happened on my first day back to Charleston, one phrase came back to me as I lay in shadows with little gratitude or appreciation for the nineteenth-century luxury that surrounded me in my room at the bed-and-breakfast.

Do you believe in a God of love?

Why had Helen asked me that?

My answer to Helen a few hours earlier would have been that I could not believe in any God unless I truly could see him in the stars.

I was an astronomer, in no small part because of that first glimpse through a telescope at the age of five. The letter that had drawn me back to Charleston had found me at a small community college in Santa Fe, teaching astronomy.

Because I'd spent my early twenties in travel, I was an older student when I finally went to college in Santa Fe, securing a bachelor's degree in science by my midtwenties. I had chosen Santa Fe because it would allow me, as a student, occasional access to its observatory, high in the clear mountain air.

I'd made friends and connections as a student — it helped that I had enough money to rent an upscale apartment and enough sense to throw semiannual discreetly lavish parties with the right people, naturally from the astronomy department. I believe I was not hampered by the traces of my southern accent or by my refusal to discuss my past except for my travel stories, for as I discovered, a one-legged man of cultivated mystery is never unattractive.

Because of my connections, when a minor teaching position opened at a nearby community college, I had no trouble getting it, despite my relative lack of academic credentials. It was only first- and second-year astronomy that I taught, well within the abilities of anyone able to read the textbooks, and the position paid poorly, so my competition for the job had not been sterling anyway. (My understanding of calculus and advanced mathematics was too pitiful for me to ever get a required Ph.D. to let me teach at a more advanced level, or better yet, involve myself in research. No, at best I was an enthusiastic layman, with sound knowledge of the workings of the sky as determined by those fortunate ones with the mathematical ability.)

I was content with my position at the college. The night sky had always fascinated me, and this gave me regular access to one of the world's most powerful telescopes.

Yet nothing I ever saw from the observatory on that New Mexico mountain ever held the place in my memory given to my first glimpse at the moon up close. I never forgot, either, the old man telling me I could see God in the stars. For what I learned showed the opposite for so long.

This was confirmed again and again for me as I continued to absorb, through books by like-minded scientists, everything possible about the cosmos.

I learned, of course, that in the early 1600s the Catholic Church had forced Galileo Galilei to drop his support of Nicolaus Copernicus's theory that Earth revolved around the sun. Theology dictated that the sun and the universe revolved around Earth, for had it not been written in Psalm 104 that God had placed the world on its foundation, never to be moved?

Even as a teenager, I found the dogmatic theology of the early Catholic Church ridiculous and, because of it, in my mind I made a clear division between faith and science, that it was one or the other. Accordingly, my reasoning went, if I had to choose between accepting the existence of God on the merit of faith or instead choose the proofs of science without God, my decision would be easy.

I was not actively agnostic, however, merely uninterested in those on the other side of science, and in particular, those on the other side of astronomy. The universe was fascinating enough without God in it.

Yet.

When I look back, I see that one of the first times God openly beckoned my soul happened in the Arizona desert.

Upon leaving Charleston, I made it my goal to circumvent the world and thought it foolish to ignore my own backyard before crossing the Pacific. I had spent three months hitchhiking westward across America. This was the time of Detroit gas-guzzlers, before the phrase *serial killer* had gained common usage in cultural parlance, when hitchhiking had a romantic innocence.

I had also determined that I would avoid the interstate highways. It seemed that I would not see much of America in an intimate way from the roaring strips of asphalt, and I had no interest in thumbing for rides at exit ramps all across the country. No, I wanted small-town cafés and quiet intersections and rides from local farmers.

This philosophy served me well.

In Arizona, I made the trek to the edge of the Grand Canyon, then headed south, through the fir-dotted mountains and finally down past Prescott and farther west until I reached the desert flats.

The rides on the narrow ribbons of isolated highway were infrequent, not because of inhospitable locals but because of the scarcity of vehicles out in the lonely heat.

At one roadside turnout, I spent five hours vainly waiting and saw no one. I did not mind. I had shade and plenty of water, and roadrunners are fascinating creatures as they scurry from mesquite to mesquite.

As dusk approached, I stuck with my policy of refusing to hitchhike in darkness, not that it was likely anyone would arrive. I pulled a picnic table far enough away from the road that I would not be detected by any passing headlights. I used my knapsack as a pillow, stretched out on top of the table, and stared upward at the dazzling show of stars.

I was looking at a four-dimensional sky,

for although we see it in two dimensions from the surface of the Earth, the tapestry of stars is woven not only in height and width, but in depth and time.

The light reaching my naked eyes on that lonely night had left some stars ten years earlier, other stars hundreds of years earlier. Had I had my telescope with me — and I purchased a small one shortly after because I regretted wasting this opportunity — I could have seen stars and galaxies of stars so far away that they had sent forth their light thousands and tens of thousands of light-years earlier.

Thus, peering into the universe is akin to peering backward into time, and this marvel alone should have given me some sense of awe of what God has done in creating something from nothing, but the shutters of my soul at that time in my life were closed tight.

Then, as if the glittering light of millions of stars on a desert night wasn't enough to nudge me toward him, God sent forth another marvel, no less wondrous than the stars above but far more rare.

Something in the early hours of the morning woke me from my sleep on that roadside picnic table fifty miles into the desert. I cannot say it was the cold, for I was not shivering. Nor was it a noise. But some instinct that alerted my body.

I struggled to my elbows and looked in all directions. When I saw what had wakened me, it took several confused moments to realize what I was seeing.

The moonlight threw silver across the coarse sand and cactus and mesquite. That silver seemed to roll across the ground, as if the sand had become a flowing live tapestry, twenty-five or thirty yards wide, just beyond the picnic table that was my bed.

I hardly dared breathe, afraid to give notice of my presence. For what I was seeing was a blanket of tarantulas, thousands upon thousands of them marching resolutely forward, surging onto the road ahead, then disappearing as my eyes lost them to shadows beyond the road.

Fully five minutes passed as this wide, heaving carpet of brown and silver streamed by me. Then they were gone, leaving me to wonder if I had imagined this vision.

In all that I have read since, I have found no explanation for this gathering of tarantulas or for the instinct that compelled them to march as one to a destination unknown to all but themselves.

I simply know that it happened, and I was there to witness it.

In a media-driven culture, it takes great effort to shake loose cynicism and view the world again with the wonder of a child. Those who do, however, will find themselves humbled and awed by all the mysteries of existence.

I sympathize with those who say it is preposterous to think that this world is moved by an invisible hand, that something or someone created it and exists beyond what we can sense. I, too, was once reluctant to accept that there might be more to life than what was visible to my eyes.

But is it a truly preposterous notion?

For without God, the universe is a place of despair.

Despair that I well knew that night in my room.

Despair that had been my companion since the summer of my tenth birthday.

For while I did not know where my mother had gone, I alone truly knew why she had abandoned me.

CHAPTER 10

The next morning in Charleston, again I decided to first check with the hostess of the bed-and-breakfast to see if anyone had left a message for me.

Although it was only 6:45 a.m., she appeared as immaculately primped as if she were ready for a dinner party. I, on the other hand, had one more day's growth of beard and wore khakis and a navy blue golf shirt.

She watched me carefully as I made my way down the curve of the staircase, noting, I'm sure, my limp.

I asked for any messages.

With a beaming smile and a covert glance over my shoulder to confirm I was still alone, she handed me an envelope. As if she had been expecting me or my request.

I turned it over and glanced at it. It had my name on the outside, in the slant of feminine handwriting.

Finally, I thought, *progress.*

I stepped onto the piazza of the elegant house before opening the envelope, fully expecting another message from the person who had sent me the airline ticket.

The envelope was unsealed. I lifted the flap and pulled out a folded piece of paper.

Lunch. 12:30 p.m. At 82 Queen. It is about your mother.

That was the total message. Same handwriting as the outside of the envelope. Unsigned. On plain paper, in a plain white envelope.

I hurried inside. "Did you see who left this?" I asked.

Her eyes widened at the possibility of intrigue. "Oh, my heavens, I did not. It was on the table just inside the door." Her eyebrows arched. "Is there anything I can help you with?"

"No," I said. I remembered where I was. The venerated South. "No, thank you, ma'am."

I walked out. I wouldn't be surprised if she had read the note herself and was as curious as I was about who had left it for me.

April had brought the low country its usual blue skies, clear as if seen through polished glass, not yet hazed by wilting summer heat; with the sunshine came the familiar fragrance of magnolias from the hidden gardens of the ancient mansions. The beauty of the morning lifted my spirits some. Much as it might hurt my leg, I chose not to take a cab; few destinations were far in this cloistered southern end of the peninsula that made old Charleston.

I walked around the rocking chairs on the mansion porch, ducked beneath a hanging basket of ferns, and stepped down to the brick path on the trimmed lawn. I headed east half a block, staying within the shadows of the oaks of White Point Gardens, until a turn took me up Church Street.

During the summer of my fourteenth birthday, I would rise early each day and take this same route up Church, following it as it changed from the narrow cobblestone south of Broad to wider pavement as it neared Market, heading ten blocks north where the carriage houses drew tourist trade for horse-and-buggy rides.

At that hour, just after the sun had burned away any mist over the tidal rivers and the marsh flats, before the bustle of cars and the clatter of horse hooves, the wind had not had a chance to build, nor had the clouds of afternoon thunderstorms. In the almost magical peace among buildings two or three centuries old, on crooked cobblestone streets disturbed only by the warbling of songbirds flitting among the branches of the blossomed trees that overhung the sidewalks, I liked to imagine I was part of an earlier time, when the ships brought in slaves and took away bales of cotton, or when soldiers in gray darted from house to house, or when the women daintily picked their way across mud streets as they fanned themselves beneath parasols. I wanted to live in any other time but the time of my boyhood, before the Barrett name had become a burden of legacy generations old.

Other times during those walks of my fourteenth summer, I would imagine that I was seven or eight years old, before I had driven my mother away, and that all I had to do was reach out with my hand and she would smile and reach for my hand in return. I would be able to point at one old building leaning into another, and she would describe to me how each had survived any of Charleston's varied tribulations — the War of Northern Aggression, the earthquake of 1886, the great hurricane of 1911, and the assorted fires of each — explaining the monstrous iron braces that workmen had used to straighten and tighten the buildings.

Those summers — before my mother had left me, when I had her to myself for a few precious hours each day — were so perfect I wasn't sure I could trust my memory of a woman so pretty sometimes she would catch me staring at her long dark hair or her flawless features or the black eyes that shone with so much life. Before I had driven her away, we would wander the old streets, and the music in her voice would cradle me as she told stories about the people and the buildings. From her, I had absorbed not only Charleston's history, but her fascination for the pirates and plantation managers and slaves and gunrunners and soldiers, seeing them through her eyes so clearly it was as if they walked the streets or sat on the piazzas of the old mansions as ghosts.

Of what little my mother had left me upon her departure, it was this gift — the knowledge and love of Charleston's history — that I traded upon during that summer. At Market Street, I would wait for the first tourists to spill out of the hotels and offer to guide them, walking them past the buildings on Church Street I knew so well, past the old Planter's Hotel that was now a stage theater, past St. Philip's Church with its wedding-cake spire, once saved from fire by a black boatman who called the alarm and was rewarded for it with a grant of freedom, past the pirate house where Blackbeard himself may have traded goods with the town's gentry.

Most of the tourists I guided were older women — Yankee schoolteachers or bored wives of rich businessmen — perhaps charmed by the earnestness of a gangly boy in a pressed shirt and ironed pants.

In looking back, I wonder if what drew them was my sorrow and innocence and southern accent. For I'm certain I was not the best guide, yet when I finished the one- or two-hour walk with my customers, they unfailingly tipped me as much as I had charged them for the tour.

Except for the memories my walk up Church Street now brought me, that four-teen-year-old boy was a stranger to me. What little I shared with that boy — and only when I permitted myself the weakness — was the remnant of that sorrow, an un-defined longing, like the nearly invisible current of a slow, deep river carrying the soul forward to an unknown destination.

CHAPTER 11

At 7:30 a.m., I walked into the office of Senator Geoffrey Alexander Gillon.

I expected the wheelchair. Senator Gillon had been in one as a high-profile public figure since my boyhood, and he shrewdly played the sympathy raised by it to his advantage during photo ops and political campaigns. What did surprise me was the size of the senator's private law office overlooking Charleston Harbor on Vendue Range, something I immediately guessed that Gillon equally shrewdly underplayed, for he met constituents in a smaller, spartan office on King Street, paid for by state funds.

The Vendue Range street name had been given in honor of the Vendue masters who had brought Charleston its first boom of wealth through their auctioneering skills. As a young lawyer still scheming for senatorship, Gillon had purchased one of the wharf's warehouses before Charleston's heritage movement had made them fashionable, before conversion of the ancient brick shells into offices and homes and restaurants had dispelled the ghostly echoes of long-dead auctioneers and slaves with the tinkle of contrived laughter and replaced the forgotten dust of cotton bales and bags of plantation rice with the burnished wax of gleaming hardwood.

Geoffrey Alexander Gillon's vanity led him to the frequent public complaint that his real ambition had been to secure something suitable on the nearby tiny street named after his distant ancestor, a complaint that gave Gillon the chance to draw attention to the historical Alexander Gillon who had captured three British vessels — two without firing a shot — during the British blockade of Charleston in 1777. Because of the Revolutionary-era Alexander Gillon, Geoffrey insisted that he always be addressed as Geoffrey Alexander, as if Geoffrey feared his continuous references to a famous ancestor might otherwise be overlooked or forgotten. Senator Gillon referred to him as the "other Alexander," suggesting a closeness that verged on ridiculous, considering the distance imposed by two centuries and a much-fragmented family tree with more than its fair share of scoundrels.

It was one of Geoffrey's favorite stories, recounting how the "other Alexander" had bested the even more famous Charles Pinckney during a convention to consider the newly proposed Constitution. Charles Pinckney, as Geoffrey Alexander told each new audience with great animation, had clarified a point of debate by using a lengthy phrase of Latin; Geoffrey Alexander's ancestor rose to thank Pinckney for his considerable erudition and went on to conclude his own remarks in high Dutch, thereby ensuring that no more Latin was quoted during the entire debate. While the story was only mildly amusing, it served a deeper purpose, allowing Geoffrey Alexander Gillon to subtly remind his audience of his family ties to the shaping of the Constitution.

"I am surprised to see you," said Geoffrey Alexander Gillon, rolling his wheelchair out from behind a massive mahogany desk. His office was the entire back half of the second floor of the converted warehouse. Walnut bookshelves lined the long walls. Diplomas, citations, honorary degrees, and separate photos of Gillon with three previous presidents filled the spaces around the bookshelves. The wall at the far end of the office was glass, mirrored to the outside, giving a spectacular panoramic view of the harbor while keeping the privacy within.

"Helen deMarionne arranged this within

the last twelve hours. I doubt you are surprised."

"Prickly, aren't you." The rubber of his wheelchair tires squeaked on the hardwood floor at his turn around the desk. Gillon continued, crossing the expanse of the office over several hand-hooked rugs until he stopped short of me. "What I meant, as you well know, was that I find it a surprise that you have returned to Charleston."

"Worried you'd made a mistake in the legal agreement I signed before I left?"

He chuckled as if I had meant the remark in good humor.

During his trial years, Gillon had learned to play it folksy in front of jurors and was unable, or unwilling, to lose his habit of dragging his vowels more deliberately than most. He also favored his own interpretation of the southern look, which, if he had worn a white suit with a dark bow tie, would have made him a replica of Colonel Sanders of KFC. He had a square, heavy head, thick white hair, a mustache almost wide enough to form handlebar curls, a trim goatee, and round spectacles. The decorum of his political office ensured, however, that he did not wear white, but instead a well-pressed gray suit with a rose-colored dress shirt and navy tie.

He had a file folder in his lap, one that I knew had been there before my arrival, because when I had entered the office, Gillon had been twiddling a pen and had not pulled anything off the desk before approaching me.

Gillon offered me the folder.

"Is the fact that you haven't offered me a chair deliberate?" I asked, ignoring the folder in Gillon's outstretched hand.

Gillon's sudden smile gave me a wide view of thousands of dollars' worth of porcelain-capped teeth. I saw, too, the powder of makeup on Gillon's nose. Smelled the wafting expensive cologne.

"Can't escape my trial-lawyer habits," Gillon said. "It's a real advantage to make the opposition uncomfortable with my handicap. And I didn't know which way this meeting would go."

"Make it easy on us," I said. "Cut the garbage. Unless you want me parading my handicap too. You do remember it, don't you?"

I stared at Gillon until he looked away. He gestured with the folder at a black leather chair behind a coffee table. The sitting area of the office.

I moved to the chair. Gillon followed with a slow roll of rubber tires. When I was settled, Gillon offered me the folder again. I took it, opened it, glanced at it briefly, and set it down on the coffee table.

"Yes," I said. "Your point?"

"That's why I am surprised that you have returned to Charleston. By breaking the conditions of agreement, you now forfeit a sizable monthly stipend. And, I might add, leave yourself open to unfiled criminal charges."

"You ever offer visitors a cigar?"

"In a humidor on the bookshelf on my desk," Gillon said. "While less hospitable than fetching one for you, it would be more expedient if you helped yourself."

"Sure," I said, rising again, "especially since a man with one good leg and half of another is faster than a man in a wheelchair."

I found the cigars — Cuban as expected — and a cutter and a silver lighter. I returned to the chair, clipped the end of the cigar, sniffed the fresh tobacco, and twisted the cigar in a slow circle as I lit the end.

"Obviously you are an aficionado," Gillon said. "You should enjoy this one. I have friends in Miami and —"

"The whole cigar image thing is a crock," I said. "I can't imagine a fouler way to pollute taste buds. Or anything more absurd than a pack of men using them as weapons of posture."

"Then why . . . ?"

"Cigars have their uses." I picked up the manila folder. I held the glowing cigar tip to the end of it and blew gently until flames curled upward around the paper. I held the folder until half of it had blackened in the rising flames, then dropped it on the coffee table.

"This table is an heirloom!" Gillon sputtered, whacking the flames out with a magazine. "Have you lost your mind!"

"Just angry." I ground out the cigar on the heirloom table. "And getting angrier. You're the first person Pendleton would have called after I visited him yesterday. You know there's nothing left to give that agreement any power. And you know why I'm angry. So I shall repeat myself. Cut the garbage."

Blackened wisps of paper floated in the air between us. Gillon stared in disbelief at the remnants of a fifty-dollar cigar on the coffee table and the circle of burned varnish where I had stubbed the cigar.

"Fine, then," Gillon said, raising his head. "No games. Helen called and said you had received a letter that brought you back to search for your mother. Tell me about this letter."

"No," I said. "I'm sure Pendleton informed you about the police report that came with that letter. That's the only thing you need to know. I'm not here to give you answers. I'm here to get answers. About my mother. You do recall my mother."

"Now you're the one playing games. I was robbed, shot, and left to die on the very same weekend your mother ran away. One of those shots hit my spine. This wheelchair reminds me every day of that weekend. And of the fact that more time and resources were spent on finding your mother than on the men who broke into my home and shot me."

"I didn't know," I said. "I was ten at the time. You were still years away from being the man behind a set of papers that put me into exile."

Gillon looked steadily into my eyes. "You were well taken care of. At least I fought them for that."

I stared back until Gillon was forced to look away.

"Tell me about my mother," I said. "Tell me about that weekend. I understand from Helen that she stopped here to get my trust fund money from you."

Gillon did not look up from the buffed fingernails of his manicured hands where they lay flat and still on the thighs of his useless legs.

"There's not much I can tell you," Gillon said. "All I can remember unusual about the afternoon — aside from her insistence on getting the trust fund money immediately for reasons that became clear soon after — was the tiny gash on her cheek. I recall it well because I remember thinking it needed one or two stitches to heal properly. And I remember she seemed upset when I asked why she wanted to leave town so suddenly."

I hid a shiver of anguish. At his recollection of the gash on her cheek. And why she was upset. That was my secret. And my sin. I would share neither.

"What seems more strange to me is that you complied with her request," I said. Helen's words of the evening before came back to me: *I do know your mother had leverage over the Barrett family. And used it.* "Why would you write her a check for such a large sum? And why on short notice as she demanded?"

Gillon's face hardened. "My advice is that you leave this alone. Your mother made her choice when she ran from

Charleston. I'm sure she now has regrets, wherever she is. She must wonder whether the money she stole was worth giving up her home, her son, her future grandchildren. But obviously the regrets haven't been strong enough to bring her back."

"You're still playing games. Helen deMarionne would not have sent me here without a reason. By disappointing me, you will disappoint her. How much does she contribute to your campaign war chests?"

"Nasty," Gillon said. "Interested in going back to school? You'd be a great lawyer."

"I'm interested in what you know about my mother. Tell me. It will keep Helen happy."

"What could I possibly help you with?"

"My mother's maid was her best friend. A Gullah woman. She'd know best what my mother was thinking before she ran away. Only she disappeared immediately after my mother left. I'd like to find her now."

A picture came into my mind. Ruby. Our maid. Laughing over a cup of tea as she sat with my mother in the kitchen. It seemed they were always laughing together. I hadn't found it strange because that's the

134

way it had always been between the two of them.

Instead of answering, Gillon backed his wheelchair away from the coffee table that separated us. He rolled to the window and looked out over the harbor for several minutes.

"Indulge me first," Gillon said. He wheeled around and faced me. Against the sunlight, he was a dark outline, a hunched figure. "The canceled cashier checks of the monthly payments you received, all of them were sent to me to keep on file. For a few years those cashier checks were returned from banks in different places across the world, then one spot repeatedly for another few years. With interest and adjustments for inflation, over two million dollars. What did you spend it on?"

"What makes you certain I spent it?" I asked. "At the beginning when you actually sent the checks. I haven't seen one for the last two years."

"I only sent what Helen gave me."

"She's broke? The great Helen deMarionne?"

He ignored my question. "I know you spent it the same way I know you don't own any real estate or a boat or anything that's a tangible asset. Until it becomes

135

cash, money leaves a trail, Nick. A musky lion spoor that trackers like me with connections into banks and government can follow like phosphorus footprints under a full moon. Where did all that cash go? Drugs? Women? Gambling?"

"What I did with it is my own business," I said. "I paid a high enough price for it."

"It has been a long time since any of my indulgences were refused." Strangely, he smiled. "The Mount Carmel African Methodist Episcopal Church."

He answered my unspoken question. "Ruby. You can find her at the church."

I knew where it was. I was in no mood to thank Gillon, so I didn't. I walked to the door, doing my best to hide my limp. When I reached the door, I stopped. "You're the one who found me, then. Through the cashier's checks that you traced."

"Yes," Gillon said from the window. "For another lawyer's client."

"Then you know who sent me the police report and letter."

"No. This lawyer insisted on keeping his client confidential. At the time, I did not care. I was well paid for finding you. Something I now regret."

"Stirrings of a conscience?" I asked.

"A conscience is too noble and too foolish," Gillon said. "Until Pendleton called me after your visit, I had no idea you would receive what you did once that client found you. Those secrets haven't been buried long enough."

I opened the door.

"Take my advice," Gillon called to me. "It's not often I offer it without my extravagant hourly fee. There are men of great power in this city who do not want the past revisited. These men may be old, but their kind of power does not necessarily diminish in tandem with hearing and eyesight and thinning hair."

"Men like you?" I asked.

"Men like me."

CHAPTER 12

"This chair," I said. "A recent acquisition?"

I'd carried it to the back of the antique shop. It was the high-back mahogany chair I'd noticed the day before, the one with talons for feet, each clutching a smooth ball.

Glennifer was in the act of pouring tea into a fine china cup. Two other cups with matching saucers waited beside it on her desk. I'd arrived a few minutes earlier, much to their unfeigned delight. They each wore a black dress; all that had changed from their appearances the day before were their necklaces. On anyone else, I would have suspected jewels that large to be fake. Not, however, on them.

"You do have a good eye for antiques, Nicholas," Elaine said in answer to my question. Pencils stuck out from various places in the netting of her piled hair. She had a habit, it appeared, of putting a pencil in, then forgetting about it as she reached for another from the desktop. "To re-member it after all these years away is a re-markable feat of —"

"Laney!" Glennifer stopped in midpour. "Remember our little talk yesterday? No more information for this young man unless he gives us some in return. If we ran our shop with this same kind of careless regard for value, we'd be even more impoverished than we are."

I smiled. "So it did belong to Helen deMarionne."

Glennifer sighed defeat and resumed pouring the tea.

"Glenny?" Elaine asked.

"Why stop now?" Glennifer answered. "The damage is already done, my dear. He was smart as a young boy and obviously that hasn't changed."

"Helen brought it in two months ago," Elaine said to me. "Really, we gave her more than we should have, but it's a fine piece. Unmistakably unique, wouldn't you agree?"

"I believe," I said, "that it must have been painful for her to sell it."

"Most definitely. We've made great profits selling her items over the years, watching her use money instead of bloodline to hold her head high. To that woman, fine furnishings are a way to purchase the heritage she never had. It is my impression they are more important to her than life."

Indeed.

I was thirteen. In the deMarionne mansion. In the dining room. A fan clicked on its bearings above me, its wide, painted wooden blades bleeding away some of the summer heat.

I was on my knees, trying to pick up the pieces of a Greek statuette, when Helen deMarionne walked into the room. From my perspective so close to the floor, I mainly saw legs perched on red high heels, for she wore a short thin-strapped summer dress. Behind her was Lorimar Barrett, Pendleton's father. They'd been sitting on a screen porch hidden from the world. He had a crew cut, matching the one in photographs of his brother, the man my mother had married, then betrayed with my conception. Lorimar wore a white shirt beneath suspenders, his tie loosened. He held a glass of bourbon, swirling it against ice and watching me with disdain as Helen interrogated me.

"What are you doing?"

"It fell," I said lamely.

The sound of it breaking against the tile floor of the dining room had brought her in.

"Obviously it fell," she said. "And obviously it broke. Do you think collecting the pieces and gluing them together will somehow restore it?"

"I —"

"You nothing. That was worth five thousand dollars. Do you hear me?"

Some of the smaller houses in Charleston sold for less than that. I knew this because Pendleton tracked real estate in an obsessive way. Already, with his father's encouragement at the Barrett dinner table, he talked about buying slum properties and renting them.

"I hear you," I said.

"Well?"

"I hear you," I repeated.

"What I meant," she said, moving her hands on her hips, "was how are you going to pay for it?"

She knew what I knew. I did not have a hope of finding five thousand dollars.

She glared at me, waiting for my reply. My humiliation was completed by the presence of Lorimar Barrett, who merely stared at me with half-lidded eyes and sipped his bourbon.

Worse, my own eyes flicked in the direction of Helen's legs, drawn by the tanned skin over smooth taut muscles. I gulped at involuntary pubescent speculations, inappropriate at any time, and certainly not somewhere I would have directed thoughts deliberately in this moment.

When I lifted my eyes to hers again, she stared directly into my eyes, as if she had read my mind.

I felt myself blush.

She spun, swirling that short skirt. "Let's go," she said to Lorimar. "We'll have the maid clean it up. I suppose one shouldn't expect much from a boy like him."

Like that, they dismissed me from their thoughts.

When the door shut behind them, Claire tiptoed in from where she'd been waiting in the kitchen.

I was still on my knees, my stomach knotted with shame and anger.

"Thank you," Claire whispered. She leaned down and kissed my forehead. "If she knew I broke it, she would have made my life unbearable."

I asked the obvious question.

"Why does Helen now need to sell her precious heritage?"

"Tsk, tsk, young man." Glennifer handed me my teacup on its saucer. "We do have questions of our own."

"I've learned that my mother was given my trust fund money before she left

Charleston. She did not steal it as the newspaper reported. That's all I can tell you for now."

Elaine clapped her hands. "I knew it. I knew it. All those years ago, right here behind this very desk, I turned to Glenny and said your mother was too good a woman to do it. Didn't I, Glenny? Didn't I?"

"It was I who told you."

"Nonsense. I told you. Remember the day. It was just before Theodore Crane, bless his soul, brought in the wardrobe with the hideous glue patch where he'd tried to repair it himself."

"Of course I remember the day. It wasn't a wardrobe, however, but a chest of drawers. And the hinges clearly showed it was fake. It was no less than an hour after he departed that I turned to you and —"

"Why does Helen now need to sell her precious heritage?" I asked again.

Each of them stopped, puzzled. It took them a moment to get their bearings in the present.

"You would have to ask Pendleton," Elaine said moments later.

"I doubt he wants to speak to Pendleton," Glennifer said in a theatrical whisper. "Remember, Laney? Claire."

To me, Glennifer said, "You did elope

143

with Claire? At least confirm that."

"I did elope with Claire."

"See, Laney? He wouldn't want to have anything to do with Pendleton."

"What would Pendleton know about Helen starting to sell off antiques?" I asked, ignoring the stab of pain.

"It's not what he knows," Glennifer said. "It's what he's done."

"Oh yes," Elaine added enthusiastically. "Some say his secret vice is gambling, but that's a rumor I won't place any stock in whatsoever. I think something he's done has caught up with him and he's paying for it. Maybe he's fathered a child in one of his numerous affairs. Maybe —"

"What we've heard," Glennifer said, "is that he's taken money from places he shouldn't. Let's leave it at that. And we won't even get started on the fact that Claire has been known to wear dark sunglasses on cloudy days and cover her face with makeup."

Was this why Claire had left him? He beat her? I wanted to ask, but the conversation continued around me, as if I weren't there.

"He's a brute," Elaine agreed. "Like his father."

"But Lorimar wasn't a thief. Or if he

144

was, he was smart enough not to get caught."

"Places he shouldn't?" I decided to go with that strand of Pendleton's character. "Pendleton's taken money from Helen deMarionne?"

"Laney, not a word," Glennifer said firmly.

"It was blackmail," I said. "Not gambling. Pendleton's been blackmailed for years. I know who's been doing it. And I know why."

"Perhaps we don't need to leave it at that," Glennifer said.

"Oodles," Elaine said. "He's taken oodles from Helen. Real estate pyramid things. But you didn't hear it here."

"Thank you." I finished my cup of tea and stood. "Perhaps I'll stop by tomorrow."

"You can't leave! You didn't tell us about the —"

"Blackmail?"

"Exactly."

"Tomorrow," I said. I had a feeling I would have more questions for them by then. "See you then."

CHAPTER 13

Lunch. 12:30 p.m. At 82 Queen. It is about your mother.

I was early and waiting at the restaurant for the person who had left the note earlier at the bed-and-breakfast. Layton had been asleep, there'd been no sign of his daughter, and a short cab ride took me back to the old quarters of Charleston.

Eighty-two Queen was a street address and also the name of an elegant restaurant in the historic core. I sat in a courtyard of the restaurant, an open sky above me, among live oaks and palmettos. Lights were strung from tree to tree on invisible wires. At night those lights would give a luxurious glow, like stars set into the darkness above. I knew this because I had brought Claire here, only once, before our elopement. As with most of the rest of Charleston, I could not escape the ghosts of memories.

Now the sky was pastel blue, and touches of a breeze reached me in the courtyard. I watched the entrance, unable to guess at who might arrive. I was convinced, however, it would be the person who had sent me the airline ticket and letter and old police report.

When I saw her, I knew my guess was wrong, for it was the daughter of one of the men I hated.

I stood to greet her, hiding my surprise at her arrival. The day before, in Edgar Layton's hospital room, this woman had made it clear she did not want to see me.

And now she was here.

* * *

Our table sat in shade, with the brightness of a clear midday providing a pleasant warmth among the perfume of flower blossoms.

"This is fine? Outside?"

"More than fine." She allowed me to move her chair for her as she sat. "Thank you."

I took my own place, glad I could look at her directly. If I had been at another table, it would have been rude to stare.

She had tied her hair back, and it showed the classic lines of her face. She had replaced the dismal browns and blacks of yesterday's clothing with a navy skirt and jacket. This woman was beautiful.

"My name is Amelia Layton," she said.

"Nicholas Barrett," I said. "Nick."

"I know." Before I could try to make

sense of that cryptic remark, she continued. "I'm sorry for yesterday's rudeness."

"The circumstances," I said, "were less than ideal. You have my sympathy."

"As you do mine."

Another cryptic remark. I wasn't sure why she thought I needed her sympathy.

"Well, Nick Barrett," she said, "I am interested in knowing how you make a living."

"It's a good way to get an immediate handle on someone," I said, trying to be flippant. "What do you do?"

By the tone of her voice, I knew immediately my attempt had not worked.

"I'm a physician. I specialize in heart problems. I'm single and work-obsessed, which hides a fear of getting hurt by yet another man. Does that let you judge me sufficiently?"

No smile from her. I wished I could understand the reason for her tension.

"I'm an astronomer of sorts," I said, trying to lighten the mood by smiling. "More to the point, I teach the subject at a community college. In Santa Fe, New Mexico."

"And I live in Chicago," she said. "Obviously neither of us wanted to add to the limited gene pool of old Charleston."

"Obviously not." I let that rest. There were too many painful memories with that remark. "Are you hungry?"

"This is why you have my sympathy," she said, pushing some papers toward me. "And no, I'm not particularly interested in lunch."

I took them from her. They were photo-copies of newspaper articles, arranged chronologically.

I scanned the progression of headlines because I did not need to read the articles.

TRUST FUND DISAPPEARS
NAVY CONFIRMS BARRETT BOYFRIEND
    IS ABSENT WITHOUT LEAVE
MISAPPROPRIATION OF NAVAL FUNDS
    LINKED TO MISSING ENSIGN
FBI BEGINS NATIONWIDE SEARCH FOR
    CHARLESTON COUPLE
FUGITIVE COUPLE NARROWLY EVADES
    FBI HOTEL SEARCH
NEW SIGHTING PLACES FUGITIVE
    COUPLE NEAR MEXICO BORDER

I gave her back the photocopied sheets.

"That was your mother," she said. "Car-olyn Barrett. Involved in this scandal."

"Yes." Although I had been facing this

since I was a boy, it hurt no less because of the passage of time.

"After you left the hospital, I went to the newspaper office," she said. "I needed to know more before I spoke with you."

"Now you know." My voice was flat.

"Why do you think my father is involved?"

"How did you know to look into the story?" I asked in return. "It happened when I was a child. In the hospital yesterday, all I told you was that I wanted to speak to your father about my mother."

"Why do you think my father is involved?" she repeated. Her face had a stubborn set. If this was poker, I had lost.

"I recently received a letter," I said. "I don't know who sent it. But it directed me to your father."

"Will you tell me the specifics of the letter?"

"I would rather not," I answered. Although its directive echoed in my mind.

Go to the hospital and speak with Edgar Layton. You must do this soon, for Edgar has advanced colon cancer and is about to die. He has answers about your mother.

"I need to know more about my father

too," she said. "Otherwise I wouldn't be here with you right now."

"Why do you need to know more? And why do you think I have any information that would help?"

She shook her head.

I could not tell if it was a gesture of amused irony or sad resignation.

"Do you believe she did it?"

"Steal the trust fund money?" I answered. "Take a train and leave with her boyfriend?"

Amelia nodded. She kept her eyes on mine.

"I don't want to believe it," I said. "Will you tell me how you know?"

"It wasn't until you mentioned my birthday that I realized why you were in the hospital room to see my father," Amelia said. "And that's why I went to the newspaper after visiting you yesterday."

"I didn't mention your birthday."

"Yes, you did. July 12. Like you, it is a date I will never forget. I was eight years old on that Friday. I remember your mother because of that. I am only telling you this because it would be extremely unfair to keep it from you."

"Keep what from me?"

"There was a witness," she answered.

"Who?" I asked.

"Me."

Amelia told me her story without emotion. She described them to me in detail, the remnants of the day of her eighth birthday. She spoke steadily, without pause, as if she had waited a long time to tell anyone.

"I can't remember a happier day in my life. My present that morning was a birthday dress made of this red velvety material that I thought was finer than anything any queen had worn. All morning, I would run to my bedroom and model it alone in front of my mirror, hardly able to wait until my neighborhood friends came for cake and candles. And long after they had left, I still wore that dress.

"Night was different than day. Because at night, the yelling would begin. I knew my mother had a bottle that she hid under the dirty clothes in the laundry room. By supper time, she would move slowly and carefully. I never needed to hear her speak to know she had spent the day with that bottle. She never spoke when he yelled at her, just smiled at him sadly, which only made the yelling worse.

"That night it hurt me more, only because my day had been so happy. So I went up to my bedroom, but I could hear everything. I went outside. His car was there, his police cruiser that he would sometimes flash the lights or hit the siren just to make me proud. He was the police chief and people treated me differently because of it. I liked that, especially because he was always so gentle and kind with me. He never yelled at me.

"I sat inside the car. In the back. I tried to think about my birthday, not that he was yelling at her more and more. I began to cry, and I lay down on the backseat.

"It was dark, of course. A hot night where the air felt like a blanket. And I fell asleep. No one came looking. They thought I was upstairs in my bedroom.

"He had this thing about the interior light of his car. He disconnected it because he hated the backdrop of light that would show his outline whenever he stepped out of the car during the night. So when he opened the door later that night, the inside of the car stayed dark.

"He didn't know I was in the back. And when I woke up, it was too late. The car was moving. I was too afraid to tell him I was there. I should have. But the longer I remained quiet, the angrier I thought he would be when he finally found out. So I crept forward and lay down on the floor.

"I remember closing my eyes, as if that would keep me hidden. The car turned a few times and when it stopped, he opened the door and left me behind. He took so long that I finally became brave enough to get on my knees on the floor of the backseat and peek through the window.

"I saw him standing in a doorway. Talking to a woman. She had a suitcase beside her. I ducked down again.

"It seemed like forever until he came back. When he did, he wasn't alone. The woman didn't say anything, but I knew it was that woman. I'll never forget it.

"Perfume filled the car. I was still wearing my red velvety birthday dress, and I was hidden on the floor of the back of the car as he drove away with a strange woman."

❋ ❋ ❋

"That's it?" I said.

Amelia had stopped, a faraway look in her eyes.

"Enough of it," she answered. "And enough that you should at least return the favor. What do you know about my father? Why did you go to the hospital?"

"How can you be sure that woman was my mother . . . ?"

"The number on the house. It was the same number as the address of the woman in the newspaper stories. I looked it up in the phone book. And I also knew because they went to the train station. The stories said that too. She ran away with her boy-friend by train."

Growing up without my mother, I'd sometimes hoped, in a way that brought me confused fear, that perhaps she had fallen victim to a violent crime. That she had died, painful as that might be to me, was less painful than thinking she had run away. Now I could not harbor that guilty hope. All that was left was the equally guilty hope that she had died sometime after leaving Charleston. That had been another of my daydreams — that she had not abandoned me, only gone elsewhere to make us a better home, then died before she could return for me.

"Did she say anything while your father was driving her there?" I asked Amelia. "Anything that would give you a hint of her intentions?"

"No," Amelia answered quickly.

Too quickly?

"Nothing at all? Nothing to tell you why

the chief of police would help her leave Charleston one day, then begin a search for her the next?"

"Nothing, I said."

Something in the set of her face told me there was more.

"Can we meet tomorrow?" I asked. "Maybe by then I'll know more that can help you."

"Noon," she said.

We decided to meet at my bed-and-breakfast. "Thank you," I said. "At least now I know my mother is alive. Or was alive when she left me."

But I was lying when I expressed this gratitude. It appeared the only alternative to her death was that she had truly abandoned me.

Because then I could only blame myself.

CHAPTER 14

It was a small white chapel, the Mount Carmel African Methodist Episcopal Church. It was located in Charleston's East Side, between upper King and the river. The neighborhood around it was a stark contrast to the exquisite mansions gracing the waterfront less than a mile south.

In this neighborhood, windows on two-bedroom houses were boarded with plywood, faded and gray. Instead of manicured grass, the yards were worn to dirt, with broken bottles as ornaments. At one point, the people of this neighborhood had been the direct descendants of slaves. Now, most of them were servants and street cleaners. Charleston's racism was never blatant, but all the more powerful because of its insidiousness.

The grounds of the church were mowed neatly; the old wood siding was coated with fresh paint. No one answered the rapping of my knuckles on the church door.

By then, I could already guess why Gillon had sent me here if I wanted to find Ruby Atkins, my mother's maid.

The ancient cemetery.

I stood at the side of the church where

the cemetery was fenced off with white pickets clear of weeds. I began to search the headstones for a name.

I stopped in front of a small, rounded gray tombstone. Decades of exposure to rain and wind had blurred the engraved letters to barely legible grooves in the granite.

It struck me that even in sunlight, cemeteries have an eerie softness of time and sound. As if those alive grow smaller in the presence of the reminder of death — some smaller with fear and some smaller with a longing driven by the soul's instinct. A longing for beyond.

Was it preposterous to think that this world was moved by an invisible hand, that something or someone created it and existed beyond what we could sense? After all — from stars a thousand light-years away to a silent march of tarantulas in the desert to the miracle of birth — life itself was a humbling mystery.

I existed because of sunlight and water and dirt. My flesh and blood and bones were nourished by bread from the wheat that drew from moisture and sunlight and soil, strengthened by the meat of animals that fed upon those plants, sustained by the water that fell from the skies and collected in rivers and lakes.

In the macrocosm, the earth turned, the moon remained its fixed distance from the earth, all of the planets spun a dance around the sun, and the sun itself maintained a delicate balance between collapse and explosion, all of this held together by gravity that we could predict but could not explain. In the microcosm, subatomic particles were held together by the faintest pulses of electromagnetism, where particles flickered into energy and energy flickered into particles, so that in a very true sense, we consisted merely of impulses of electricity.

What an incredible, inconceivable process, dulled simply because we saw it and lived it every day.

That night in the desert, seeing the carpet of tarantulas move to an unknown destination, I still would have rejected any argument that God might be behind my existence, for I was blind, determined to live the illusion of self-sufficiency.

Now, when I stopped to consider all these mysteries, it seems equally preposterous to think such a world could exist without the unseen hand of a Creator.

In the sunshine, in the cemetery, I felt cold. Alone. With my hope for Claire gone, all I had left was to find the answer to my mother's absence. At best I would find she was dead. At worst, that she was alive somewhere and had no love or curiosity for me. But until I found these answers, I saw no place to go with my life.

I continued to search for Ruby Atkins, and when I found her, I understood why Geoffrey Alexander Gillon had smiled in that strange manner when he had informed me where to find her.

She'd been buried here.

I should have wondered how Gillon knew. But that wouldn't occur to me until it was much too late.

I was staring at the letters chiseled into granite as a large woman rounded the corner of the church. She was an old black woman, who moved as if her shoes fit too tightly against corns and bunions. She wore a loose, multicolored dress that gave indication of her bulk yet concealed the exact lines of her massive body.

"What bidness you got here?" she demanded. "What you doing amongst all those dead folk?"

She covered the distance from the church to the graveyard and stood close enough for me to hear her labored breathing as she continued to squint at me in suspicion.

"I was looking for someone I was told I could find at this church."

"Middle of the week? Only two people here is my husband Samuel and me. He's pastor of this fine church, gone today to visit his ailing brother. And I just stopped by to practice at the organ."

Her hands went to her hips. "I know you ain't here for me or him. So's whoever told you to come here looking is as big a fool as the person what listened. And I guess I'm looking at one of those two fools right now."

I smiled. "Yes, ma'am. I'd agree with you, except I did find who I was looking for. Ruby Atkins. Trouble is, I didn't expect to find she was resting in peace."

"What bidness you got, looking for Ruby? It's been years since the Lord took her home."

"She worked in my mother's household," I said.

"She was your mama's maid is what you're saying. Don't need to pretty it up for me, like there was some shame in what Ruby did to get bread for her family."

"Yes, ma'am. I do apologize."

"Your mama's maid. What call you got

to look for your mama's maid?"

"I was hoping to ask her some questions."

"C'ain't ask a dead person questions."

"Yes, ma'am. I didn't realize she was dead until I found the tombstone."

The old woman would have none of my excuses. "Who you be?" she demanded.

"Nick Barrett."

The old woman gave a groan of surprise. "Your mama was Carolyn Barrett!"

She tottered closer and grabbed my wrist. "Tomorrow. Come back tomorrow when my Samuel is here. Me and my Samuel's been waiting a long time for you."

CHAPTER 15

During lunch, Amelia had given me permission to visit her father. She'd suggested late afternoon. So it was, with the day beginning to lose its heat, that I walked down the hallway to his room once again.

This time, when I politely rapped my knuckles against the door to room 2553, I found Edgar Layton awake and sitting in bed, dressed in dark blue silk pajamas and watching ESPN on the color television mounted from the ceiling above his bed.

The old man gave his attention to me. His eyes glowed from beneath the bony brows of his large head.

"You some sort of preacher or charity worker? I thought I'd scared all of you away. It's been a week since anybody tried to save me from eternal damnation." Layton's legs were covered by a blanket. Beside his left leg, on top of the blanket, was the remote control for the television. Layton lifted the remote and clicked off the television. "But go ahead, sit down. One form of entertainment is as good as the next."

I had tried this scene out in my head a dozen different ways. In the end, I had decided this depended on Layton's vulnerability to the close approach of death. Wondered if Layton actually had the answers in the first place.

In all the ways I had gone through it, I'd not once expected to find myself so skittish, filled with nervous adrenaline.

I pulled up a chair. "No preacher," I said. "Nicholas Barrett."

Layton's intense glowing eyes stared at me, like lit candles from the depths of a carved-out pumpkin.

I stared back at the formidable bone structure of the man's face and head. The man had been there for both of the tragedies in my life. Looming way above me when I was ten, his chief of police's hat throwing a big shadow, the deep raspy voice telling me I was better off without a no-good tramp of a mother. And when I was nineteen, helping the ambulance driver pull me out from behind the steering wheel of a wrecked Plymouth Valiant, shining a flashlight hard in my eyes, the same deep raspy voice boring into me from behind that light and cussing me out for stupidity and drunkenness.

"Nicholas Barrett." A slow, lazy, triumphant smile crossed his face, his intended effect ruined immediately by a painful cough that shook his body as if he were a rag doll in the grip of a terrier. "I thought I'd sent you running for good."

❋ ❋ ❋

After the car accident, while I was in the hospital and an hour before Helen had arrived to give me a legal agreement to sign, I'd heard the door open. There was a slight squeal in the hinges; I knew to listen for it.

Even though the sound of the hinges thrilled me with hope, I left my eyes closed.

This time, I told myself without opening my eyes, *it will be Claire. She is my wife. Surely the footsteps I hear are hers, not from a nurse or doctor.*

I had not seen Claire since the night of the accident. More accurately, I had not seen her since falling asleep in the car. She was not there when pain called me forth from internal darkness to the darkness of the night, my head and chest leaning against the steering wheel. She was not there when I was loaded onto the ambulance stretcher. She was not there waiting for me at the emergency room. All I knew was that she survived with little injury; that she had not appeared once in the two days I'd been in the hospital; that my lower right leg had been neatly sheared off by a surgeon — just below the knee — and that nurses changed the dressing twice daily.

Once again, I was disappointed when I opened my eyes.

It was not Claire. But a large, square-headed man in a police uniform who had reminded me of Frankenstein's monster when I was a boy.

I licked my lips. I was in constant thirst and constant pain.

Edgar Layton sat beside me and stared at me.

I had been hoping for Claire but also expecting the police, so I was not surprised at this man's arrival.

I licked my lips again and reached for a glass of water at my bedside. Just before my fingers closed around the glass, the large, square-headed man pulled the glass away. He drank the water in several gulps and set the empty glass down near my fingers. Layton smiled the smile of complete control.

"I am Chief Edgar Layton," the man said. "I am in charge of the investigation of the accident that put you here in the hospital."

He introduced himself as if I wouldn't know him. As if he hadn't turned me away from his office when I was a boy, stopping by to ask him if he had news about my mother.

Chief Edgar Layton lifted the blanket off my legs. "I understand you lost part of a leg," he said. "Tough break for a kid. But then stupidity has its price."

I was angry that this man was trying to bully me. Anger gave me the courage to remain silent.

"I also understand that one of the passengers is still in a coma," he continued. "The deMarionne kid."

"Claire's brother, right? Philip. Not Claire."

I had been reassured a dozen times a day by nurses that Claire was not hurt. Still, I wanted to hear it from the man in charge of investigating the accident.

"Does this mean you can't remember much of what happened?"

"Just tell me it isn't Claire."

"It's her brother. I doubt he's going to live when they pull the tubes out of him. And if he does live, he'll be a vegetable."

"I'm very sorry to hear that," I said.

"Tell me about the accident," Layton said. "Start from the beginning."

"I don't remember a thing."

"Don't lie to me, son."

"I don't remember a thing."

167

"I found you behind the steering wheel. At the hospital they found high levels of alcohol in your blood. If the deMarionne kid dies, you'll be charged with manslaughter. That family has got a lot of money, a lot of connections. You'll do some hard time. Especially since you stole their daughter."

"I don't remember a thing."

The man in the police uniform reached inside his shirt, pulled out a black-and-white photo, held it in front of my face. It showed me, slumped behind the steering wheel of the Plymouth Valiant. "All the jury needs to see is this. It'll be an open-and-shut case. In front of a judge who is the next-door neighbor to the deMarionnes. A judge out to hang you if he could."

"I don't remember a thing."

The man in the police uniform slid the photo back inside his shirt. He dug into a shirt pocket for a toothpick. Leaned back, chewed on the toothpick.

"Fact is, taking all of this to court won't bring back the deMarionne kid. It will just add to the hell that his parents are already facing. It won't help the Barrett family to be involved in another scandal involving white trash in their own backyard."

Another scandal involving white trash in their own backyard.

Edgar Layton let those words hang there, accusatory. I understood the implication. And could say nothing in my own defense. I wondered if he remembered me as a pitiful ten-year-old kid, pleading at the police station for any answers about my mother.

Layton said, more or less grunting, "If this goes to court, the newspapers will splash the deMarionne name and the Barrett name across headlines for a week, maybe two. Neither family wants to see that. I'm here to help them. Which means today is your lucky day. I'm going to give you a get-out-of-jail-free card."

Layton leaned forward. He pulled a small notepad out of his other shirt pocket.

"Yup, kid, all you have to do is write and sign your confession, and this little matter will drop right out of sight."

Another grunt. "At least for as long as you stay away from our fine city."

❋ ❋ ❋

"Tell me about my mother," I said to Edgar Layton. "The truth."

"You've come back for that? For some grand deathbed confession?"

I felt a thrill of discovery. His answer had revealed more than perhaps he intended. It was not a denial that he knew the truth. But an affirmation that what he knew needed confessing. For the first time since arriving in Charleston, hope filled the sails of my journey.

"Some people in your situation," I said, keeping emotion out of my face, "would take that opportunity."

"My situation. Say it the way it is. I'm dying. My insides are eating me up. I vomit blood and pieces of my stomach. I'll be dead in a week. Probably less. Too bad, so sad."

"Some people vomiting blood and pieces of their stomach in the last couple days of dying," I said, "just want to talk to someone."

He tried propping himself on his elbows. Failed. Fell back. "Not me. All I want is morphine."

"I hold copies of two police reports that describe the same accident," I said. "The one you released officially. And the one that sent me away."

"Are you threatening me? As if I would care if anyone knows about something I did that long ago?"

"You owe me," I said, disgusted at the whine in my voice.

Layton pressed the buzzer at his bedside. "Unless you're here to give me morphine, go away."

I saw no choice. I went.

CHAPTER 16

On my return to the bed-and-breakfast, I passed the Barrett mansion on South Battery. It was the opposite direction from the deMarionne residence, with the bed-and-breakfast roughly in the middle of the two mansions, so I'd had no need to pass it as I made trips from the inn, and until this moment, I had avoided it.

Now, however, I wanted to test myself. Had I managed to toughen myself enough that it and its memories would not affect me?

It was three-storied with the prerequisite ponderous columns in front, columns that supported a long, wide second-floor balcony above the entrance. Aside from those columns and the massive twin steps leading up to the mansion, the box-shaped architecture itself showed no imagination, only a blatant display of the prodigious amount of money it had cost the merchant who originally built it centuries earlier.

I had lived there — the unwanted nephew and cousin — from the day my mother ran from Charleston.

I had lived there until my elopement with Claire.

I had lived there with Pendleton.

Thursday my mother left Charleston by train. Left me by train.

The following Monday, I was back from the beach house with the other Barretts, and they had taken me to the mansion.

Not to my home. Not to my mother.

Constantly for three days earlier — the Friday, Saturday, and Sunday — I'd asked when my mother was going to return to pick me up as promised. My questions had been met with evasions that I did not understand until arriving at the Barrett mansion that Monday.

My suitcase was in one of the upper bedrooms, and I sat on the bed, staring at the dim, musty oil paintings that I had no inkling were to surround me for the rest of my adolescence.

Pendleton arrived and stood in the doorway of the bedroom. "Nicholas," he said.

His voice was oddly muffled by the nose I had broken a few days earlier. His nose was still plastered, the flesh around his eyes had settled to a puffy, deep blue. He'd avoided me until then, not wanting me to see how much I had injured him. Whatever pride he might lose by allowing me to see my handiwork, however, was more than offset by the value of the article on the front page of the folded newspaper in his hand.

He threw it at me. It landed on the bed. I picked it up. I was too naive to understand the value of this article for Pendleton and foolishly read it in his presence.

TRUST FUND DISAPPEARS: Local attorney Geoffrey Alexander Gillon has reported that $300,000 is missing from a trust fund established for a child in Charleston's prominent Barrett family.

While details of the fraud have been withheld to protect the Barrett family, police confirm that other family members have filed a missing person report on Carolyn Barrett, widow of deceased war hero David Collin Barrett. Police also confirm that a search of her town house in the Ansonborough district shows that a departure had been planned.

"Her suitcases are gone and by all indications most of her clothes and personal belongings are no longer at home," said Charleston Police Chief Edgar Layton. "Furthermore, records show that she purchased two train tickets for a midnight departure on Friday, and witnesses confirm she was on the train with a naval ensign named Jonathan Britt."

The missing money had been put into a trust fund for her son, Nicholas William Barrett, other family members say.

"We believe she not only ran away from her son," says Lorimar Barrett, a fifth-generation Charlestonian and uncle to the motherless boy, "but she took his inheritance too. She has literally left him a penniless orphan. But our own family will not abandon him as she has."

Charges have been filed against Carolyn Barrett, and a warrant has been issued for her arrest.

Pendleton, standing there in my room on the second floor, had waited until I fully comprehended what I was reading.

When I looked up at him, he was ready with his reason for bringing the newspaper to my attention.

"So," he said, pointing at the plaster on his nose, "do you think I deserved this? Or that maybe I was telling the truth?"

He was also ready to flee. He reached

the stairs at the end of the hallway as I roared out of the bedroom. There, within sight of the adult world below, he was safe from me.

"What is it, Pen?" his mother called from the sofa, where she was reading a romance novel.

"Nothing," he said. He gave me a smirk before sauntering down the stairs. "Nothing at all."

❊ ❊ ❊

I stood on the sidewalk, washed by the perfume of the immaculately tended flowers and honeysuckle and climbing vines.

I probed my soul for any reaction to the sight of the mansion. This was where I had endured the death of my childhood. This was where Pendleton had taken his new bride, Claire, assuming lordship of the estate following the deaths of his parents.

I stared at the mansion and felt nothing.

Apathy, it has been said, is a much more damaging emotion than hatred. When you hate, you are on the far side of love.

It pleased me, this apathy.

As I congratulated myself on my emotional distance from my past, the purring of an automobile engine disturbed my thoughts.

I looked to my left to see a late-model BMW slow and turn up the drive of the Barrett mansion. It was black with tinted side windows. As it turned, however, I saw a flash of the driver through the windshield.

Pendleton.

I stumbled as I turned away in haste.

I walked as quickly as I could.

I told myself that Pendleton had not looked at my face, that our eyes had not met, that he hadn't seen me in front of the mansion like a boy looking through a window into a candy store.

And I chose to believe my lie.

CHAPTER 17

"Mizz deMarionne is expecting you."

Behind me, coming in from the harbor and sweeping across East Battery through the open door of the deMarionne mansion, the wind had picked up. Down the street, a man with a large dog was out, leaning into the wind, trouser legs whipping against his shins. The day's cloudless sky had been replaced by evening thunderheads, reaching upward in black, towering mushrooms. A few stray pellets of rain smacked the columns of the piazza. Ella's face and voice were colder than the approaching storm.

I followed her, silent. I met Helen in the great room. Helen stood at a window overlooking East Battery. She was in darkness, her face invisible to me. Rain began to come in off the ocean, kicking up whitecaps on slate gray water barely visible in the streetlights at the seawall.

"I spoke to Geoffrey Alexander by telephone," Helen said. "He informs me that he met with you this morning. I have also arranged another meeting for you. Tomorrow morning. At nine-thirty. With a retired navy man. Admiral McLean Robertson. I've written down his address. You shouldn't have any trouble finding it. He lives on Murray Boulevard."

"Admiral Robertson."

"Yes. His former assistant is the one who left Charleston with your mother. I imagine you remember the newspaper articles. If you insist on continuing this futile search for her, the admiral would be a logical person to visit."

"You are too kind," I said. Helen had always been a controlling person. I found it amusing that she now felt she needed to control my search.

"Kindness has nothing to do with it," Helen said, unaware of my amusement. "I simply want to know about the accident that took my son's life. I have helped you as much as I can. I expect, then, that you will honor our agreement. I want to see what you promised me."

I moved no closer. Helen did not turn from the window.

"With certain conditions."

"This is my son's death we are speaking of. I will not accept conditions."

"You have no choice. I gave a copy of the police report to a Charleston attorney. If Pendleton and Claire finalize their divorce, and if she becomes mayor, this attorney will deliver it to you. If not, the report will remain in confidence."

"Why? At least tell me that."

"No." I found I enjoyed speaking to Helen in abrupt tones.

Helen continued to speak to the window. "Geoffrey Alexander told me you want to find your mother's former personal maid. Perhaps I can help you with that."

"No." I added nothing more. She might think she was in control, like earlier when she had engineered my exile. But not anymore. I was dangerous now, simply because I cared so little about anything.

"It has been years since I added the word *please* to any of my requests. Please tell me about my son."

"No," I said again. "Good-bye."

I did not wait for Ella to escort me to the main door.

I had another destination in mind.

I walked from Helen's in anger and frustration, walked through the familiar elegant halls, walked through the garden. In the last light of day, the carriage house appeared much shabbier than it had in the glow of lantern flames of the previous evening. Where climbing ivy failed to cover the exterior walls, the brick was chipped in places, weathered and bleached of color.

Wood window frames showed cracks and splinters beneath peeling paint. The roof sagged slightly and was exposed in places where shingles had blown away.

I knocked on the door to the carriage house. Heard footsteps inside. Stepped back as the door opened. And tried not to flinch at impulse of surprise.

"Yes?"

She was Claire. But wasn't.

For a heartrending moment, I thought I was ten again, shyly lost in my innocent crush on Claire. The girl in front of me could have stepped out of one of the photo albums of my childhood, before my mother left, when Claire and I were two children playing at the beach.

"Yes?" the girl in front of me repeated, an arch in her eyebrows, as if even at this young age, she were accustomed and amused to reducing men to clumsy speechlessness. She took me in from toe to head, slowly. I felt very middle-aged.

"I'm here to see Claire," I said. "I'm wondering if . . ."

"Mother," she called behind her, "there's a man at the door for you."

She turned back to me. Total self-possession, total self-confidence. "I'm Michelle. Claire's daughter. Is this a date?"

Before I could introduce myself or reply to her question, Claire appeared directly behind Michelle, holding a glass of white wine.

"Go away," Claire told me.

"Go away?" Michelle echoed. "Mother, Pendleton goes on dates all the time. You should take your turn too."

I thought it was sad that a girl who could have been no older than ten or eleven spoke with such adult clarity.

"Shut the door, Michelle."

"No," I said. "Claire, I need to ask you one thing."

"Who is this man?" Michelle asked. "What is this?"

"His name is Thomas," Claire said, using my middle name. "He's from an antique shop on King. We had a particularly difficult disagreement the other day, and I find it incredible that he would appear on my doorstep to continue it."

"You're lying, Mother," Michelle said. "And not very well."

"So be it," Claire said. "Regardless, I am not interested in any discussion with him. Or you."

"I am," Michelle said. "He looks familiar."

Claire handed her glass of wine to

Michelle. She steered Michelle toward the interior of the house, which was an open floor plan and a mixture of old and new furniture beneath oil paintings and framed prints.

Claire returned almost immediately, stepped outside, and closed the door behind her. Even with the wind that swirled through the garden, scattering dried leaves of untended and unpruned trees, I smelled the plum-sweet warmth of wine on Claire's breath. But this night she was not drunk.

"How dare you do this to me. How dare you involve my daughter in this melodramatic appearance of yours." Gone was the stumbling slur of her previous evening's speech. "Speak now. Speak quickly. Then leave. If you ever do this again, I will call the police."

"You and Pendleton live apart," I said.

"Brilliant. You deduced this by the fact that I am forced to live in my stepmother's servants' quarters?"

"Are you divorcing?"

"We are legally separated. Divorce may be the final result. Either way, I don't want you in my life."

"What if I told you there was a good reason for all that happened?"

"Give me the reason."

"I can't. I can only ask you to trust me until the day I can tell."

"You are a fool," she said. "With no idea of how much a fool you are."

I stared at her. Short as her hair was, the wind plucked at it, the way sand-filled wind had done on the beach in another lifetime.

"I can look back and understand something," she said. "When I fell in love with you, it was because of rebellion and sympathy. I knew marrying you would be as good a protest as anything against the stranglehold of my step-mother's wealth. And you were a lost little boy, wanting so badly to be part of the rest of us. You did anything for me, just to belong, and I was young enough to enjoy that kind of control, without knowing how tedious it might have become had we stayed married. Pendleton, for all his faults, at least made life interesting. Nor does Pendleton try to fool himself with what he wants. You? You want to believe you're above all of our ways. But you want Charleston badly."

She smiled, knowing the effect of her smile. And knowing the effect her words had on me.

"Nick, I've grown up. I don't hate the establishment. I'm going to be the mayor. I don't have a teenage urge to thumb my nose at Charleston by sheltering an outcast."

Her tongue flicked her lips, as if there was some pleasure in emasculating me. "Nor do I want the kind of man who is an eager puppy, following at my feet in hopes of my attention or approval from the rest of us. That was then, Nick. This is now."

"I've changed," I said. My face felt set in stone.

She laughed. "That's just it, Nick. You haven't. Otherwise why would you be here?"

CHAPTER 18

I left the deMarionne mansion. Most of the storm had passed. All that remained was wind and scattered rain coming in almost sideways from the waters. The dark empty streets suited my mood; except for that familiar man walking a dog among the oaks along East Battery, I was alone as I passed the antebellum mansions with their warm yellow lights within, lights as in a Kinkade painting, taunting me with their promise of a home and peace longed for, which I might never have.

I dreaded the prospect of an evening alone in my room. I toyed with calling Amelia, for she had given me her hotel number, but I told myself it was the coward's way, seeking the company of one woman to replace another.

I decided to walk until I was tired and thoroughly cold and hungry. I would stuff myself with pasta at an Italian restaurant until I was drowsy. I would take a taxi back to the inn. I would soak in a hot bath until my muscles were totally relaxed. I would collapse into bed and hope for sleep without dreams. Tomorrow would bring what it would bring.

And then what? I asked myself.

I walked along East Battery. My golf shirt gave little protection against the wind, and the skin of my exposed arms was tight with goose bumps. I allowed myself that question again.

And then what?

I could not strike back at Pendleton without hurting Claire. Nor would Claire return to me. As for my mother, Amelia had answered enough; my mother truly had gone to the train station and truly had abandoned me.

What other truth would I want to know? There was no point in visiting the admiral, or even in returning to the church for more information about Ruby.

I knew that in the morning I would leave Charleston again.

This time, however, all my heart ties had been severed.

At least I had accomplished that.

Fueled by anger and depression, I walked as hard as my plastic limb would permit. My walk took me past the turn on East Battery, past the Barrett mansion, past the Yacht Club, and north again to the waterfront wharves, with only the occasional car splashing the puddles in the streets to break into my morose thoughts.

I reached the park at the end of Vendue Range. The storm had left the adjoining pier empty. A long, deserted path out on the pier drew me to the waters of the Cooper River, where as a boy I had watched container ships pass under the bridges during the nights I had escaped the Barrett house and had no other place to go.

Now, like then, I enjoyed the sight of the large ships gliding soundlessly forward.

Halfway to the end of the pier, I stopped to watch a ship approaching from the yards upriver. Because of the trick perspective of distance, the lights of its tower seemed to merge as the ocean-bound hulk eased through the shipping channel.

I saw a movement to my left. Between me and the street, at the beginning of the pier, was the man with the dog, moving closer to me. Not until then did I realize they had stayed with me the entire ten minutes it had taken me to walk this far from the deMarionne mansion.

Although the man's face was lost beneath the shadow of a fedora above his overcoat, the gap between us had closed enough that beneath the lights of the pier, I could recognize the large dog on the leash as a Rottweiler, massive across the shoulders, with a head broad like a bear. This was the same man I had seen earlier at the deMarionne mansion.

It seemed eerie, their purposeful walk toward me. Especially in light of the coincidence of their appearance the other times. I continued to watch. The man and dog passed beneath one streetlight into the shadows before the next, with only two more lights between them and me. Still, they moved closer. They stopped, only fifty feet away, in the pool of shadows on the other side of the streetlight between us.

I wondered if I knew them or if they knew me. I was about to call out a greeting when the man squatted beside his dog. I wasn't certain because of the darkness, but it looked like the man reached for the dog's collar.

The man straightened. The end of the leash dangled toward the ground. The big black dog stood, expectant, its head trained in total focus on me.

"You should have left it alone," the man said. Then casually he spoke one more word. "Kill."

The dog erupted into motion, launching forward like a silent, savage rocket of teeth and muscle, passing beneath the wash of the streetlight with a blur of tan and black.

The edge of the pier was only a dozen steps away, but I lost any chance to turn and dive for water in the first few heartbeats of frozen fear, my mind flashing images of my bare forearms torn as I raised them in protection. My mind moved past that and even before I realized I was thinking it, I was pushing the heel of one shoe with the toes of my other shoe and stepping out of the shoe with a snap of shoelaces and reaching down and rising with it in both hands just before the Rottweiler hurled itself upward at my throat.

I brought my arms upward into myself, shoving the shoe into the dog's face with the desperation of raw, unthinking panic. The momentum of the beast flung me onto my back, cracking my head against the pavement of the pier.

The shoe saved me for the first few moments of the attack. It had wedged into the dog's mouth. I clung to that shoe as the dog, in his daze, tried to shake it back and forth, finally breaking the horrible silence with a muffled snarl of frustration.

The dog weighed as much as a man. Its front claws raked at my chest. Rear claws scrabbled for traction against my pants legs.

I rolled, forearms between my chest and the dog, still clutching the shoe that was the only barrier against the leverage of the dog's bone-cracking jaws. The dog kicked and scraped, gathering its rear legs to gouge at the softness of my belly.

I rolled again, frantic from the pain and terror, frantic the dog might release its grip on the shoe and tear into my throat. The rough pavement banged the points of my shoulders, banged my elbows, scouring skin to the bone.

And still I rolled, hoping I had guessed right, hoping the attack hadn't disoriented me. The edge of the pier was too far away and what I needed was one chance at safety, a chance that would come if only I could roll beneath the safety chains of the railing on the near edge of the pier.

Then the pavement dropped away. For a breathless second, there was only weightlessness. I had been prepared for this drop, hoping for it. I had time to gulp in air. Then came the icy shock of oily harbor water.

It was high tide, and the plunge threw the dog and me below the surface, still locked in a macabre embrace of a primal death fight between man and animal.

I felt the dog's legs push against me. Not

in attack. But in its own panic at the depth of the water. And my fear became a gush of hot, unthinking rage. My hands found the slick skin of the dog's neck. Keeping my grip, I slid around the dog's body so that those gouging claws pushed vainly against churning water instead of my chest and belly and groin. Still underwater and almost riding the dog now, I squeezed my fingers into its neck, in my rage trying to rip into the cartilage and flesh.

My advantage was that one gulp of air. The extra thirty seconds of oxygen. The dog sagged, and still I tore at the dog's neck in total fury, feeling the animal's windpipe like a hose in the grip of my fingers, reveling in my own savagery. I held tight until blackness began to burn inward from the edges of my brain. And then, finally, I pushed away the limp mass of fur and muscle and with my last few moments of consciousness, fought for the surface of the water.

I found night and air and took a heaving gasp of renewed life. I paddled for a few moments to orient myself.

The lights of cars on the bridge showed me I was pointed upstream, and with another turn, I saw the dark form of the pier. On top, I saw the outline of the man, sharp against the streetlight, leash still hanging from his hand. Beneath his hat, the man's head was focused on the water, as if he was straining to see me.

The man held a pistol, had it trained on the water.

I paddled silently and slipped backward. Exhausted, I let the slow current take me away. Farther down, I would angle back toward land, toward moored yachts, and pull myself up in safety.

CHAPTER 19

I woke the next morning with my bedsheets stuck to the crusted blood on the skin of my belly and chest. Upon returning to the bed-and-breakfast the night before, I'd soaked in the bathtub in darkness, for I never enjoyed the sight of my half leg ending so abruptly. Soap and hot water had stung the scratches badly, but most of the bleeding had stopped before I'd gone to bed for a night of broken sleep.

Yes, it hurt to pull away the bedsheets, but a person can take savage satisfaction in pain in the heat of battle.

I was that person.

Somewhere along the way, my actions and questions since my return had prodded this attempt on my life. In finding the truth about my mother, I could also smash those who had smashed my life. My pain was secondary; the pain I would inflict was primary.

I folded the blood-encrusted sheets so that the stains did not show and left them on the bedcover. I hardly cared what questions or suspicions they might raise among the genteel owners of the bed-and-breakfast if the laundry maid happened to open the sheets before washing.

After showering — try that someday on only one leg — I blotted the fresh blood off my belly and chest with tissue paper and flushed it away. Where the bleeding had stopped, angry red ridges showed where I had been clawed.

I put on a fresh T-shirt to soak what blood might seep out during the day and covered it with a loose oxford shirt.

I spent my usual awkward few moments adjusting my plastic limb, then finished clothing myself.

I was ready.

Half an hour later, I sat in the cool dim quiet of the Mount Carmel African Methodist Episcopal Church. Pastor Samuel's wife, Etta, had gone to get him from the church office.

I turned at the scuffling of footsteps.

It was the old woman's Samuel, standing in front of his wife just inside the entrance to the sanctuary, leaning on a pew. The bald center of his head cleanly divided white, curly fringes on each side. He wore thick glasses that magnified his eyes into bulging eggs. His black pants hung loose on him, supported by suspenders over a white starched shirt.

He took a step closer to me, reaching for the back of the next pew for support again. His progress was almost like a baby's learning to walk for the first time. Etta followed behind, towering over him in the aisle.

I rose, waiting for him. To walk toward him would be a disrespect of impatience.

"I knew your mama well," Samuel said. The vitality of his baritone was such a contrast to his appearance that I found myself staring at the man's mouth as he spoke. "From the time she was a little one."

I took Samuel's extended hand and gently shook it in greeting. I was afraid of hurting the delicate bones in the old man's hand. "A pleasure to meet you, sir."

"Pleasure's mine. Fact is, I thought I'd see the pearly gates before I'd see you. We never thought it would have been proper to try to talk to you when you was living with the Barretts and always intended to have this talk when you was grown. But you left Charleston. . . ."

"Yes, sir, I did." I left it at that. Either they knew about the accident or they didn't. Either way, I was here about my mother.

I gestured at a nearby pew. "Shall we sit? I'm interested in what you might tell me about my mama. And why it is you've been waiting for me."

Samuel eased himself down. Let out a sigh. "Etta, why don't you sit opposite. You remember as much as I do."

The old woman moved up and took a seat on the opposite side of the aisle. I turned around to face Etta and Samuel from where I sat in the pew in front of them.

"You knew my mama since she was little?" I prompted.

"She grew up just down the road," Samuel said. "Before they put in the expressway. Sat here in this church, every Sunday, singing and praying. Couldn't carry a tune, as I recall, the only white person amongst all us black. Her face stuck out whilst I preached, and her voice stuck out whilst all of us sang. And our good Lord knows, we loved that girl, best friends as she was with Ruby Atkins."

"They was thick as blood," Etta chimed in. "Ruby came from good stock. Her folks loved her, raised her to be respectful. Your mama, well let's just say she'd have been better off if someone clubbed her daddy in the head and drowned him face first in his own bathtub."

"That's how he died, Etta," Pastor

Samuel snorted. "Police said it was a jealous husband what followed him home. No one ever found out exactly, but no one really cared either. He was that kind of man."

"I was getting to that," she told Samuel with irritation. "But he's first got to know how it was when Ruby and her family started taking her in 'cause she wasn't even getting fed and clothed proper."

I listened, as much fascinated by the ebb and flow of conversation between a man and a woman who had lived together for half a century as I was by the description of my mother's childhood. I hadn't known much; whenever I'd asked my mother, she had found something else to talk about, and I was always left with the impression that somehow she was ashamed of it.

"Weren't for Ruby," Samuel said, "who knows what might have happened to your mama when she was a little girl. Carolyn's own mama barely made ends meet and was more interested in men and whiskey than putting food on the table. Sure, your mama had an older sister that worked some and helped the family, but shortly after their daddy died in the bathtub, that girl run off. No one knew to where, and no one heard from her again. Ruby and her family, well, they took your mama in and treated her like one of their own."

"Our good Lord blessed your mama with looks," Etta said. "She didn't put on airs about it, but she could turn a man's head. When that Barrett boy saw her working as a waitress down at the grill, he didn't care how much his family stood against him marrying a lower-class girl. He swept her off her feet."

"We didn't see your mama much after she left and got married," Samuel said. "We all knew she married into old Charleston money, and we figured she was spending her Sundays in her husband's church."

"That's good and proper," Etta said. "A woman's got to do what her husband says, unless he tells her to do something stupid or ungodly, and thank our Lord he gave women the common sense to decide when a husband's wrong."

Etta squinted at Samuel, waiting for him to disagree.

Samuel cleared his throat. "She always kept Ruby in her life," he said quickly, filling in the silence. "They were best friends and the way the world was back then, seemed easiest for them to pretend

Ruby was her maid. She helped your mama through some hard times too."

Etta frowned at Samuel. "Tell him."

"I was easing into it."

"Tell him. We agreed it was all right to tell him. Ain't no one else in the world who knows but us and Ruby's sister Opal. Now that he's come back, he's got a right to know."

I looked back and forth between the two of them.

Samuel sighed heavily. "Your mama ended up coming back here on a rainy night, out of the blue, the worst night of her life."

He stopped and stared off at a stained-glass window, where sunshine sparkled on dust motes. When he resumed, face back toward mine, his voice had quiet pain.

"There ain't no easy way to say it." The large eyes behind the thick glasses didn't blink. "It hurts me just to tell you. Someone had violated your mama, and she had nowhere to go but back to us."

The words and implications of what they meant pinned me into helpless silence.

"Seems she was afraid to go to the police. She weren't going to tell us his name, said it was to protect us, said the man what had done it was rich and powerful and owned the police. She said wasn't nothing we could do but hold her close to us and help her get through the night."

I bowed my head.

"She swore us to secrecy. Said if anyone found out, specially if anyone guessed who'd done it, it would break her husband's heart. Broke our hearts, seeing her in such pain, and thinking more 'bout the man she loved than 'bout herself."

Samuel sighed long and hard. "If she never got the chance to tell you, I'm telling you now. We saw her off and on over the first few years after you were born. People were rough on her, thinking she'd been unfaithful to her husband, a war hero who died without coming home. Every time we saw her, she told us how much she loved you, despite what it had cost her reputation. She told us time and again it didn't matter who had fathered you, only who had mothered you. Take that to heart son; she loved you more than life."

Samuel squinted and stared hard at me. "Son, you all right? Son?"

I was remembering.

"Yes," I lied. "I'm all right."

"Son, your mama was a good woman," he said. His hand on my shoulder was a comfort. "When she started to show in the months after that rainy night, it was far too late to tell the world it weren't her fault, that she'd been violated. She held her head high, even with folks in Charleston saying she was white trash, just like where she'd come from. It was only here in this church that she was welcomed. We loved your mama. You was baptized here."

She held her head high, even with folks in Charleston saying she was white trash. I dropped my head to hide my eyes from this gentle preacher in front of me.

"It's all right, son. It's all right."

It wasn't all right. To discover now she'd been raped, not unfaithful. To discover I was the product of an act of her helplessness, not betrayal.

Pastor Samuel had no idea of my last words to her.

※ ※ ※

"Why did you hit Pendleton?" my mother asked four hours after I had punched my cousin with all the might of my ten-year-old biceps and forearm and fist. "His mother tells me you were standing on the beach and hit him for no reason at all. But I can't believe that."

This was Wednesday. The day before my mother abandoned me and left a scandal in her wake.

My mother's question had not been a surprise. Nor her entrance into the upstairs bedroom of the beach house, with its westward inland view of Folly Island and the one road that ran down its narrow length past all the houses that lined the beach. I had seen my mother's Chevrolet approach the Barrett house, shadows of palmettos falling across its hood as she turned into the drive. I had heard the angry murmuring of adults below as my mother first faced the Barrett wrath before trekking up the stairs, had smelled my mother's perfume as the door opened with a swoosh of air drawn to the screen of the open window in front of me.

Lost in the confusion and pain and doubt that had tortured me since punching Pendleton in the face for calling her a tramp, I refused to turn to face her.

"Why?" She repeated her question softly, moving closer to me and resting her hands on my shoulders. "I know you must have had a good reason."

When Pendleton's mother had first demanded I explain why I had punched her dearly beloved son, I had refused to answer, unable to repeat the horrible accusations that now pushed down on my heart like anvils of dread. As for Pendleton, he had enough political sense to realize it would not play well if the adults in his world knew what had prompted my spectacular punch. We both held our silence for the day, something that was mistakenly interpreted in our favor as an honorable code of brotherhood.

Still, my deed could not go unpunished. I'd been banished to upstairs solitude until my mother, summoned for this emergency, could arrive at the Folly Island beach house after her shift at the museum.

By the time she arrived, Pendleton had returned from the hospital. He chose to sit in a living-room recliner, head leaned back, ice bag on his forehead, where his dramatic pose ensured that his aunt would be forced to acknowledge the plaster on his nose and his noble fight against pain caused by her son.

"Talk to me, my love," my mother said to me in the bedroom. "What's the matter?"

I could not bear to look at her face, as if I might for the first time see the betrayal that had lain waiting for me all along.

She turned my head gently and lifted my chin. A tear trickled down alongside my nose. She wiped it away.

The last rays of sunset cast soft yellow light across her face. It was a beauty that I ached to touch. I wanted to throw myself into her arms. I wanted the return of innocence that would allow me to sob away my fear and sadness as I clung to her for comfort. But if what Pendleton said was true, how could there be any comfort from her again?

The cold emptiness that gave me strength all afternoon grew as I fought against my love for her; I flinched at her touch and pushed away her embrace, something she pretended not to notice.

The silver chain with a cross that has always hung from my neck was clenched in my right hand. This, too, was something she pretended not to notice.

"Nick," she said, "I believe that you believe you had good reason to hit your cousin. But it's not right under any circumstances to hit anyone."

For the first time since she entered the room, I looked at her squarely. I spoke bitterly. "What if someone was trying to hurt you? And the only way I could stop him was by hitting until he stopped?"

"No one was trying to hurt me. Were they? And if they were, I would be glad you protected me."

Her sweet smile was reward for my question. My resolve to hate my mother faltered, but against the world-shattering disappointment of my new knowledge, her smile only served as scattered raindrops useless against a raging fire. I could not tell her that I was defending her, for then I would have to tell her why.

"Nick," she said to my silence, "I am required to find a way to punish you suitably or have you apologize and make up with Pendleton."

What she wanted to tell me was that the Barretts made the rules and that she and I either lived by them or left. And if we left, then I might never have the chance to rise out of the poverty she had faced during her own childhood. She wanted to explain to me that she had bound her soul in the silk of the Barrett riches, not for her, but for me and my future. But then, at age ten, I was too young to understand.

"I will never apologize to Pendleton. If he comes near me again, I'll hit him harder. Maybe I'll use a baseball bat."

She took my clenched fists in her hands. "What happened, Nick?"

"Leave me alone."

How could I explain that I was too afraid to tell her? I knew I'd done right, defending her. But if I told her why, I might discover that Pendleton had not lied. That would be worse, far worse, than the injustice of being punished for doing something right.

I pulled my hands away from her.

She studied the rigidness of my shoulders, the stiffness of my neck beneath the ragged edges of my hair. Again, I would not understand until later how it filled her with sorrow that the divide had arrived. She knew, as all mothers instinctively know from the first moment of separation as the umbilical cord was cut, that the baby's destination was to become a man, and to do so would mean rejection, small rejections sometimes, then larger rejections — slashing against the intimate bond of a mother's fierce proprietary love with tiny cuts and escalating larger cuts — until finally the tiny creature that had depended on her very blood in the womb, depended on the milk from her breasts, depended on her love every waking moment of babyhood, depended on her stories and acceptance all through childhood, was no longer a tiny creature and would eventually walk away to find his own place in the world. But because we were so close, this moment had always seemed so far away. Until now, with me determined to keep my first real secret from her.

Worse, she could not in this moment be my friend. Because I had punched *the* Pendleton Barrett, she was forced to accept her role as parent.

"I know how much you like your vacation here every summer," she said. "But Pendleton's parents now wonder if it is suitable that you remain."

"I don't want to stay here," I said. "Not if Pendleton is here too."

"I'll take you home then."

"I don't want to go home either."

What I really wanted was the home I'd felt was mine before Pendleton's words.

She rested her hands on my shoulders again. "Where would you like to be?"

"Away." I pushed her hands off my shoulders. "Just away."

A long, long silence held us, until my continued rejection forced her to speak.

"Away from me?" she asked softly.

"Yes," I said. "Away from you."

❋ ❋ ❋

It took several moments for me to realize that Pastor Samuel had lapsed into silence.

I took a deep breath, looked up, saw tears running down the leathered black cheeks of Pastor Samuel.

"You got to know, son, your mama loved you fierce. She told me more than once it didn't matter how you were conceived, you were still a child of God, given to her. After Ruby died, Etta and me, we might be the only two people in the world who didn't believe she run out on you. She loved you too much."

"Oh, God . . . ," I said. Pastor Samuel bore the tears that should have run down my own face, but it was the first time I had uttered those words with that need.

"Yes, sir. Oh, God . . . the Lord's the only place we can turn."

Unasked, Pastor Samuel began to pray, giving me the answer to redemption, his baritone softly filling the peace of the church. "Lord, you sent us Jesus, just a man and much more than a man, willing to die for the message of love you placed upon his shoulders to deliver to us. Lord, through Jesus, you promised us a home beyond these tired, pained bodies of ours, to give us hope and forgiveness when things look darkest here on Earth. Thank you, Lord, for the love of your Spirit that fills us when we turn to you. In Jesus' name we pray. Amen."

I had closed my eyes. When I opened them, I saw that Pastor Samuel had risen. He nodded at me, as if giving me permission to be alone. He made his awkward way back down the aisle.

I remained in the silence of the sanctuary for five minutes, trying to understand what I'd learned, fighting the emotions I'd spent my adult life trying to keep separate from my heart.

I forced them back and found strength to rise from the pew.

❊ ❊ ❊

Pastor Samuel was waiting for me outside the church, sitting on the steps, looking over the low grass of the cemetery.

"Who?" I asked. "Who was my father?"

"If anyone knew, it was Ruby. But she died a day after your mama disappeared." Samuel bowed his head briefly, then raised it again. "Someone run her over with a car and left her to die on the side of the road. Charleston police said it was an accident, but in my heart I knew it was murder. I always feared she was killed because she knew something she shouldn't."

"You talked to the police?"

"Sure 'nuff. The only time in my life I ever spoke to the chief of police himself. Big fellow. Don't recall his name, but I do recall he was big and looked like someone had worked him over good with a stick of ugly. He hated black folks."

"Layton," I said. "Edgar Layton."

"That was his name. Edgar Layton. He's the one. Told me it was an accident and that I shouldn't trouble him no more unless I wanted to get run over by accident someday too."

CHAPTER 20

I took a taxi back to the Two Meeting Street Inn. From there, it was a short walk to the south seawall that protected the houses from the tides. The water was flat in the aftermath of the previous evening's storm. Morning automobile traffic was light along the promenade. It gave the old houses to my right an illusion of serenity that seemed to put me into the century before, when the poor freemen would get to the seawall early and hang bait in the waters and tell stories to each other in low voices as they drew on cigarettes and discreetly handled flasks of raw whiskey.

The fishermen were out this morning too; the only difference that time had given was that the rods were made of nylon and graphite instead of bamboo, and the buckets at the feet of their stools were plastic.

I nodded as I passed them. Some returned my nod; others did not. Regardless of the changes in the world outside of Charleston, here the class differences were still punctuated clearly by color of skin.

I walked slowly along Murray Boulevard with these thoughts. Even so, I reached the address early and chose to stand at the seawall and stare at the water for ten minutes rather than knock on the door before my appointed time.

Brown pelicans, majestic in their massive ugliness, silently passed overhead. It seemed I was a boy again, staring and wondering what unknown destination called them with such certainty.

❊ ❊ ❊

Once, during my travels, I spent an entire day seated in front of a rock wall in the Tassili N' Ajjer mountains of Algeria, simply staring at a rock face carved with figures of cattle. During those years, deserts drew me, for the night air tends to be clear and cloudless, perfect for viewing through a telescope.

I'd arrived by camel and guide, mesmerized on the journey by the endless dunes of the northern Sahara, broken only by desolate outcroppings of rock. Our world was a world of rippled tan and brown, framed by the clear edge of distant hills that shimmered against a pale blue sky and the glare of the constant brutal sun.

Except for the wheezing of camels and the occasional grunt of the guide, it was a world of heat and silence. In fact, at one point during the journey, I asked the guide to go ahead with our camels, leaving me alone in the immense silence of the desert.

For the first time in my life, I heard no sound. It was eerie, away from the comfort of the noises that break even the stillest of nights in the company of other humans.

After ten minutes of glaring sun, I began to wish for wind so that I could hear the rattle of sand grains. After twenty minutes, I began to wonder about my own existence, for without sound to confirm reality, it was too easy for my mind to wander into strange caves.

At that realization, I began to whistle. Partly to create sound where there was none and partly to comfort myself. For in this silence and desolation, I was as alone as a man could be. I did not know my guide well. My telescope was in its case, and all of my other possessions and money were on the camel with him. For all I knew, he had not stopped over the next hill as I had requested but had fled at no risk to himself, abandoning me where my long undiscovered body would eventually dry to parchment.

He did return, of course, and took me farther into the cliffs of the dry mountains to show what I had been promised.

I was there, as always in my travels, to

view the night skies away from the pollution of the light of civilization, and I was there to view in daylight ancient rock art of which I had heard much about in Morocco. But more truly, I was there for the reason I had spent the previous years in travel.

Escape, under the guise of seeing the world.

I did not want to merely find work somewhere and begin the life of a mortgage and car payments. I wanted to be a learned, sophisticated eclectic Renaissance man; I wanted a certain nobleness to my pain. I had the luxury of a monthly stipend, and careful budgeting let me wander wherever I desired, for as long as I wanted.

Unencumbered by a relationship or family ties, the only disadvantage I faced during all my travels was my artificial limb. To accommodate the physical restrictions imposed on me, I carried little luggage and kept my walking to a minimum. Yet the dangers and difficulties of traveling alone in strange countries as an incomplete man were more than balanced by the apathy I bore because of the events that had taken my leg from me. I had myself convinced that I cared little if fate would take away my life, a suitably melodramatic illusion for a suitably melodramatic wanderer. The carelessness of this attitude took away most of my fear; the romance of the melodrama added vibrancy and color to the dullest and grungiest of bars or cafés, for all that mattered was that I was in an exotic location away from Charleston and the pain of lost love. Self-pity, after all, mixes well with bitter coffee, stale pastries, and indifferent service in a foreign language.

On this journey, at different stops over a period of ten days, I was to see a procession of giraffes across a cliff face, engraved into the rock some six to seven feet tall, their sense of movement given by a long-dead artist utterly uncanny. On a sandstone wall, I saw the lone figure of an archer painted with pigments, only nine inches tall but with such detail I could make out the string of the bow and muscles of the archer's legs. I saw a life-size crocodile etched into a giant, cracking boulder, the two-inch-deep grooves still triumphant over wind and sand after millennia of exposure.

Eight thousand years earlier, this desert had been a great grassland — the crocodile serving as evidence that those who peopled it lived in a wetter climate — until the rains stopped and the land began to shrivel. Where dunes now rippled in isolation, there had been rivers and shallow lakes and green grass to support cattle and nomads. The people had vanished like the rivers and had left behind the stories painted and engraved into the rock.

My favorite of the primitive art scenes was the cattle, which seemed to emerge from the rock face at my approach. The surface that this artist had chosen caught the sun's rays perfectly. I watched all day because I had little else to do and it had taken so long to arrive. I watched all day because as the sun moved, so did the shadows across the rock face, giving the illusion of depth and motion to the long-horned cattle.

It was in this quiet that, had I been so inclined, I might have felt the tugging of God's call to my soul.

Only now, looking back, can I understand the mixture of vague unease and peace that filled me to behold this timeless art.

The unknown artist, I believe, had been seeking immortality. For we are the only species that face the curse of knowing that someday death will steal from us everything we have earned in love and in knowledge.

In the sun that day, watching the shadows and desert spiders move, I did feel the blackness of the futility of human existence. Instead of embracing this futility as evidence of the soul within me, I chose then to concentrate on the sun and shadow as a way to deny my loneliness and yearning.

Now, in argument for the existence of the soul, I begin with the observation that to be human means to be alone. However great the love I might find, I cannot merge my being into the being of the other. I will die alone — many may be gathered as I draw my last breath, yet in drawing that last breath, I will be a solitary and tiny figure on that journey through the curtain to whatever lies beyond this life.

As a human, too, I yearn. It is a feeling impossible to define well. I remember once stepping out of a theater in Charleston on a warm summer night, filled with the emotions of a sad movie, holding Claire's hand. Above us was a clear dark night and the brightness of the stars, a backdrop of vastness against the emotions in my heart, and something unknown in me responded to this like a harp string plucked by an invisible hand. I yearned with a homesickness to be somewhere else, an unknown place as difficult to define as the yearning itself.

As a human, too, I dream. I laugh. I cry.

There are those who believe that because the soul cannot be measured or seen or found through experiment, then the human body is merely a complicated package of protein that exists without a soul.

Then, at that rock, in front of the engraved cattle by a long-dead artist, I was among those who would deny the soul exists. I was unwilling to let that artist reach across time and speak to me of his longings and his loves and his hates and his fears. I was unwilling to let that artist reach to me from beyond his death to speak to me of his own soul.

Now I understand all that makes us human — courage in the face of death, loneliness, yearning, the sources of laughter and tears, dreams, love — is as invisible as the soul and equally impossible to place in a test tube or on a scale. I now understand that all of what makes us human defies the notion of body and mind without soul.

For anyone willing to consider the matter, it comes down to this: either we have a soul, or we do not.

If we do not, death is an eternal void of

darkness, and life's brief dim flash against a span of eternity is next to meaningless. If we do not have a soul, then all the hatred and suspicion and greed that was hidden in the society of Charleston as I grew up was justified, for every person should seek what he or she can during this brief life.

If, however, we do have a soul — something of essence that will exist beyond the life of the body — then come the awesome mysteries of what lies behind the existence of our soul.

Why? How? Where will it lead beyond this life?

What is it that calls us forward to our destination?

❊ ❊ ❊

The pelicans that had led me to my melancholy musings had long since silently passed when I turned away from the seawall and walked across the street to the address that Helen had given me the night before.

The retired admiral's residence was two stories high. Colonial columns dominated the front facade. It was pastel yellow, not as large as the ten thousand-square-foot mansions of East Battery, but still easily big enough and prestigious enough to command over a million dollars. It said something for Admiral McLean Robertson's naval pension that he could afford to retire on the Charleston Harbor.

It said more that the entrance was gated and secured with electronic surveillance. I pushed the intercom buzzer. I stared steadily into the video monitor. I expected to have to state my name and reason for visiting into the intercom. Instead, the gate swung open.

The sidewalk wound past lush gardens, immaculately manicured. I stepped up to the columned entrance to the mansion. The front door opened as I approached. The man behind the door easily stood six feet four, dressed in a well-tailored suit. He had a navy-style crew cut and an impassive face.

"I'm here to see Admiral Robertson," I said. "He is expecting me."

Without a word, the bodyguard led me across marbled floors into a den beyond the kitchen.

Swords hung on the magnificent walnut panels of the den walls. As did ink engravings of Civil War battle scenes. The desk held an old cannonball as a paperweight. In the corner of the room was a full-size mannequin dressed in a Confederate uniform, complete with musket and sword.

A man stood posed at the window of the den, surveying the harbor. Smoke drifted around his head. He turned to me, sucking on a long-stemmed pipe. He wore black slacks and a black sweater and was tall and thin. When he stepped away from the window to ease himself down into a leather armchair, sunlight played across an intense face withered by age, jowls held in place only by the discipline of exercise.

"I have always loved noting the geographical accident of the island of Fort Sumter," Admiral Robertson said. "So perfectly situated in the center of the mouth of the harbor. It meant that ships on both sides of the harbor entrance were within cannon-fire distance of that ancient technology. Not that it would matter today, of course, when the distance we fire shells is measured in miles, not hundreds of yards. Still, it always seems to me as if a military mind had placed the island there eons earlier, anticipating not only the limitations of gunfire during the revolutions, but the importance of this city in American history, ensuring that the island was one of the most significant features in the events that formed the character of this nation."

The admiral drew on his pipe. "That island tells much of the secrets to military success. Understand the limitations of all weapons at one's disposal. Use them to maximum effect. Remain aware of one's flanks at all times. Keep the resolution to do what is necessary to guard those flanks."

I wondered if this was an oblique warning.

"Helen tells me you insisted on seeing me," Admiral Robertson said. "I assured her it would be a waste of your time."

"I want to know about my mother, Carolyn Barrett."

"Why would I be able to tell you anything about her?"

"It was your assistant, Jonathan Britt, who disappeared with her and a sizable amount of navy funds. What can you tell me about the night he and she fled Charleston on a train?"

Admiral Robertson bent his head as he relit his pipe. He drew on it hard, cupping the bowl of the pipe with both hands. After several puffs, he spoke again. "Jonathan's private life was his private life. Obviously it was a surprise when he stole the money; otherwise I would have prevented it. To me, your mother was a name in a newspaper. Why should I know anything else about her?"

"You had such a lack of understanding of your own people that it came as a total surprise when your assistant did what he did? As a military man, your awareness of your unprotected flanks was that incomplete?"

"Do not insult me." His voice turned savage so quickly that I wondered if he would step across the room and strike me.

If so, I was ready to strike back.

"It's only an insult," I said calmly, "if it has any truth in it."

"There is no truth in it. Perhaps now you should leave. Unless you have any evidence regarding your mother that demands further examination, our time together is finished."

My silence gave him the answer. No evidence. No position of strength.

"Good-bye," the admiral said.

That is why he agreed to see me, I thought. *This is a strategic assessment on the admiral's part.* Which meant he *did* have something to hide.

I departed the room without a sense of defeat.

I believed I had heard more than one lie. But among them was at least one lie that I knew to be a lie: the admiral had said Helen sent me to him at my insistence.

But I knew differently.

Helen had made the appointment without consulting me.

The admiral had enough to hide that he'd agreed to see me.

I needed to learn why.

CHAPTER 21

"Tazo Chai," I announced.

Glennifer and Elaine, it seemed, had not moved from where I'd left them the day before. In one hand, I held a tray with cups from the Starbucks down the street. In the other hand, I held a bag with danishes.

"Tazo Chai to you too," Elaine answered. "I hope that means hello."

I shook my head gravely. *"Tazo Chai* is a tea. The formula for this ancient beverage will soothe your psyche and enlighten your spirit, if you trust the advertising."

They still looked puzzled.

I set the tray on the desk. "My turn for tea. Starbucks."

"Hmmph," Elaine said. "Our tea costs two cents a bag. You probably paid two dollars a cup. The only person guaranteed a soothed psyche and enlightened spirit is the person making all that profit."

"Well, I think Nick is sweet for caring," Glennifer said. "Even if we both know he has only returned to get what he can from us."

"Yes," Elaine sighed theatrically, "he's going to use us, then discard us."

"Trading," I said. "You give. I give. Remember? The great American way of life."

I handed each of them a cup. I pulled up a chair while they adjusted the milk and sugar levels.

Glennifer sipped at her tea. "Elegant bouquet." She giggled. "Oops. That's a wine term, right?"

"Glenny, don't try to fool him into thinking you know nothing about alcohol." Elaine smiled at me and made a motion of tilting a bottle into her mouth. "She's a sucker for huckleberry wine. More of a sucker for any man brave enough to come calling with a bottle of it in his hand."

"Oh, hush." Glennifer giggled again.

"I need to know about a dog owner," I said, turning them to the business at hand. "I'm guessing he travels in the circles you find familiar. And his dog, a Rottweiler, isn't easy to forget."

Their smiles faded.

Not, I think, because of my question. But because I had little time for anything else but business.

Perhaps I should have felt guilt for my bluntness. These two old women obviously enjoyed the chance for company. Perhaps I should have listened more to their stories, bantered in return, asked them about memories important to them.

But I was conscious of my desire to strike back at those who had struck me down. And, I reminded myself, these two women had agreed to my terms.

"I can't think of anyone offhand," Elaine said. "Most of our customers run with poodles."

"But we can ask," Glennifer said.

"Not without payment," Elaine corrected her. "Nick has not told us nearly enough."

"Can you tell me about Lorimar Barrett?" I asked. "I remember he spent a great deal of time with Helen deMarionne."

"He and she had a longtime affair," Elaine said.

Now I sighed theatrically. "You didn't mention this earlier."

"You give. We give," Elaine said. "Remember? Surely you can't expect us to divulge everything. Not for free. Have you learned anything interesting since yesterday?"

Instead of answering, I rose and unbuttoned my oxford shirt all the way down the front.

"Oh, my." Glennifer fanned herself.

"Oh, my." Elaine patted her chest above her heart. "Glenny, avert your eyes."

"I'll do no such thing!" Glennifer said.

With my shirttails out, I pulled my T-shirt out from my pants and lifted it high enough to show the raw, bloody scratches that the Rottweiler had left behind.

"Last night," I said, "someone tried to have me killed. I was attacked by a large dog."

They exchanged their characteristic glances.

Elaine stared at me thoughtfully. "Any scratches on your back?"

"No."

"You didn't run, then." She sounded angry on my behalf. "This person must have called the dog off the attack then."

"No."

Elaine continued to stare at me with that same thoughtfulness and spoke soberly. "I would not have guessed this about you."

"Laney?" Glennifer said.

"Glenny, think about it. Nicholas did not run from the dog. The owner did not call off the dog. Nicholas is standing here. What do you think happened to the dog?"

"Oh, my," Glennifer said. But it wasn't with the same tone she'd playfully used when I was unbuttoning my shirt.

"I think I could be frightened of you," Elaine said to me. Quietly.

"You shouldn't be," I said.

"Once, when Glennifer and I were much younger, we witnessed Lorimar Barrett at a beach party." Elaine spoke as if I hadn't answered her. "Another young man had crossed him — I can't recall the reason, nor does it matter to this story — and Lorimar knocked this man down with three blows to the face. When the man was down in the sand, Lorimar kicked him brutally again and again and again. Two others had to tackle Lorimar to stop the beating. Charges should have been laid. Your uncle should have spent time in prison. But the chief of police who arrived after the ambulance had departed was Edgar Layton. The Barretts had other connections, of course. Still, I believe it was Edgar Layton who helped Lorimar the most. It didn't surprise me when in the years that followed, I heard they did business together."

She paused. "Though he's dead, I've never forgotten Lorimar's ruthlessness."

❋ ❋ ❋

The September after my mother ran from Charleston, I bicycled to the police station after school.

I was short. I could hardly look over the counter to ask my question. I pulled myself up, my knees rubbing against the varnished wood of the counter.

"I want to speak to the chief of police," I said to the police officer on the other side, sitting behind a typewriter.

I couldn't remember the chief of police's name. I remembered he had asked me questions about my mother. I remembered his large, ugly head. I remembered the menace in his eyes.

I was terrified of my memories of the chief of police, terrified at the thought of seeing him again.

I was more terrified my mother might never return.

No one in the Barrett mansion wanted to discuss my mother.

So I was here.

The officer came around the counter and squatted down slightly so that I could look him in the eyes. Middle-aged, he had a lightly freckled face that gave him a young, trustworthy appearance.

"What is it, son?" This police officer didn't sneer at me as he spoke. Not like the chief of police had. Instead, this police officer smiled. "Broken window? Lost dog?"

"I want to know about my mother. She's lost. I want to know why no one can find her."

His smile flickered. His eyes shifted, as if he suddenly recognized me. "Sheriff

Layton isn't here, son. I'm sorry." The police officer straightened.

"I need to speak to the chief of police," I said. "I'll wait."

I sat on a bench at the side of the office and waited. I listened to methodical clacking of a typewriter, to static hissing of a police radio.

Chief Layton didn't arrive. But my uncle Lorimar Barrett did.

He stormed in, hurling the door shut behind him. He wore a dark suit. The jacket was unbuttoned, giving me a glimpse of the familiar suspenders. He grabbed me by the arm and shook me. "What are you doing here?"

"I want to know about my mother."

He shook me harder. "You do not, I repeat, you do not embarrass me like this again. The Barrett family has suffered enough humiliation because of her."

"I want to know about my mother."

He slapped me. The only reason I did not yelp was because shock sucked all the breath from me. He slapped me again. "You impudent little illegitimate stray. You —"

"Mr. Barrett," the police officer said. He'd stepped away from his typewriter and stood beside us. "He's only a boy."

231

Lorimar spun on the man and shoved him against the counter. "You stay out of this. Remember who owns you."

The officer blinked several times. Stayed silent.

Lorimar spun on me. Slapped me again. "Am I understood?"

"I want to know about my mother."

"Shut your mouth." Again, he slapped me. Harder yet. I felt my lip split.

"I want to know about my mother." All my frustrations and fear and guilt were summed up in those few words.

His next blow drove me to my knees.

"I want to know about my mother." I pushed my tears inside. I would not cry in front of these men. "I want to know about my mother."

Another blow. Now I was on my hands and knees, staring at the dull wax of the yellowed floor.

"I want to know about my mother." From my mouth and nose, blood and saliva dribbled onto the floor. I could hardly form the words. It felt like something inside me was breaking. "I want to know about my mother."

"Shut up."

A boot in my ribs. Another.

"I want to know about my mother. I

want to know about my mother."

"Shut up. Shut your mouth before I kill you."

I waited to be struck again. Instead, I heard another man speak. "Enough, Lorimar. You've made your point. I called you here to take him away, not to kill him."

Chief Edgar Layton. Had the police officer lied to me? Had he been here the entire time?

Layton's massive hand grabbed the back of my shirt collar. He yanked me to my feet. "Stupid boy," he said. "Don't come here again."

Layton barked an order at the officer now behind the counter. "Lou, get a towel and give it to this boy. And, Lou, you'll keep your mouth shut. Won't you?"

Layton spoke to Lorimar. "Take this boy home. Make sure he does not come back."

Lou, the police officer who returned with a towel, had been kind enough to soak it in cold water first. I pressed it against my face and stumbled along as Lorimar Barrett shoved me step-by-step toward his car.

Lorimar left the bicycle behind at the police station. It was never returned to me. It was one of the last objects in my possession that had been given to me by my mother. Nor was I given another bicycle by the Barretts, although Pendleton received a new one each birthday.

Lorimar Barrett did not speak to me as he drove me home. Behind the cold wet towel pressed to my face, I was resolute. I would show no pain again. Not to him. Not to the world. Not about my mother. I muffled my sobs with the cold wet towel.

The bruises and cuts on my face were ignored by the rest of the household over the next two weeks, dinner conversation flowing around me as it always did.

When the bruises and cuts were finally gone, when my face showed no signs of the beating, I was permitted to go back to school. The other injury, my cracked ribs that stabbed me with each breath for another month, was invisible to the teachers, who expressed sympathy that such a bad flu at such an unseasonable time of year had kept me home for so long.

I didn't ask about my mother again.

* * *

"Someone really tried to kill you?" Glennifer asked, her tea virtually untouched. "It was deliberate, this dog set upon you?"

"It was deliberate."

"Who did it?"

"I don't know."

"Obviously, someone is desperate to keep you silent," Glennifer said. "Will you quit asking questions because of it?"

Not this time, I thought.

"He won't," Elaine answered for me. "Not this man, Glenny. He's not the innocent little boy who once came in here with his mother anymore." She faced me squarely. "You don't care that someone might get hurt as you try to uncover something so long buried?"

"I've already been hurt," I said. "I'm not afraid."

"I didn't mean you," she said. "I meant others."

CHAPTER 22

Just before noon, I returned to the bed-and-breakfast.

What I had discovered in the cool quiet of the church profoundly changed what I understood about my mother and added heavily to the burden of guilt I had carried since the day she stepped out of my life.

I was on the porch of the bed-and-breakfast, waiting for Amelia to meet me as we'd agreed upon the day before, lost in those sad, dark thoughts, when Claire's daughter, Michelle, walked up the brick path from the sidewalk. I watched her approach, thinking that she, too, was lost in sad, dark thoughts.

I gave her a small smile that I'm sure reflected the sad emptiness inside me.

Michelle was in retro fashion — platform shoes, bell-bottom jeans, and a tie-dyed T-shirt — and it made her look like a little woman. Once again, I was struck at how little childishness she allowed the world to see.

"Helen said I could find you here," Michelle said. "I need to talk to you."

Such directness was disconcerting for

someone so young. "Shouldn't you be in school?"

"I call in sick whenever I want. Mother signs whatever note I ask her to write."

"Oh."

"I need to talk to you," she reminded me with no sign of impatience.

"I'll listen." I looked out through the tress of the park toward the harbor. It seemed everybody I saw strolling past were couples, holding hands.

Michelle sat on a nearby bench. She handed me a photo that she pulled from her back pocket. "I knew I had seen you before. This was in Helen's photo album."

Claire, with me, on the beach. During our honeymoon. We'd asked an old man in swimming trunks to take the photo. I handed it back to Michelle.

"Who are you?" she asked. "Really, who are you?"

I turned my eyes back on her and finally saw signs of the ten-year-old in her. She was hunched forward with worry lines on her crinkled forehead.

"Ask your mother," I said, not unkindly. "If she wants you to know, she'll tell you."

"She won't. That's why I'm here."

"I wouldn't feel good about breaking her trust, then."

"And you'll feel good about getting her beaten?"

My turn to lurch forward in surprise.

"Pendleton showed up at the carriage house sometime this morning. I was in the bathroom, getting ready to go out. He didn't know I was in the house. He began shouting at Mother, demanding to know what you had told her."

I held up a hand, stopping her quick bursts of words. "He knew I'd visited?"

Michelle took a deep breath. "From me. Last night. After you left. He called to see how I was doing and I asked if he knew someone named Nick. I told him about your visit. I didn't know he'd go ballistic on Mother."

She hugged herself and shivered. "He slapped her in the face. Two or three times. I heard it from the bathroom. That's when I came out. He didn't apologize. Not to me. Not to her."

"I'm sorry," I said. "Very sorry."

"Your fault my father hits my mother?"

"I'm sorry I put you and your mother into the situation. I'll call Pendleton and —"

"No!"

I waited, surprised at her alarm.

"He must hate you real bad. If you call

Pendleton, he'll know I told you. Or maybe that Mother told you. And you haven't seen him when he really loses his temper."

"I'm not sure I can make that promise," I said.

She stared at my face. "You're ready to kill Pendleton, aren't you?"

I didn't answer.

"Will you tell me about you and Mother?"

I shook my head.

"Will you tell me about the police report?"

I frowned.

"Pendleton shouted over and over again, demanding that Mother tell him what she knew about the police report. She didn't answer. That's when he began to slap her. He must be really worried about it."

"Walk with me," I said. "I need to talk to Claire."

CHAPTER 23

There was an awkward moment as Michelle and I approached the carriage house.

Helen stepped completely out of the doorway. She immediately averted her face from me and walked past both of us as if we didn't exist.

It didn't bother me. At least now, unlike during my childhood years, I had given her good reason to be cold and angry with me.

❊ ❊ ❊

Michelle had been correct when she'd warned me during our walk that Claire would be drunk. Not yet noon.

"Oh, you," Claire said, wearily, when Michelle escorted me into the carriage house. "I imagine I should be grateful —" she stopped to collect her thoughts more fully — "for this diversion. Helen wanted a serious talk with me until she saw you stepping into the garden."

"Thank you, Michelle," I said.

"I want to stay," Michelle answered.

I shook my head. Reluctantly, Michelle stepped back outside.

I sat on the sofa and spoke to Claire in a low voice. I wanted to reach out and gently touch the fresh bruise on her face.

"Why are you protecting him?" I asked. "Do you want to be mayor that badly?"

"Shut up." She poured a glass of wine from the bottle on the table in front of her, emptying it. "Go away."

"So you don't deny you are protecting him."

"Your hearing must be impaired. I've said quite distinctly —" she stumbled on the word *distinctly,* getting it out quite indistinctly — "that this is none of your business."

"He beats you and from what I've heard, he cheats on you, takes your money. Does a political career demand that much of an illusion of a good marriage?"

"You should go now." She focused dreamily on her wineglass, swirling the liquid slowly. "You should leave Charleston. Please leave Charleston. Your return has made it very difficult on me. Go away. I'll deal with my life."

I grabbed her wineglass and set it down. "Like this?"

"I'll take my pleasure whatever way I want." She picked up the glass again, took several large gulps, and smiled. "Please, go away. Leave Charleston."

"I need to know about my mother."

"And you accuse —" Claire hiccuped —

"you accuse me of being single-minded."

"Helen knows something. I'm certain of it. I have been asking questions about her. Today I called an old school friend who is now a banker here in Charleston. Your stepmother's financial situation is, let me say, precarious. Her credit is in shambles. I've heard she's been selling antiques on King Street."

"I have my own trust fund. She can't touch that."

"She had an affair with Lorimar Barrett." I wanted to confirm some of the gossip I'd gotten from Elaine and Glennifer.

"Old news, Nick. Small city. They lived just down the street from each other. All the social gatherings are so inbred. People around here have affairs all the time."

She paused for more wine. "Do I care that my husband's father spent time with my stepmother? Besides, it's not like either of them were having affairs on anyone. Pendleton's mother was long dead. And Helen's been a widow almost as long as I've been alive."

She tossed more wine back. "Satisfied, Mr. Detective?"

"No. I don't like it that you have to live like this."

"Why start caring now after all these years? When you left me, it sent a clear message."

"A message that you should marry Pendleton in less than two months?"

Claire started to laugh. A quiet, drunken laugh. She finished her glass of wine. "Just remember you started this. You're the one who opened the lid to the . . . the . . . panorama's box."

She giggled. "The lid to the Pandora's box. I've told you to go away and still you're here. So now I'll tell you, but you're going to have to imagine what it was like back then here in Charleston. Remember? Proper society. When a single girl could not be pregnant?"

Claire lapsed into silence. Her drunken laughter had drained her of energy. When she lifted her face to me, her eyes were filled with tears.

"I was desperate. No one knew that you and I had been married. We had only been gone four days. The marriage was annulled in secrecy, and I wasn't going to tell anyone that you had abandoned me for a monthly payment from my stepmother."

She put her hands into my hands. "I was not going to give up our baby. It was all that I had left of you, and at the time I was foolishly romantic about the love I'd thought we had. So I did the next best thing. Found someone I thought I could live with and married him. Pendleton always wanted us to be married. So did our families. I thought he was the best solution. I was wrong."

Claire moved close to me, crying freely. She rested her head against my chest. "Why did you have to leave me?"

I hardly realized I'd put my arms around her shoulders. I hardly felt the pain of her pressing against the lacerations on my chest. I was still trying to comprehend.

As she wept, Claire stroked my hair. My face. "Pendleton has a lot of things to hate you for. By the time he realized the due date was two months earlier than it should have been, it was too late. He and I were married."

"Michelle," I said. "Michelle is my daughter?"

"No." I'd never heard a voice hold such tired sadness. "You and I, we had a son."

"He's . . . he's . . ." I couldn't finish my question.

"St. Michael's."

I didn't understand.

"He was stillborn, Nick. The doctors . . . they said it sometimes happens. But in my

244

heart, I know it was from the times Pendleton hit me in the last month before . . . before . . ."

I held Claire, conscious of the fact that I was holding another man's wife. She continued to stroke my face, her fingertips gentle against my nose and my lips. "It was like I died inside, Nick. I know that's a cliché, but I understand it because I lived it. All those hours of labor, knowing he would be born dead. All those hours, not knowing how hard it would hit me when I finally held that little baby with his perfectly formed fingers and toes and his quiet, beautiful face. I don't remember much after. They tell me they had to give me drugs to calm me down. I was a zombie at the funeral service. A zombie for the next several months. Then I settled into a life of not caring. It was easy. We had money. We had our name. No one cared if I drank too much. All of us have our vices."

St. Michael's graveyard.

She pulled closer to me, a bundle of soft vulnerability. She pulled my head down toward her face.

I loved her. I deserved her. I wanted her. I ached to protect her. I'd dreamed of this. But she was another man's wife. Whatever might happen next would be poisoned by that inescapable fact.

That was the reason, I told myself, that I could not let this continue. But her accusations of a day before made my heart feel like frozen wood. *You were a lost little boy, wanting so bad to be part of the rest of us. You did anything for me, just to belong, and I was young enough to enjoy that kind of control without knowing how tedious it might have become had we stayed married.*

Those words were another reason I pulled away. "No," I said. If she could hurt me, I could hurt her.

"No?" Her fingertips brushed my lips again.

"No."

She straightened. Wiped her face. "Go away," she said.

"Claire . . ." I was remembering the last time I had pushed someone away to spite myself. Already I regretted this. Claire had been this close to giving herself to me. She was separated from Pendleton. How much would it take for her to leave him completely and come back to me? Especially when she learned the truth about why I'd left. "I'm sorry, Claire."

Too late. She'd moved away from me, hugged herself with her arms. Her face was cold again. "Go away. Don't come back. Tomorrow, I'll forgive myself for this drunken weakness. But I don't want to ever see you again."

CHAPTER 24

Amelia was waiting on the porch of the bed-and-breakfast when I returned. Standing at the rails. Staring coldly at my approach.

She did not sit on one of the rockers when I reached her.

"I'm sorry I'm late," I said. It was a quarter past noon.

"Not important," she answered. "Your life is not my business. With the exception, perhaps, of one area. I won't even apologize for asking."

"Ask."

"Have you heard of the phrase *remittance man?*"

I raised an eyebrow. "That is a strange question. Will you tell me why you asked?"

"Remittance man," Amelia continued, face suddenly scornful. "During the mid- to late-1800s, aristocratic English families rid themselves of sons with embarrassing habits by shipping them across the ocean to the frontiers of the new America, where it would not matter how openly they displayed drunkenness or gambling, providing them with monthly remittance payments as a guarantee to keep them from returning to

England to spoil the family name."

"I am familiar with the phrase," I said. Too familiar. I could guess where she was going with this, why she was so edgy.

"I learned that phrase today from Geoffrey Alexander Gillon."

"Gillon!" I leaned forward. "Why would he call you? How did he know where to find you? How —"

"He's our family attorney," she said icily. "Has been for years. Because of my father, there are arrangements to make, difficult in these circumstances."

I leaned back.

She remained icy. "He told me you eloped with Claire deMarionne. The deMarionnes would have done anything to get rid of you because your background was white trash — his words, not mine — and you gave them the excuse they needed in less than a week. He said my father found you drunk behind the steering wheel of an accident that left Claire's brother in a coma and eventually killed him. Said Helen deMarionne gave you an offer: Stay in Charleston and face criminal charges for the accident. Or annul the marriage and accept a monthly settlement. He said you dumped your new wife for the money and left the hospital as soon as you could."

"Why would my name come up in a conversation with Gillon?" I asked.

"So you don't deny it?"

"I won't deny it," I said.

"That's all I need to hear." Without another word, without looking back, she walked off the porch, down the sidewalk, and past all the magnificent mansions that lined the waterfront.

Pastor Samuel had only been able to tell me where Ruby's sister Opal had last worked as a maid. I was very familiar with the mansion where the family lived. It was near the bed-and-breakfast, and I found it intolerable after Amelia's departure to continue to sit on the piazza and torture myself with memories.

So I tried to find solace in movement.

I walked. I took a degree of savage satisfaction in the biting pain of my plastic limb.

Five minutes later, I arrived at the Ellison mansion.

Honeysuckle and magnolia perfumed me as I approached the front door.

Without hesitation, I knocked.

I heard footsteps. The footsteps stopped.

I knew I was being scrutinized through the peephole by whoever had approached the door.

The footsteps moved away.

I knocked again.

Then I began to pound. Doors like this had been a barrier to me all of my childhood.

Finally, the door swung open.

"Go away. We don't offer tours." The old woman was dressed formally, down to her white gloves. Her dull red skirt was conservative, and her jacket was discreetly ornamented by a gold pin holding a carnation. Her blue-rinsed hair had been set and sprayed, her cheeks rouged, and her eyebrows penciled in.

"I need to ask a question," I said.

"Read a guidebook. Now go away."

She began to shut the door. I inserted my foot. My right foot.

She slammed the door, hoping I would yelp. I did not. I was grimly amused that my plastic limb finally had a use.

"Remove your foot and go away." She was unintimidated by my stoic response to the slammed door. She spoke in soft, long southern vowels, her voice filled with the supreme politeness that in her circles meant just the opposite.

"No guidebook will have the answer I need," I said.

"Please try to understand." She spoke to me as if I could not possibly understand, using the tone she might have chosen for a colored person, before it had become out of fashion to call servants that. "If you do not leave immediately, I will call the police."

"A maid once worked in this household," I said. "Opal Atkins. It would help me greatly if you could give me her address."

I spoke clearly, biting off each syllable, something I had consciously taught myself as part of my effort to leave everything of Charleston behind.

"The business of this household is of no matter to anyone except those of this household."

For a moment, I felt thirteen again, as though facing the collective disapproval at the family's nightly meals in the Barrett place, with a haunting perfume of wisteria and jasmine wafting in from the garden through open windows.

"Sordid business usually is," I said. I allowed the polite southern drawl back into my voice. "Wasn't it your husband, Edmund Ellison, who resigned as college dean to take a job in your daddy's bank? Marijuana and two coeds at a private after-curfew party in their dormitory room, I believe, which would have been forgivable if he hadn't also used scholarship foundation money to fund the trips he took to Bermuda with those two coeds. Your daddy replaced the money and had a talk with someone at the newspaper and none of your husband's activities became public. It helped that your daddy and his bank held a million-dollar demand loan against the newspaper, which, of course, was a lot of money at the time."

Wide as Lauren Ellison's eyes suddenly opened, I was confident she wouldn't recognize me. These people never saw beyond themselves, and anyway, too many years had passed since I'd been in Charleston.

To her credit, she did not back down. "I have suffered your rudeness long enough. Go anywhere with those rumors and face a slander suit."

"You have Opal's address," I said calmly. "If not, you know of someone who does."

She pushed the door, squeezing my foot into the frame. I could like this old woman's stubbornness. But I, too, had that quality.

"Your son Fraser dismembered animals

in the carriage house at the back of your fine property," I said. "Other people south of Broad wondered what happened to their dogs and cats, but I knew. And I think you did too. How is Fraser these days?"

"I should be able to find something that has her address," she said. "Will you wait a moment?"

CHAPTER 25

"Who do you know who owns a Rottweiler?"
I asked.

"Another bedside visit," Edgar Layton
said. His head trembled as he spoke. Although I did not want to be, I was impressed at the effort he put into keeping
his voice strong and under control.
"Haven't you given up hope of some kind
of deathbed confession?"

Implying that there is something to confess.
It strengthened my resolve to be here, re-
gardless of how much acrimony I risked if
Amelia appeared in the next few minutes.

I repeated my question. "Who do you
know who owns a Rottweiler?"

"What a stupid question."

"Where is my mother? You took her to
the train station the night she left Charleston."

"Say I could tell you right now where to
find her." Layton's grin was a death mask,
his skin stretched tight across his forehead,
his nostrils large, dark openings into his
skull. "How would you force it from me?"

By his reply, I found it interesting that he
did not care that I knew. Or how I knew. I
did not flinch at his smirk. I looked di-

rectly into the man's glowing eyes. "You've got a day, maybe two, to live. No matter what happened that night, no one can hurt you for it. Telling me won't cost you a single thing. Please, help me."

"The mercy route." Layton had to take several deep breaths to continue. "Is that it? You've dropped all pride and you're on your knees, begging. Do it more. I'll consider telling you."

He does know.

"I've dropped all pride. I'm on my knees. I'm begging. Please help me."

Layton studied me. "Nope. That doesn't do it. But I enjoyed watching you."

I stared steadily back at Layton.

"Maybe try force," Layton said. "Threaten to kill me. I'd suggest a pillow over my face. I doubt there'd be an autopsy. No one would suspect murder, not with me this close to dead anyway. You could get away with it."

"I'll kill you if you don't tell me," I said tonelessly.

"Nope. That threat doesn't frighten me. You'd be doing me a favor. Like you said, I'll be gone in a day or two. You'll save me a lot of pain. And, trust me, time goes slow when every breath is agony."

I continued to stare at the skeleton of a

man in the bed in front of me.

"See? With me, you have no leverage. When a man cares about nothing, nothing controls him. He is free. On the other hand, you care so much about finding your mother that it gives me control over you." Layton cackled. "Me, an old dying man with the power to make you beg."

Layton recovered his breath again. "I've always known that. This city is filled with fools who gave me power because they had something they wanted to protect. Reputation, money, loved ones. I could always find what was important to them and use it against them. Like plucking cherries from a tree. Rich, juicy cherries that I sucked dry. But me? I don't even care to live. I'm not even afraid of God. There's not a single thing you can use against me."

"No, there is nothing to use against you," I said. "But I can make you a promise."

"What could you give me that I would care about?"

"Protection for Amelia."

He blinked.

"Why did I ask you about a Rottweiler? Someone tried to kill me last night. Only a day after Geoffrey Alexander Gillon made a threat that I should leave all of this alone.

There is something terrible that I may bring to light. And you are part of it."

I was just guessing. But what did I have to lose? And Edgar's focused stillness told me I wasn't totally wrong in my guess. About the threat. Or about the love for his daughter.

"Whoever is trying to stop me might believe Amelia knows what you know. What if they go after her next? The truth about my mother is a hornet's nest. I know this from Senator Gillon. He's already warned me about swinging a stick at it. But I'm not going to stop my search. If you help me find the truth, I may be able to prevent the hornets from stinging innocent bystanders. Like Amelia. You do care about her, don't you?"

"Go away," he croaked. "Go away." His face formed into lines of anger.

I pressed harder. "You blackmailed Pendleton. To how many others have you done the same? When you die, people with power are going to want what you once held over them. Even if it means hurting her."

"Shut up," he said. He spoke with strength that surprised me. "Shut your mouth."

"Oh," I said, "you do care about something."

I taunted him, a dying man. "Suddenly you are no longer free. And, after you lived this life of yours, does your precious daughter love you as you love her?"

He rang the nurse's bell, rolled over, and faced away from me.

I left him there. I walked away, feeling diminished.

❀ ❀ ❀

I was standing at the elevator doors when I heard my name called.

I turned and saw a nurse hurrying toward me. Middle-aged, huffing from the effort.

"Yes?"

She slowed. "Nicholas Barrett?"

The elevator chimed. The door opened.

"Yes."

"Mr. Layton asked me to catch you. He wanted me to tell you something from him."

I let the elevator door shut behind me.

"It doesn't make much sense to me," she said. "So if you don't understand it either, don't feel bad. Sometimes patients on morphine . . ."

"Yes." I tried to hide my impatience.

"McLean Robertson owns a Rottweiler," she said. "That's what Mr. Layton asked me to tell you. McLean Robertson owns a Rottweiler."

CHAPTER 26

"Nicholas Barrett?" Opal Atkins said after I introduced myself at the doorway, drawing a hand to her mouth with a gasp. "Lord, have mercy. The devil's finally come around to make me pay for my sins."

While her ground-floor condominium spoke against any stereotype of the elderly, Opal Atkins resembled the short, flower-patterned-dress-wearing, pie-baking grand-mother of any television commercial. The curls of her short white hair framed a deeply wrinkled face. She wore wire-rimmed bifocals. Age had begun to hunch her back.

She retreated into the apartment, word-lessly beckoning me to follow. She pointed me to the couch and, still without speak-ing, filled a kettle with water and set it on the stove to boil.

This interlude gave me time to look around the interior.

I cannot comment, of course, on the quality of retirement of all maids who spent a lifetime of service in the homes south of Broad, but moments earlier, from the side-walk, it had appeared to me that Opal Atkins had not fared badly in her pension years.

By taxi, I'd traveled from the old quarter over the Cooper River to the opposite side in Mt. Pleasant. The address I'd been given for her was a seniors' complex of one-level condominiums. By the new brick exterior, large grounds of trimmed grass, and expansive flower beds, this was no depressing prison where the elderly were sent to await death.

The interior of her condominium confirmed it. The layout was open and filled with midafternoon sunlight from generous windows; her kitchen was separated from the living room by a half wall inset with glass blocks. The furniture was modern, as was the taste in paint colors. All that betrayed her age and sense of fashion were the profusion of knickknacks and dozens of family photos scattered throughout, filling the spaces on every shelf, ledge, and windowsill.

The wait for the water to boil gave me time to ponder her words of greeting: *Lord, have mercy. The devil's finally come around to make me pay for my sins.*

Was I the devil?

Or had he appeared with me?

I did not ask. Not immediately. Opal did not seem to be in a hurry to banish me. Over the half wall that separated us — me on the sofa, she in the kitchen — I saw that she was cutting slices of chocolate cake and setting them on a plate.

When she was ready, she came around the corner with a tray, carrying a teapot and the prepared cake. She poured the tea. Her tiny, shaking hand paused over a bowl of sugar lumps.

"If I remember right," she said, "when you were a boy, you took sugar and some milk. Has that changed?"

I shook my head.

She added the sugar and milk and stirred the tea before handing me the cup on a saucer.

I sipped and smiled a thank-you. "This is a nice place to live."

She pointed at two nearby wedding photos. Each showed a young proud man beside a beautiful woman. "My oldest boy is an engineer. The other, an architect. I helped them get through college, and they haven't forgotten. Some do, you know. I know plenty of old folks who don't get help from their children."

I sipped and nodded, then asked the obvious question. "You remember me as a boy?"

She looked up from her task of lifting a slice of cake onto a plate. "Sure do. It was my sister Ruby who looked after you, but there were times, especially when you were younger, that she brought you over when she was looking after you and wanted to get out of your mama's house."

I dimly remembered a clanky ceiling fan in a small house that always smelled of gingerroot. "That was you? In the house on Amherst?"

"None other. You were a handsome boy. Nice and polite. I'm glad to see you grew up the same."

I accepted the cake.

"I know what's on your mind," she sighed. "You heard me say the devil's come around to make me pay."

I nodded.

"You want to ask me about your mama, right? About Ruby, right?"

Again, I nodded.

"Lord, Lord, Lord," she said. "The guilt I've suffered since that night. I'm almost glad you're here to give me the chance to confess."

"That night?"

"The night your mama left Charleston. See, when all the newspapers went on and on about her leaving like she did, I should have stepped forward and told it different. At least, the part that I knew was different."

I leaned forward.

"What you need to understand," Opal said, "is that Ruby should have been there. But it was me instead. I'm the one he saw from the doorway. Not her. She died instead of me."

Opal told me what she saw that night. And finally I understood why my mother had left with Edgar Layton. It began with four packed suitcases on the hardwood floor, just inside the door of the town house where I was raised. . . .

❋ ❋ ❋

My mother was carrying the fifth suitcase down the stairs when the doorbell rang.

She set the suitcase beside the others. She opened the door to see the large unsmiling face of Chief Edgar Layton.

He filled the entire doorway, looking even taller with the hat on his head. He took it off, showing the flattop brush cut that added intimidation to his ugly features. He held the hat against his chest, faking respect for her that they both knew he did not have. The light from behind her spilled over her head and onto his face, showing thickened scars on his eyebrows, scars from his legendary boxing days. Her shadow fell across his chest, like a small black paper cutout against his uniform.

"Hello," she said.

"Mrs. Barrett," he said. He didn't blink, his eyes dull dark rocks in his enormous head. "I'm sorry to intrude."

There were stories about Layton. How he'd beaten a black prisoner to death with his bare hands. How he knew every prostitute in town. How his position as chief was a brokered deal between the mayor and the old Charleston aristocracy. How Layton used his position to help those people keep their power, always mindful to set aside more than a little something for himself.

"No intrusion . . . ," she said, lying as a southerner is required. She gestured at the suitcases. "I'd invite you inside, but as you can see . . ."

"Yes, ma'am," he said. "Looks like you're going on a trip. Which makes it even more difficult to tell you why I have stopped by instead of calling on the telephone."

Beyond him, she saw the chief of police's car. The motor was running, the headlights throwing twin circles of yellow on the cars parked in front.

"You see," he said, "there is some news I believe can only be delivered in person."

"Yes?" Her voice was high and strained.

"It's Nick," he said.

Her world was reduced to watching his lower face, the way his lips moved as he talked, as if her eyes might actually see the words enter the air as he told her more. She reached up to her face and touched the deep cut on her cheekbone.

"There's been an accident out at the beach house," he continued. "I'll take you there myself."

She nodded, numb. "Is . . . is he dead?"

"No." Layton gestured for my mother to step outside to the waiting car. "My instructions are to take you there as quickly as possible."

"Mizz Barrett? Ever'ting be all right?" It was a voice from the top of the stairs, from a black woman carrying another suitcase. Opal, who was there instead of Ruby.

"I'm not sure," my mother said. "I'll be back when I can. Finish up and go on home when you are ready."

Layton's eyes met the eyes of the black maid. Only briefly. His predatory look chilled her, and she turned around.

Layton led my mother into the night, to the car where Amelia lay hidden on the floor in the back.

❅ ❅ ❅

My cup of tea was half empty and cold by the time Opal finished.

"I don't understand," I said. "Your sister Ruby. I thought she was my mother's maid. But you said you were there at the top of —"

"She was your mama's maid all right. They'd been friends all their lives. But Ruby took sick that day. Your mama needed someone to help her pack. Ruby asked me to go in her place. Your mama needed it. She was in some kind of mood that day. Not much use getting everything together. She was crying hard, telling me that she wanted to leave this hateful city. Wouldn't even go to the doctor to get her face looked at, even though a half dozen times it started bleeding again."

I dropped my eyes to stare at my shoes. That was my last image of my mother, of the deep cut on her cheek.

"What it was," Opal said, unaware of the renewed surge of the guilt I always carried, "was that I should have gone to the police as soon as folks said your mama had run off. Because I knew different. She never came back for those suitcases I helped her pack."

"But you didn't . . ."

"I was afraid. Of that man. The chief of police."

Opal poured more tea for me. She stood.

She walked around the room, straightening pictures on the wall that did not need straightening.

I added more sugar and milk to my tea and waited until she returned.

"People think we're stupid," she said. "They look at the color of our skin. They look at the part of the city we come from. They look at how and where we work, and they think we're stupid. I fought all my life against that. I went back and got my high school diploma after my boys were grown. I go to college for night classes now that my husband's passed on and this place is too empty. I'm old and I'm black, but it doesn't mean I'm stupid."

She lifted the teapot to pour yet again, so distracted she forgot she'd just filled my cup. She set the pot down.

"That night long ago, I saw that man in your mama's doorway. I saw him, too, in the car that run down my sister. Sure I did. It was a rainy day, the next day, a Friday. I'd gone with Ruby to get a sack of groceries. Halfway home, I remembered I'd forgotten some vanilla for a cake I wanted to bake that night. I ran back to the store and was just about caught up with her when that car passed me and run into her ahead of me. Think I didn't recognize that big ugly head of the one and only chief of police of Charleston? Think I was so stupid I couldn't figure it out? He thought it was Ruby at the top of the stairs. She and I had a strong family resemblance. To a man like him, I'd bet all of us look pretty much the same anyway. I remembered the way he'd looked at me when I was looking down on him. It was the look of death, and the next day my sister Ruby was dead. Now who you think I could go to and tell that story? Me, a young black woman in the South in a city like this, up against a man like him? And how long you think before I get run over myself and leave behind two young boys? No, sir, I kept my mouth shut and have suffered with that secret ever since. My own sister dead and I couldn't do a thing about it except keep my mouth shut."

Opal began to cry silently.

I lifted a napkin from the serving tray and handed it to her. "I understand," I said.

"Don't tell me you understand!" It was a quick moment of savageness, a glimpse of the strength and willpower that had taken her through life. "You won't ever know what it feels like to keep that kind of poison inside."

I thought of my mother's face as Opal had seen it. I thought of the tiny, deep cut. In truth, I could have disagreed with Opal. I knew how the poison ate.

* * *

I moved from the sofa and stared out the window at the quietness of life outside. Elderly men and women walked slowly on the brick sidewalks that cut attractive paths across the grounds. Some used canes or walkers. Others did not but were betrayed by stooped backs or uncertain steps.

"I'm sorry," Opal called out to me. "I had no right to talk to you that way. It's not your fault this happened."

Again, in truth, I could have disagreed with her.

As I turned toward Opal, I forced myself to keep my own shame and guilt and regret out of my face. Because of me, her sister had been killed. Unlike Opal, however, I would not confess.

"Thank you for your help," I said. "Perhaps it would be best if I left now."

Opal made no effort to offer me more tea. In the South, that was a firm good-bye.

She escorted me to the door. "I hope you find your mama," she said, just before opening the door. "I didn't know her like

Ruby did. I'm not sure there's anything else I can tell you that might help."

"It's been a long time," I said. "I'm not expecting much."

"All of it has been a real shame. A real shame. My Ruby gone. You growing up like you did." She frowned and shook her head. "Your mama's sister is the one that should have took you in, especially with all the money she had and how your mama helped her get it."

"My mama's sister?"

I recalled what Pastor Samuel had told me this morning: *Sure, your mama had an older sister that worked some and helped the family, but shortly after their daddy died in the bathtub, that girl run off. No one knew to where, and no one heard from her again.*

Opal was nodding gravely as I continued. "Her sister," I said, "ran away when she was a little girl. I never met my aunt once when I was growing up."

Opal's eyes widened. "I thought you knew. I thought your mama would have told you sometime before she left."

"Knew?"

Opal grabbed my elbow. Firmly.

"Come inside," she said. "Maybe I can help you after all."

CHAPTER 27

I stood on a brick walkway in a garden dominated by three oak trees draped with Spanish moss. The shade of those trees covered a profusion of subtropical flowers and foliage plants. Hummingbirds darted in tight circles around a feeder. The buzz of bees was soothing on a windless day, the heat pleasant in the late afternoon.

Paradise. If a person could set aside who owned the garden.

That owner of the garden knelt in front of me as she weeded among ginger lilies. She knew I stood behind her but had refused to rise and greet me.

"A few days ago," I began, speaking to her back, "I was in an antique shop on King. I saw a chair I was tempted to buy. Italian craftsmanship, if my relatively untutored guess is correct. A very striking piece. What made it memorable were the feet of the chair. Each one was a talon clutching a smooth ball. I can't imagine how many hours it took to carve this chair of beauty. In the end, I didn't purchase it."

"No?" She finally spoke, the woman kneeling in front of me. Her hands, however, kept busy. They were protected by garden gloves, and with precise, calculated fury, they struck at weeds. The right hand jabbed with a tiny hand spade; the left hand plucked the offending plant.

"It was far beyond my price range," I said. "Still, I seriously considered it. Sentimental value and all that."

"Really."

I couldn't see her face. She wore a wide-brimmed garden hat with dark protective netting that wrapped down and under her chin. The rest of her clothes consisted of overalls. I'd interrupted what looked like a seriously planned gardening session.

"Really. You see, I was certain this chair once belonged to the mother of the woman I married. I'd seen it in the family mansion countless times. It saddened me to think that this once proud family had been reduced to the common plight of selling household furnishings."

"Perhaps," the woman said, "they simply tired of the chair. That happens, you know."

"I find that hard to believe," I said. "You've always been vain, almost triumphant about the fine furnishings of your household."

Helen deMarionne sighed. She set aside her garden tools. She rolled off her knees and sat with her legs tucked behind her. I still saw little of her face, screened as it was by the dark netting and the shade of the wide-brimmed hat.

"Have you come to gloat? Come to inquire what has happened to our family fortunes?"

"I just want truth."

"Read the Bible. I've been told it has all the truth you need."

"I need to know what happened to my mother."

"This is becoming tedious," Helen said, settling against the soil. "We've been through this already. I want the truth about how my son died. Which you refuse to give me. And I've told you everything I can about your mother."

Helen appeared comfortable, reclining as she was on the warmth of the soil. I was not.

I took a bamboo chair from a sitting area nearby and moved it close to Helen. I sat.

"I believe there is much more you can tell me about my mother." I hoped my voice hid all of the conflicting emotions I felt. I thought of the letter I had received, and those ten cryptic words.

Ask Helen deMarionne the truth. She knew your mother best.

"As her sister, perhaps you did know her best."

Helen's stillness became utterly rigid. "You know," she said softly.

"You ran away when she was a child. You returned. She introduced you to Maurice deMarionne. I imagine it was your idea, not hers."

"She owed me because I kept our father from her. I have no regret about making my sister make payment for that. I found out who she'd married, how she was living. So, yes, I returned. It would have done me no good for anyone here to know where I'd been or how I had lived. I made her vow to keep it a secret that we were sisters. Your mother owed me and she knew it."

Helen's head did not move while she spoke. She kept her face resolutely away from me. Her voice had no inflection.

"I was the oldest," Helen said. "The first to develop. I could see my father begin to watch her like he had watched me. With that ugly want on his face. I couldn't let it happen to her, the way he'd been with me. She was sweet, innocent. She didn't yet think of the world as a place of the users and the used, not like I had learned. So one night, he was drunk, taking a bath. He called for me. When I opened the door, I had a bat in my hand. Hitting him, I started to cry, because it was as good as I had ever felt. I hate him for the fact that I enjoyed hitting him until he died. The police knew who had killed him. And why. But in that section of town, sometimes it was better for justice to take its own course. After that, I ran away. Atlanta. I had learned a lot from my father about men. It helped me survive. Here in Charleston, marrying Maurice was no different than what I'd done in Atlanta. Except the money was better and I had respectability."

"I am not here to judge you," I said. "At least not for that. I was orphaned. You were my only family. You could have taken me in."

"So that the entire world would wonder why? I liked my past where it was. Behind me. There was no need to have people doubt the fictional past I had created for myself. You were already taken care of by the Barretts. You didn't need me."

"Claire is your stepdaughter. Not your daughter. There was nothing to stop us from marriage. You destroyed that for me."

She sighed. "I had it planned so well. Claire would marry Pendleton. Even then, I foresaw the day that the deMarionne funds would become a dry well. Pendleton's family had money. You didn't. It was that simple. If Claire married into the Barrett fortune, which Pendleton would someday control, I would never lose this house and this life. I'd sold my soul for this life. I wasn't going to lose it to keep you happy."

"Except now the IRS has frozen Pendleton's accounts and you have started selling your antiques."

"I am very aware of the irony," she said. "Everything that I had planned so carefully now in tatters. If only I would have known then what I know now."

"Which is . . . ?"

She answered me with a long, long silence.

As for me, I didn't know what else to say. Her choices had become irrevocable acts. Screaming in anger at her would change nothing. Asking her again and again would not gain me any knowledge about my mother, not if she refused to tell me more. I had no leverage against her. And her sense of moral obligation seemed so cold and weak that I held little hope of appeal.

I stood from the chair.

"You love her still?" Helen asked, her head still hidden and facing away from me.

"Claire? She is a married woman."

"Last night, I wanted to talk to her, but you appeared. So I talked with her today. She'll divorce Pendleton for you."

"And we can become yet another tawdry couple playing out a soap opera of affairs among the upper crust of Charleston?"

"Leave Charleston with her. You're rich. You can afford it."

"I am not rich," I said. "I have not kept any of the money you sent me."

She snorted. "Truly?"

"You can't understand that, can you? I didn't sign that annulment for the money. I only took it because it would cost you. I hope you find it amusing that aside from my monthly needs, you supported orphanages wherever I traveled."

Helen stood too. She dusted off her knees by slapping them with the garden gloves she'd removed from her hands.

"Leave Charleston with her," she repeated, her back to me, staring at the high hedge that fenced in this garden. "You're a rich man. Not from what I've sent. But from your inheritance."

"My trust fund money disappeared with my mother."

"Perhaps," she said, "but that's nothing compared to the Barrett fortune. That's the irony. You're entitled to half. By law, you'll get what's owed to you before the IRS can take it from Pendleton."

"I don't understand," I said.

"Let me give you some priceless knowledge, Nick."

"I'm listening."

"First of all, I want you to know I did not discover this until recently. Had I known from the beginning . . ." Her voice drifted.

It was surreal. The prettiness of the garden. The butterflies and hummingbirds. The flower blossoms. The light rustling of leaves as a breeze began to caress Charleston. All of the world's life continued, while Helen and I were frozen in this moment.

"You were not the love child of an affair," Helen said.

"I know that now," I said. "My mother was —"

"Yes," Helen said. "There was a reason why Carolyn held her silence about that horrible night as she did. Her husband, David, adored his older brother, Lorimar. Think about it. How could she tell her husband that his own brother betrayed him in such a way? Especially if it would be Lorimar's word against hers, the poor girl from a bad part of town? By the time she knew she was pregnant, it was too late. Then David was killed in action. She demanded that Lorimar pay monthly into your trust fund. She wanted Lorimar to be reminded every month what he'd done, how he'd betrayed his brother. Much as she hated it among the aristocrats of Charleston, she wanted you raised with all the advantages she never had."

I could hardly comprehend what she was telling me. "Lorimar Barrett was my father?"

"Lorimar Barrett was your father, Nick. You and Pendleton are half brothers."

CHAPTER 28

"Nick, I need to see you."

It was a whispered voice over the telephone. Ten o'clock. I had been half asleep, trying to lose my misery in the escape of exhaustion, and at first my hopes fooled me.

"Claire?"

"No." Long pause. "Amelia Layton. We have to talk. Right away."

I rubbed my eyes. "Sure. Where?"

"My father's house. I'll give you the address. You can walk here from Meeting Street."

In the old quarters of Charleston, you can walk nearly anywhere else within twenty minutes. I made it in less than ten, for Edgar Layton's house was south of Broad, naturally among all the other moneyed houses clustered near the tip of the peninsula.

It was a stone building, rising high and narrow with similar darkened houses on both sides. The previous night's storm had long since cleared, and while the glow of the city lights obliterated any but the brightest stars, the moon fought through the haze, pale blue, hanging just above the roofline of the house, casting a shadow directly in front of the piazza that ran along the back side. In the flower beds, dead stalks of last year's marigolds cast thin lines of black against the dim backdrop thrown on the ground by the light of the moon; it seemed like they were tall, crippled soldiers waiting wearily for the reaper's scythe to take them down.

Amelia explained to me later that this house was not her childhood home; that had been a bungalow north of 17, a highway that essentially bisected the haves on the south from the almost-haves on the north. It was so close to the Citadel that on Friday mornings the cadence of military marches rolled among the live oaks of her yard like a breeze shimmering the leaves, the sounds of the school reaching her as surely as the tangy salt air off the swampy lowlands of the Cooper River beside it.

Amelia had been thirteen when her mother died, the same year that Edgar Layton moved south of Broad among Charleston's rich. By then, her hatred for her father had escalated into a cold war with occasional skirmishes of hot-blooded teenage rebellion that he always won on the surface but lost on a much deeper level because his unyielding punishments scourged further her diminishing love and respect for him. Amelia lived like a stranger in that cold, empty house, waiting no longer than the morning after her final day of high school to move from her father, never visiting again.

As I was about to find out, she had her own childhood ghosts of guilt that she'd never quite been able to bury.

❋ ❋ ❋

The back door was unlocked. I found Amelia in the large luxurious kitchen. Copper-bottomed pots and pans hung from hooks above an island with a granite countertop; it was definitely a cook's paradise, obvious even in candlelight.

For the ceiling light was not on. Amelia was illuminated by those candles, as if she wanted the comfort of near darkness to hide alone in her thoughts. She sat at a small dining table in the corner of the kitchen that overlooked the backyard. She wore black jeans and a black turtleneck.

As I entered the kitchen, she smoothed her long thick hair by running her hands through it.

I sat opposite her. Papers were spread across the table. There was a Ziploc bag that held a pistol. I made no comments.

Because Amelia was staring at the table, I, in turn, was able to study her. Despite the burden inside me, I acknowledged to myself the understated beauty of her face. Then I realized my assessment was not that impartial. It was my first awareness of a current between us.

She lifted her eyes and caught me staring.

More of that electricity.

"Hello," I said.

"I am so sorry, Nick. Sorry about what you've gone through. And sorry that I assumed the worst about you."

She sighed. "I told you earlier that I'd met with Senator Gillon," she said. "I didn't tell you he'd asked if I'd found my father's collection. I asked Gillon what he meant by a collection. He told me not to play dumb and warned me that hiding my father's collection could put me in great danger. So, of course, after I left Gillon's office, I began to wonder what he had meant. That's why I came here tonight." She smiled wanly. "I found it."

Amelia picked up a yellowed sheet of paper from the table and gave it to me. "I was wrong about you. The accident when you were nineteen. Tell me about it."

"Not much to tell," I said. I took the sheet of paper. I was holding a copy of an accident report. That involved me. "Where did you find this?"

"Why did you tell me you were driving?"

"I didn't. I told you I was found behind the steering wheel."

"But you weren't driving. I know that now. This report. And the photographs of the accident scene. I'm not a detective, but even I can tell you weren't driving. The front passenger side door is buckled in where it would have crushed your right leg. Blood on the floorboard on the passenger side. Yet the photograph of you behind the steering wheel doesn't indicate any damage to the car that might have hurt your leg. It's obvious from the photos that someone dragged you over from the passenger side and left you behind the steering wheel. Yet you took the blame. Why?"

"Where did you find this?" I asked, deliberately ignoring her question. I held up the report. I indicated the contents on the table. "What is the rest of this?"

The flickering light of the candles showed the sadness on her face. "Why did you let everyone think you were driving? Just tell me that."

"The accident is a closed subject," I

said. "It's my mother I want to find."

I picked up the plastic bag. The pistol inside sagged heavily in the bag as I held it by the top and read the label, knowing I would see the date of Amelia's eighth birthday — the date that my mother stepped onto a train and abandoned me in Charleston — starkly written behind the initials M.W.R. & C.L.B.

C.L.B. Carolyn Leah Barrett. My mother's initials. How was this pistol linked to her? Had she witnessed or been part of a murder?

"This pistol . . . that night . . ."

"You'll understand better," Amelia said, "when you see where I found it."

"Sure," I said. My heart was heavy. Had I really wanted to learn this about my mother? That she had left behind her son and left behind a murder?

"It's been since high school that I last visited my father," Amelia said. "Do you see any irony in the fact that my first return has technically been a break-and-enter?"

It wasn't a question that needed an answer.

She stood. "Are you curious?"

I answered by standing.

I followed her out of the kitchen and

down the hallway. She snapped on some lights. "You know," she said, "my father cared little for cooking, but he hired an interior decorator to provide the appearance of those with rich tastes he aspired to imitate. You'll see the rest of the house is the same."

She was right. Antiques, rugs, and furnishings straight from a home decorator's magazine.

"This house has no soul," she said. "Money can buy a house, but it won't make it a home. Trust me, I know."

I continued to follow as Amelia moved upstairs, shutting off lights behind her as she turned on lights ahead. The floors were all hardwood, the walls and ceilings smooth plaster with ponderous moldings at the joints. There was no place for dust to hide, no place for anything to settle without the knowledge of Edgar Layton and his disapproving attention to detail. Despite the age of the house, the renovations he had directed had sterilized it so thoroughly with his determination to make it proper that with one single exception, the entire house was devoid of any interesting nooks and crannies that might provide an illusion of character, give it a personality that a person could grow to love as much as an eccentric aunt.

We reached the top of the stairs. She pointed at a linen closet at the end of the hallway on the second floor.

"When I was a teenager, I caught my father there once," she said. "Caught him in the act of stepping, crouched and backward, out of the tiny closet, although it was half his size.

"It was weird. I'd returned home after forgetting my purse and knew he didn't expect me to be in the house at all. It was so weird, I immediately turned around in silence and sneaked down the stairs and out the back again without letting him know what I had seen."

She led me to the closet. "A few weeks later, when I was sure he was on duty, I explored the interior of the closet, poking and prodding and tapping at the walls and shelves. I couldn't find anything. Still, I never forgot the sight of his huge body, bent and folded, as he backed out from the inside of the closet. My father never did anything without a coldly calculated reason. I knew something was hidden inside."

We neared the closet.

"When Gillon asked me about the collection, I decided it must be hidden there."

She laughed softly. A hammer and crowbar rested on the floor. "Unlike during my teenage years, tonight I wasn't afraid of leaving any damage behind as I searched it."

She pointed upward. "I replaced the ceiling panel, but that was before I made my decision to call you. You'll find it moves aside easily. And the shelves are built sturdy enough to use as a ladder. I'd like you to see what I saw. That way you'll more easily believe my story."

I was very conscious of the prosthesis that served as my lower right leg. While it served me fine for walking, climbing was another thing.

She misunderstood my hesitation for the politeness of someone who wasn't going to pry unnecessarily. "Go on," she said. "I'll wait for you in the kitchen."

There was a flashlight resting on a stack of towels on one of the shelves. She handed it to me. "Go on," she repeated. "You want to learn about your mother, don't you?"

❋ ❋ ❋

Alone, I studied the inside of the linen closet. The shelves were wrapped around the walls in a U-shape. Left wall, rear wall, right wall. Some of the linens stacked on the shelves showed the imprints of shoes where Amelia had climbed.

Above, the interior of the closet ceiling was lined with crown molding at the joints of the wall and ceiling, just like the rest of the house. But why would anyone bother to spend money on expensive molded wood when the decorative effect would never be seen? Unless the ceiling, as Amelia had discovered, rested on top of the molding.

I stepped on the bottom shelf of the rear wall, holding shelves on each side for balance. Like a rock climber moving up the inside of a chute, I reached the ceiling with the top of my head; my feet were now on the shelves some four feet off the floor.

I tensed my neck muscles and pushed. The ceiling popped loose from where it rested on the crown molding. A draft of cooler air hit my face.

I slid the piece of ceiling ahead, resting it on crossbeams. I climbed one set of shelves higher, so that my upper body was now thrust into the opening. All of this movement was difficult and slow for me — I was grateful that Amelia did not witness my crippled awkwardness.

With my upper body in the opening, my hands were free to shine the flashlight beam around me. All that separated me from the roof of the house were trusses, five feet of space, and cobwebs between the trusses. Shredded insulation filled the floor of the attic between the crossbeams. The end of the house was some five feet away from here, a patch of bare stone the color of old bones in my flashlight beam, with some exposed wiring that ran down into the insulation and out of sight.

Just in front of me, I saw where Amelia had pulled up strips of insulation to expose a large ring handle on a square cover of plywood. I took the ring and pulled, lifting the square of plywood and sliding it onto the crossbeams of the ceiling below my waist. My flashlight beam showed the interior of the storage area hidden behind the linen closet. Primitive wooden ladder rungs ran down one wall. It took me five minutes to clamber down the back side of the linen closet.

The total area of the hidden storage space was double the interior of the linen closet. The front half was empty; the back half held a large — almost antique — safe, the black exterior pitted and chipped.

The safe door was open.

I scanned with my flashlight.

The interior of the safe was compartmentalized, with perhaps two dozen rectangular shelves made of thin steel. The tiny alcoves held plastic bags, and I pulled one out.

It held a small knife with a smear of blackened, dried blood across the blade and bottom half of the handle, a blurred fingerprint trapped in the blood. There was handwriting on a white label on the outside of the bag: *C.W.Y., 08-10-69.*

I pulled out another bag. It held two misshapen bullets labeled *A.N., 02-02-65.*

One by one, I pulled out more plastic bags. A pair of scissors, one blade broken: *O.H.G., 09-11-72.* A derringer: *K.I.T.W., 12-11-63.* Other plastic bags with photographs, some showing sprawled bodies at a crime scene, others showing surprised couples in bed, pulling blankets up to protect themselves against the camera, invariably against a backdrop of a cheap hotel room.

Another caught my eye. A folded piece of paper within the clear plastic, handwritten ink blotchy across the paper, labeled *C.J.R., 05-09-68.* I opened that bag, half knowing already what this macabre collection meant and wondering if the writing on the letter would confirm my suspicions.

Dated May 5, 1968. I, Clifford James

Ritchell, deputy mayor of Charleston, confess by my free will that I was engaged in an adulterous affair with Laura Lynn Swanson, secretary of the Public Works Department, and that said affair included secret liaisons at City Hall. Our first encounter took place at . . .

Somehow Edgar Layton had once leveraged a confession out of this man, then held the confession.

I understood. These labeled plastic bags, heaped around me like explosives from the past, were able to detonate shock waves into families and generations unaware of the past horrors hidden among them. This collection had given Edgar Layton his famed and, to outsiders, almost unfathomable power base. Crimes covered but never forgotten. The guilty, never free of their guilt, and like me, always beholden to Edgar Layton.

A collection of the sins of the city.

CHAPTER 29

In the kitchen, Amelia was motionless and seated at the table again. In her hands was a large scrapbook.

I touched her shoulder lightly. I wanted her to know I had returned, but I didn't want my voice to intrude on her thoughts.

She gently set the scrapbook down on the papers of the table, just to the side of the sealed plastic bag. She reached up and held my hand in place on her shoulder.

"It's a scrapbook of my life," she said. "He documented everything about me. Even my graduation from med school. I didn't know he was in the audience, but there's a photo of me accepting my diploma and a photo of him at the banquet hall, as if he was trying to fool himself that he had been part of it."

She dropped her hand from mine and wiped her eyes. "The combination to the safe? My birthday. I had tried my father's date of birth, my mother's date of birth, the date of her death, the date of their marriage. But it was my birthday that he used. I thought he'd learned to hate me as much as I hated him. But I was wrong. He just hid his love from me, because when he showed it, I let it bounce off me like garbage thrown into the street."

Her voice had been rising with her emotions. She stopped suddenly and became very calm.

"In his den — you don't have to look — there's a film projector set up. And a screen. For the old eight-millimeter films. I ran the film before I went upstairs. It's family stuff. Me as a little girl on my bicycle. Me at the swimming pool. Me at the Grand Canyon. All the dumb boring stuff that no one would find interesting except your own family. Beside the chair in his den, there's probably two dozen empty bags of chips. He'd been sitting there, night after night, watching the films. Of me as a little girl. Before I started hating him."

She took a deep breath, trying not to cry. "And now he's dying. Alone. Holding inside how much he loves me because he knows I'd just throw it away."

The sobs came. She muffled them in her hands. "Oh, God. I don't want him to die like that!"

I gave her time and silence. I moved to the window and stared at the darkness of the garden, thinking that all of us were vulnerable to something that had no source in body chemicals, body glands, body organs.

Love.

We all needed it. Even a man like Edgar Layton, who hid that need from the world and perhaps from himself.

"Nick?"

Amelia's voice trembled.

I moved back to the kitchen table.

"I was eight years old," Amelia said. "I knew it was wrong. But I couldn't tell anyone. Not Mother. It would hurt her. Not my father. After what I saw him do, I was terrified of him. Not the police. He was the police. And even if there had been someone to tell, my secret would put my father in jail. I knew that. How could I put him in jail and hurt him and hurt my mother, who would then know what he had done? So I had to hold that secret. And I began to hate him."

Amelia began to cry again. "I'm so sorry. I'm sorry I knew. I never felt like I had a father after that night. And I began to hate myself because I knew it was wrong not to tell anyone."

Sometimes, I believe, trying to comfort someone is no comfort at all. I did not try to stop her tears.

How much time passed, I could only guess.

When her breathing stopped coming in short hitches and gulps, she placed her right hand on the table. She'd made a fist and did not open it.

"All along," she said, "I thought he didn't know that I knew about that night. It was among his stuff in the closet upstairs. When I was a girl, I thought I'd lost it. I was wrong. He'd taken it from me. He knew there was only one place I would have found it. That night in the car."

She continued to cry. "All these years, he knew that I knew."

Again, I waited, not sure what she meant, for her fist was still closed.

She reached across the table to offer it to me. I stretched out an open palm. She opened her hand and the object fell onto my palm.

A silver cross on a silver chain.

I knew whom it had belonged to. At least it was confirmation, if I had needed it, that the woman in her father's car was my mother. But that was the least of it.

I pulled my hand back before Amelia might notice any trembling. I squeezed so hard on the cross that the points bit into my skin.

"Your mother's?"

I shook my head, not trusting my voice. I

rose, found a glass in a cupboard, filled it with water from the tap, returned to the table.

"She had it with her that night," Amelia said. "Did you know that?"

It was not something I wanted to answer. "Where did you find it?" I asked.

CHAPTER 30

Amelia told me the rest of the night of her eighth birthday.

All of it.

After my mother stepped into the police cruiser, Amelia understood the longer she remained unknown to her father, the greater his anger would become if she was discovered.

I can picture her curled into a ball on the floor of the back of the cruiser, eyes closed in fear, straining with all her other senses to judge the progress of the car, as if the metal skin of the car had become her skin, every bump of the road transmitted to the marrow of her bones.

She heard nothing from her father or my mother until they were well outside of Charleston, when the blur of streetlights no longer washed over her and when the vibrations of the car had increased as it gathered speed on the open road.

Then my mother spoke. "Can you turn on the siren, then? Can you go faster?"

"I'd rather not. No sense risking an accident."

In her father's voice, Amelia heard the

beginning trace of anger that always frightened her.

The woman's voice was urgent. Young as Amelia was, she was able to sense it, and my mother would not let Amelia's father's anger deter her. "But I thought you had to get us there as soon as possible."

"Don't tell me how to do my job."

The rising anger in Amelia's father's voice must have finally frightened my mother, for Amelia told me the silence returned to the car.

Amelia pushed herself as deeply as possible into the pool of darkness on the floor. When the car slowed again, Amelia remembered hearing crunching as the tires hit gravel.

"This is not the way to the beach house," my mother said.

No answer from Amelia's father. By now, silent tears ran down Amelia's face. She knew something bad was happening.

Farther down the road, my mother repeated herself. "This is not the way."

"You're right," Amelia heard her father answer. "This is not the way."

The car stopped.

"Out," her father said to my mother.

Both front doors opened. Both front doors closed.

They left Amelia alone in the car and too afraid to move.

✳ ✳ ✳

Twenty minutes huddled on the floor after my mother and her father had left the car, Amelia's bladder betrayed her. She could not wait huddled on the floor any longer.

She reached to open the rear door, but because the car was occasionally used to transport desperate or dangerous men, there were no door or window handles on the inside. Amelia crawled over the seat back, tumbled onto the passenger side, her feet kicking the steering wheel. Her face pressed briefly against the fabric of the back of the front seat. It still held the perfumed scent of the unknown woman.

Amelia slowly opened the door. After the terror of her silence, the croaking of bullfrogs in the nearby swamp seemed deafening. Immediately, mosquitoes attacked her bare arms and her face and her neck.

She was afraid of snakes in the long grass in the dark. She squatted and lifted her dress, making water at the side of the car, the half-open door protecting her. There were no lights aside from the stars in a night sky as black as her fear. Nothing to give her any clue of where she was in the darkness.

Beneath the immensity of the ceiling of stars and crushed by her fear, Amelia had never felt so small. She was barely aware of the function of her body, not until she finished. She hurried back into the front of the car, easing the door shut behind her.

As she leaned on the front seat to begin to crawl over to the rear, her hand pressed on something faintly cold. The silver cross on the silver chain. She grabbed it and pushed herself up and over the seat, huddling on the floor again.

She was nearly asleep from exhaustion when the car rocked with motion again.

It was the trunk lid of the car.

Opening.

The car sagged as a heavy weight was placed inside the trunk. Then sagged again with a second heavy weight.

The trunk lid closed.

Amelia curled against herself.

A new voice reached her from the open window on the front driver's side. Cigarette smoke drifted into the car.

This new voice belonged to a man Amelia did not know either.

"Think Gillon is going to make it?"

"I don't care," her father answered.

"One way or another, the admiral will take care of it. We've got our own worries. We'll go to the train station. You head home. I'll meet you there."

"This makes me nervous," said the unknown man. "I mean, going right back into town with what you have in the trunk."

"What?" her father asked. "A cop is going to pull me over?"

Amelia heard the second man giggle nervously. "I guess not. But why are you going to meet me at my house?"

"I happen to like insurance," Amelia's father said. "Like the gun the admiral used. I'll be keeping it in my collection for as long as we need it."

"What's that got to do with my house? I mean, we can't just . . ."

"Remember the cuff links you lent me for the last charity ball?"

"Yes, but . . ."

"Anyone finds her, they find your cuff links."

"At my house," the unknown man said. "Not a chance."

"You're in this too far to say no now."

Amelia heard the audible sigh from the unknown man. He lit another cigarette. The smoke itched Amelia's eyes.

"Trust me. It's a very safe place. Unless

you decide to talk. Or try to blackmail me."

"*Me* blackmail *you?* What guarantee do I have that you won't blackmail *me?*"

"None," Amelia's father said. "None at all. But when you make a deal with the devil, you've got to expect that."

✳ ✳ ✳

The driver's door opened. It was her father, grunting as he slipped behind the wheel.

The front passenger door opened. Amelia heard a woman's voice, very low and very soft.

"You should not have killed them," she said. "You should not have killed them."

Hidden on the floor, Amelia put a tiny fist in her mouth, as if this action would keep her from making the slightest noise. The next words she heard came from her father. His voice was thickened by an animal hatred she did not know could come from any human, and this frightened her even more than her fear of being discovered.

"Listen, you tramp," her father said. The hoarse whisper seemed to come from right above Amelia. She squeezed her eyes tighter shut, but she could not block the sounds from her ears. "I know where you came from. I think I even know who killed your father. White trash."

"Touch me and someday when you least expect it, I will find a way to kill you," the woman said. "And you're right. It won't be the first time I've killed a man who deserved it. Now get us into town so I can get away from you."

From there, Edgar Layton drove her to the train station, where she got out.

❋ ❋ ❋

The car made one more stop after the train station.

Amelia could not resist her curiosity. After her father stepped out of the car, after he opened the trunk of the car, after she heard the quiet voice of another man greeting her father, after the heavy weights were removed from the trunk, and after ten minutes of terrified waiting, she found the courage to push up on her knees to look out the window of the back of the car.

She allowed herself a brief glimpse of lights in the upper stories of a mansion on the other side of a dark garden. Saw the yellow beam of flashlights. Then she ducked, afraid she might have been seen. But this brief glimpse burned into her memory like a photograph.

Although she was only eight, she knew she was witnessing the beginning of a burial.

When the chief of police's car finally returned up the drive to their home, Amelia waited until her father left the car. She waited until he entered the house. Amelia was not worried if her mother had noticed her absence. Amelia's mother noticed very little by the time evening had settled on the household. But she knew her father would immediately go into her bedroom. Her father checked on her nightly and would often wake her to give her a hug and a kiss.

So Amelia knew she had little time.

She snuck out of the car. She hurried past the familiar bushes of the yard and climbed into the hammock between two oaks. She fell back into the hammock.

From the hammock, she saw the light go on in her bedroom.

The light flicked off.

Moments later, her father appeared in the light as the back door opened. He turned on a light that bathed most of the yard in yellow, throwing shadows of the oaks down on Amelia like grotesque stickmen.

"Amelia," he called.

Amelia let him call twice more.

"Yes?" she said, finally.

"What are you doing out there?" Her father walked toward her.

Amelia was only eight, but she was smart. She waited until he was close enough to see her. Then she yawned and rubbed her eyes as if she had just awoken.

"You and Mama were yelling," Amelia said. "I came out here to get away because I was a little afraid. Is it bedtime?"

"Yes, my little sugar pill," her father said with great affection.

Her father carried her to the house. Once she delighted in his strength, delighted in the sensation of his complete control. Now it terrified her.

The night before, only one night before, his words and tone and arms around her were a security like the comfort of a fuzzy flannel blanket. Now the sights and sounds in her memory made that security a mockery.

This was the night when she learned to hate and fear her father.

She knew then that he had two faces, and she knew which one was real. The one that belonged to the devil who made deals.

CHAPTER 31

After she told me all of this, Amelia composed herself and asked if we might go for a walk. There was something she wanted to show me.

I wanted time alone to think about all that I had just learned, and I nearly declined. But I was touched at her vulnerability, and so it was we stepped away from her father's house and walked, slowly, in the Charleston night air, framed by the ancient buildings crowding the street.

"Tonight, when you answered the phone," she said quietly, matching the mood of the city around us, "you thought I was . . ."

"Claire," I said. "Claire deMarionne."

"You and Claire are now . . ."

I took so long to reply that Amelia spoke again. "I'm sorry," she said. "Not my business."

"I would guess," I said, "with what we've been sharing in terms of secrets, a question like that is minor."

Again, we met eyes. Again, that unspoken current I'd felt upon first entering the kitchen earlier.

"I'm reasonably sure," I said, "all of

what Claire and I once had has been re-solved."

"Oh."

We both heard one word in what I had just answered, the one word that a lawyer would pounce on as a qualifier. *Reasonably* sure. As in there was some room to not be sure.

"Does she know," Amelia asked with hes-itation, "the truth behind the accident?"

"I will repeat myself." I did not want to hurt Amelia by appearing harsh. So I reached across the darkness and touched her face. I enjoyed the sensation of the softness of her skin. "The accident is a closed subject."

I took my hand away. "You'll under-stand?"

She nodded. I wanted to reach across again and push back some hair from her forehead.

It was not a long walk from her father's house over to South Battery. We chose to go along the waterfront and took a longer route than necessary.

Amelia seemed in no mood to talk, and I was lost in thought. What did I now know about the night my mother disappeared from Charleston?

According to Amelia, while I was at the Barretts' summer house on Folly Island, Edgar Layton had stopped at our Charleston town house to pick up my mother. It was my mother because Amelia had found the silver cross in the front seat. If that wasn't enough proof, I had confirmation of this from Opal, who had seen Layton from the top of the stairs that night. And, if Opal was right about the man who had killed her sister Ruby by a hit-and-run, then Layton had wanted no witnesses to that fact.

Seen from the point of view of a frightened eight-year-old on the floor of the cruiser, the rest of the night unfolded like this:

My mother and Edgar Layton had driven out somewhere in the country. They walked out into the darkness, leaving Amelia behind. When they returned, it was with a body or bodies, placed into the trunk of the cruiser. Then Amelia had watched, back in Charleston, as the woman from the cruiser walked to the train station. And from there, Edgar Layton had found a place to dispose of the bodies. A place that Amelia was about to show me.

I found myself with mixed guilt and

hope. If that night of confusion for Amelia had happened as she remembered and if my mother had left Charleston because of a murder, I could absolve myself, allow myself to believe I had no part in her departure, no reason for the guilt I carried. Yet what kind of son would wish his mother to be a murderer?

As we walked past the old buildings, it finally dawned on me that in these circumstances my sorrow was extremely self-indulgent. While for me there was still a question about my mother and her past, for Amelia there was no doubt about her father's conduct. Now Amelia's father had only days or hours until death took him from her.

I stopped.

She stopped, puzzled. I held out both my hands. Slowly, still puzzled, she took them.

"I'm so sorry," I said. "All of this. It can't be easy for you."

She understood what I meant. She squeezed my hands briefly in gratitude.

That's all I said.

We began walking again.

❃ ❃ ❃

Ten minutes later, Amelia and I reached East Bay and turned right. We continued south on Broad.

We passed by the postcard-perfect restoration of Rainbow Row, town homes that in daylight would show bright pastel colors, giving tourists a flavor of the Caribbean that had once been important to the seafaring trade of Charleston. Built in the mid-eighteenth century, the ancient town houses were originally stores on the first floor with living quarters for merchants above; Amelia probably already knew that once they had fronted the water, giving the merchants easy access to ships on the wharves. If she did, she listened patiently as I explained, giving her the stories my mother had once given me.

In this vein we walked south, I pretending to be a tour guide, and she pretending to be a tourist with no fears or concerns for a father about to die from colon cancer.

In the warm night air perfumed with the flowers of the expensive landscaping, it was a pleasant distraction from the matters that had drawn us together.

To our left was the Carolina Yacht Club, the farthest point south for moored boats, and then we reached the beginning of the mansions on our right that faced the seawall and the convergence of the Cooper and Ashley Rivers.

Our grim journey did not take much

longer. We passed the bed-and-breakfast, then came to the mansions of South Battery.

"Here," she said to me. She pointed at the three-story antebellum mansion in front of us. "It's here. The place that my father stopped that night after dropping your mother off at the train station. Where I think they buried someone."

"Here?"

"When I was a girl, I would ride my bicycle past this place, trying to see who lived here," Amelia said. "But the hedges and fence keep the yard hidden. From the street there is nothing to see. Now I know that my father knew that. With these houses, so much is hidden from the world."

She turned her face upward, and the streetlights showed her vulnerability to me all over again.

"Once," she said, "I think I saw you near this house. You were alone. On the steps, looking out at the harbor. I remembered your face because I wanted so desperately to know more about what happened that night. But now I don't know if I trust that memory. It was so many years ago, and it was only once that I saw that boy. It might be my imagination that his face grew into yours. That's why I was so startled to see you at the hospital."

"It's not your imagination," I said. "This is where I grew up after my mother ran away. The Barrett place."

CHAPTER 32

I stood in the churchyard beneath a steeple that had once been painted black.

St. Michael's.

A gray veil of early dawn mist hung over the city, shrouding the upper part of the steeple. The chilly air darkened the tombstones with moisture. Every step I took among them as I searched the names crushed the grass blades that had hung perfectly balanced with heavy dew, and I left behind a trail that plainly showed my intrusion. The city had not yet risen, and the hush of gray wrapped me in an aching loneliness.

I had slept poorly during the night. Not because of what I had learned about Helen or about Lorimar Barrett.

But because of what I had learned about myself, from Claire.

I had been a father but responsible twofold for the reason I had been denied a chance to embrace my son's entrance into the world. I had abandoned him before his birth, and in so doing, allowed the circumstances that took his life.

I had dreamed of his soft cries reaching across the city to me from the cold ground of St. Michael's churchyard, and I had not been able to fall back to sleep. The innocence in those cries echoed in the room, haunting me with such tender reproach that I had dressed in darkness and sat outside on the balcony until the black of night had ebbed and I could see through the mist to the sentinel trees of the park across the street.

I joined my son, here at St. Michael's ten minutes after beginning my slow walk down the deserted cobblestone streets, when I found his small tombstone.

I stood, then kneeled, uncaring of the dew that soaked through the knees of my pants. I leaned on my hands on the tombstone, balancing on my good leg.

I tried and failed in my attempt to not think of my son's tiny perfection at birth, of a hand that could have wrapped its grip around my finger, of eyes that would have stared up with unblinking trust, of first laughter and first steps and first words.

"I am sorry," I whispered to him. "I am so, so sorry."

Consequences.

For years I had read the Bible, not as a believer, but because I felt any man of education needed to be familiar with the one book that has most affected the history and direction of mankind. I wanted to be familiar with it so that when tedious evangelists quoted pieces out of context, applying fanaticism to make up for lack of knowledge, I could at least reply from safe and studied grounds. Even before my return to Charleston, I would have always admitted without hesitation that the Bible truly is the most impressive piece of literature produced in the history of man. Drama. Pain. Hope. Beautiful language that has not suffered through translation.

It is a glorious book, and when I finally understood how the Spirit of God infused it with so much of what we as humans need to live complete lives, my response went from intellectual appreciation to profound gratitude.

Consequences.

After my mother had run from Charleston, I was still required to go to church with Pendleton and his parents, who swallowed their hangovers from the inevitable Saturday night parties and gave a wonderful show of devotion as they let the soft drone of the sermons lull away the pain of their headaches. Although the four of us shared the same pew, even when pressed from the other side by elderly

women who fussed to set their purses beside them, I always made sure there was a
gap between the three of them and me, a
small space of varnished hardwood just
wide enough to establish that I did not
want to be part of that family.

I was guilty, too, of ignoring the sermons, and my pretended devotion came as
I kept my head bowed and read through
the Bible. I particularly loved the Old Tes-
tament, with its fascinating descriptions of
savage battles and the dramas of undis-
guised passionate human sins.

One passage in Exodus, however, disturbed me greatly. In reading this passage,
I had keenly felt the bitter pain of aban-
donment and wondered, if there was a
God unfailing in love as he claimed and as
my mother had claimed, why he would
choose to make me suffer for her sins.

*I am the Lord, I am the Lord, the merciful
and gracious God. I am slow to anger and
rich in unfailing love and faithfulness. I
show this unfailing love to many thousands
by forgiving every kind of sin and rebellion. Even so I do not leave sin unpunished,
but I punish the children for the sins of
their parents to the third and fourth generations.*

I had always believed this meant that God had chosen to prescribe this arbitrary punishment because whatever he did to the parents could not be enough, that he wanted to be able to condemn their children too.

That kind of anger, I could understand. It was anger without forgiveness.

❊ ❊ ❊

In St. Michael's graveyard, shrouded by the light fog that the sun had yet to burn away, my revelation was this: it is not God's anger that casts punishment onto the next generations, but the consequences of our own selfishness.

This was not a special revelation, nor a difficult one to see or understand. But I had been blinded by a humanist philosophy that kept me in the prison of seeing this world in terms of relative good, not the absolute good of God's wisdom.

At my stillborn son's grave, I suddenly knew why that passage was in Exodus. God understands — surely in a sadness we cannot comprehend — that children and grandchildren suffer as an inevitable consequence of their parents' actions. Those abused in childhood become abusers themselves, and their children abuse so that the cycle continues. Children raised in

319

the shadow of the greed or selfishness of their parents learn that greed and selfishness themselves.

Indeed, my hollow existence without God's presence was a testimony to the repercussions of events that had begun before I was born, just as the baby put into the earth here had been born dead because of the choices of the people responsible for its conception.

Yet, and this was important for me to later understand, I still had a choice. Remain victim. Or find a way to drop the chains from my body.

But where would I find that redemption?

I thought of Samuel and his tear-soaked prayer of gratitude and sadness in his church the day before.

"Is that the answer?" I spoke clearly, looking upward in the shroud that covered the steeple that had once been painted black.

I stood. "I'm ready, then," I said. "I believe. Reach me. Touch me. I believe."

Nothing answered my challenge.

No sight or sound. No sensation. No change in my heart. The gray shroud did not part to show sudden sunshine.

I stared down at the tombstone again.

Even if God would not reply, what I wanted more were tears. My tears. For not once following my mother's departure had I allowed myself to cry.

I opened my mind to the images that I had tried to block before. I thought of my son's inert body, the softness of his pale skin as he was wrapped to be placed in the coffin. I thought of how it might have been had he lived, had I not abandoned him, of his arms wrapped around my neck and his face buried in my chest as I held him and comforted his tears. I thought of his hand, reaching up to mine as we walked down the street. I thought of Claire's pain. I thought of my pain.

But I could not cry.

So I walked away.

CHAPTER 33

I stood in the presence of the Confederate
soldier mannequin once more, surrounded
by those swords that hung on the magnificent
walnut panels of the admiral's den walls. I'd
arrived in front of his video camera at the
front entrance only a minute earlier; knowing
what I learned since visiting him a day earlier,
I wasn't surprised that he had agreed to let
me inside. Nor was I surprised that he now
gazed at me with thoughtfulness, as if waiting
to see what weapons I would fire, and what
counteraction he should take.

I wasn't going to waste time.

"You were there the night my mother
disappeared," I said to him. "You were
there with her."

Admiral Robertson took his pipe from
its stand and worked tobacco into the
bowl. I knew this was a delay tactic. I
pressed my advantage.

"You know more than you told me yesterday," I said. "I am certain of this because
of a Colt .45 sealed in a plastic bag, labeled
with the date of my mother's disappearance
and your initials — M.W.R. When the fingerprints are analyzed, they will be yours."

The admiral bit hard on the stem of his

pipe, confirming my hunch that McLean Robertson had a middle name that began with a *W*.

"Edgar Layton will die soon," I said. I thought of Senator Gillon's warning to Amelia. "How long do you think before an investigation opens into what he leaves behind?"

"A Navy Colt .45 with my fingerprints on it and what else?" the admiral said. "You come bursting in like Sherlock Holmes with a dramatic confrontation. Surely you have a way to link the gun to your mother. Her body, perhaps, with a bullet matching the gun? And an eyewitness placing the two of us together. Something that will hold up in court."

I heard the subtext. *"Her body, perhaps, with a bullet matching the gun. An eyewitness placing us together."* Was my mother dead? Had it happened after Amelia watched a woman leave her father's car at the train station? I could not help my vulnerability in this moment.

"I was ten," I said. "I just want to know what happened to my mother. You haven't asked me where that gun came from, which tells me you know at least something."

He lit a match and sucked hard on the pipe to draw flame into the bowl. When he was satisfied with his efforts and the smoke rose in thick curls, he unclamped his mouth from the stem and smiled. "Say I did know something. So what? My point stands. With nothing that will hold up in court, you and I have nothing more to talk about. Ever again."

"Not quite true. I understand you have a Rottweiler as a guard dog," I said. "Am I correct?"

The admiral lifted his head and stared at me. We each understood what the other knew.

"I no longer have it," the admiral said. He bit down on his pipe but did not inhale. "I took it for a walk two nights ago, as I normally do. He was struck by a car and killed. The driver kept going."

The admiral made a point of continuing to lock eyes with me, playing this game of liars' poker like a veteran with a winning hand.

"I'm sure witnesses can confirm this," I said.

"Why would I need it confirmed?"

"Say you did. I'm sure your veterinarian can confirm this."

"The dog was killed instantly," Admiral Roberston said, pipe still in his teeth. "There was no need for a vet."

"You filed a report with the police about

the hit-and-run driver?"

"They couldn't find your mother. Why would I expect them to find the driver of a car that hit a dog?"

"They might be interested in seeing your dog's body if I reported to the police that two nights ago a man of your height and build instructed a Rottweiler to attack me. But I'd much rather learn about my mother than go to the police."

The admiral smiled from behind a new cloud of pipe smoke. "Your Sherlock Holmes approach is wearisome. I would tell the police the same thing I'll tell you. I'm a navy man. I was fond of that dog. Yesterday morning I gave it a burial at sea. I'm afraid there's no chance of finding its body. Even if they did find it, how could they prove it attacked you?"

"Of course," I said.

As if summoned, the large bodyguard appeared in the doorway.

"Good-bye," Admiral Robertson said. "Please don't trouble me anymore."

"Next Rottweiler you get," I said, "make sure it's not such a gutless pansy."

I was rewarded with a tightening of the admiral's jaw muscles, a subtle flinch. It wasn't much satisfaction, but it was the best that I could do.

CHAPTER 34

When I arrived back at the inn at Two Meeting Street, Amelia was already on the porch, leaning against a column, staring without focus at the beauty of the flowers just past the porch railing.

She smiled as I walked the cobblestone path to the mansion.

With that smile, fresh tears filled her eyes, as if she had been waiting for someone to share her sadness with before allowing herself this grief.

"My father," she said. "He . . . he . . . it happened early this morning."

"I am sorry for you," I said when I reached her.

She stepped forward into my arms, naturally, and let me hold her.

Human nature is treacherous. She needed comfort. Yet against my will, my mind turned not to her sadness but to how wonderful she felt against me, even with the dull pain of the lacerations on my chest and belly far from healed.

As Amelia continued to cling to me, and even then, fully aware that I was betraying her childlike trust, I could not turn my thoughts or emotions back to her needs. I dwelt selfishly on mine, enjoying the sensation of wisps of her hair against my cheek.

And I thought of Claire.

With some shame, I allowed Amelia to sob against me, the sounds of her pain muffled against my chest.

I closed my eyes and waited. Laughter from the park reached my ears. An army propeller cargo plane droned overhead. A car horn beeped in the distance.

"Thank you," she said. She delicately stepped back from me and began the task of composing herself.

I stared down at the flower blossoms she had not noticed earlier.

"May we sit?" she asked moments later.

"Of course," I said, realizing how formal each of us suddenly sounded.

We did not face each other. There were many chairs on the porch, including several rockers. We sat side by side and looked out at the park. Charleston had provided us with postcard-perfect weather — no breeze, an achingly blue sky. The distant white specks of seagulls drifted high above the harbor.

"I don't remember much of getting home from the hospital," she said. "I thought I was ready for his death. I thought I was strong enough. I'd known he would die. Yet when it actually happened, I felt suspended in a zone of disbelief."

She trusted me enough to talk.

"I wish it could have been different," Amelia whispered. "My whole life with him, I wish it could have been different. But after that night . . . and he knew, all the time, that I'd been in the car. He couldn't talk to me about it. I couldn't talk to him. It drove us apart.

"His breath was going. He asked me to remember him for how he taught me to ride a bicycle, how he took me fishing.

"That's when it hit me. My daddy was about to die. It seems ridiculous that I hadn't understood it until that moment. As a doctor, of all people, I should know it best. All the clinical signs . . . the daily degeneration . . .

"I finally started to cry. How can a person contain such evil but also have that ray of love? This man loved me so much that in the end, it was me who hurt him. I continued to cry and . . .

"He cried too. Not much. His body wouldn't let him. I held his hand and the tears came down his face. The last thing he said to me was, 'I'm sorry for that night. Losing you wasn't worth anything I ever gained instead.' I told him I was sorry, too, but I'm not sure he heard me. And then Daddy was gone."

I wondered if she had heard herself call him Daddy.

When she finished, she was in tears again. This time without my arms around her to give her the illusion that my heart shared the emotions of her heart.

I felt more treacherous because my thoughts were not on her pain. But on my needs.

He was dead. Edgar Layton now existed simply as old bones and old skin, and soon those too would be gone. He was somewhere on a hospital gurney, about to be shipped to a funeral home. No chance for me to learn anything from him about my mother.

I caught my thoughts and loathed myself for them. I had become like Edgar Layton. Concerned only for what a person could give me.

"He said something earlier," Amelia told me. She didn't bother to wipe her tears. "Something about you."

"Your father?"

Amelia nodded. " 'Tell Nick he promised.' That's what he said. 'Tell Nick he promised.' Does that make sense to you?"

I shook my head. Slowly. Trying to be a convincing liar. I'd tried to make a deal with Edgar Layton. Protection for Amelia if he helped me. That's all. He hadn't helped. There was nothing now to promise.

"He said something else too. Three times. 'Dry sister. Dry sister. Dry sister.' Does that make any sense to you?"

I shook my head again. And again, it was a lie.

Dry sister.

I think I knew what he meant. Although I had found it without his help.

Not dry sister. *Try the sister.*

Which I had already done.

Now that Edgar Layton was dead, and the admiral safe behind his silence, who was left to ever tell the truth about the night my mother left Charleston?

CHAPTER 35

Amelia leaned back in her rocker and closed her eyes.

"It kills me," she said, eyes still closed, tears on her cheeks, "to think that he wouldn't listen even once to what I so desperately wanted him to understand. As he was dying, all I could think about was a man named William Carruthers. He died in my care. Then came back to life."

I nodded. A statement like that would get anyone's attention.

She described it so well that I could imagine I was there.

❋ ❋ ❋

It happened her first year out of residency. During a shift in the emergency department.

She'd entered the acute room, holding a clipboard chart for a sixty-three-year-old patient named William Carruthers, who was dressed in a hospital gown, sitting on the edge of a bed, hooked to a heart monitor. He was short and balding, with a triple chin, and flesh that looked like sludge piled on bones. Prime candidate for a heart attack. Standing beside him was Rachel Kritt, the charge nurse. Taller than

Amelia and heavy boned, she wore her red hair tied back in a ponytail.

"Rachel?" Amelia asked.

"Pulse is 93. Blood pressure 110 over 80."

Amelia took William Carruthers's hand. It was limp, warm. "Mr. Carruthers," Amelia said, "when did the pain begin?"

"A few hours ago." William stopped to gulp air. The effort of speaking had winded him. "I'm living alone, so I called my son Joseph and asked him to bring me here."

He was sweating badly, his skin gray like old paper. The EKG looked normal, but Amelia didn't like the man's symptoms. "Rachel, let's get Mr. Carruthers hooked up on IV."

Suddenly, the monitor hummed loudly and unexpectedly. Rachel froze halfway out of the room. Amelia snapped her head back to the monitor with its bursts of white lines on the green screen that indicated the fast, dangerous heartbeats of ventricular tachycardia.

"Rachel . . . ," Amelia said. Rachel stepped back toward the patient on the bed.

As they all stared at the screen, there was abrupt silence as the beat stopped for a long pause.

"Doctor?" William asked. "Doctor!"

Amelia didn't have a chance to explain. It was happening too fast. The heartbeat monitor picked up again, in slow, widened beats, then flat-lined.

Amelia had heard of this happening to heart doctors. A patient on the treadmill, walking and talking, not aware that the heart monitor showed his death, walking and talking for four or five seconds after the flat line, finally falling in surprise and getting swept off the treadmill. Sometimes a simple whack on the chest brought them back. Sometimes not.

"Come on, Doctor," William Carruthers said, still conscious and unaware his heart had stopped. "That computer screen. It —"

The old man's eyes rolled in his head. He fell backward, landing softly on the bed, faceup.

"Give him CPR," Amelia commanded Rachel. "I'll call for IV!"

She barked a command into the phone on the wall and returned to see that the monitor showed that the heartbeat had returned, but with an underlying block.

The beat was improper. She needed to bring it back. Now.

"Keep it going," she told Rachel, then bent over the man, rhythmically pressing hard on his chest. "Don't give up on him."

This man needed oxygen. Rachel continued with the sequential chest and abdominal compressions. It was all that would keep William Carruthers alive until Amelia could get him hooked into a temporary pacemaker and restore the heartbeat to normal rhythm.

Amelia tore into the supply drawer. Found what she needed. Because he'd complained about chest pains, the man had been brought into a room that held the necessary equipment.

She took a large-bore needle and found the big vein under his collarbone. She threaded the pacemaker wire into the right side of the heart.

"I'll take CPR," Amelia told Rachel. Now the extra set of hands would just mean more confusion. "Get the IV. We need him on meds."

Blood spurted upward with every misfired beat of the old man's heart. Amelia stopped CPR to adjust the temporary pacemaker, and the man's heart stopped. He began to convulse.

Amelia started him up again, pushing so hard she wondered if his ribs would crack. More blood spurted.

She shouldn't have sent Rachel away so

soon. Amelia frantically worked between CPR and adjusting the pacemaker. Every time she stopped pushing on his chest, the heart would stop and his eyes would roll back into his head. Every time she squeezed his heart with CPR compressions, it jump-started him back to life.

Blood covered her forearms.

William found his voice again, his yell a croak of horror. "Get me out of hell! Get me out of hell! Don't stop! Don't stop! When you stop, you send me back to hell!"

Rachel had made it back into the room.

"Take over again," Amelia said.

During the exchange of her hands on his chest to Rachel's hands, the CPR stopped briefly and William Carruthers convulsed again.

Died again.

Rachel's sure, quick movements brought him back. This time he bellowed with greater strength. "For the love of God, don't let me back! Keep me out of hell!"

Amelia's first thought was hallucination.

"Pray for me!" he begged. "Please pray for me. Before I die! For God's sake. Someone pray before I go. Don't let me back in hell! I'm burning! I'm burning! Demons! Demons!"

Amelia wasn't a minister. But as a

doctor, she'd do what it took to calm a patient in this much fear, even if it was a self-induced hallucination. She remembered phrases from a Sunday morning television ministry.

As Rachel kept applying CPR, Amelia adjusted the pacemaker and fumbled out words. "Take me, Jesus," she said, feeling ridiculous. "Say it after me; take me, Jesus."

"Take me," William Carruthers moaned, his neck and face slimy with his own blood. "Jesus, please, please take me."

"I believe you are the Son of God, Jesus," Amelia said. The heart monitor showed renewed ventricular tachycardia. "Repeat it after me."

"Jesus, you are the Son of God," William Carruthers crooned. "Jesus, Jesus, Jesus."

The heart monitor hummed eerily in the background.

"Forgive my sins and keep me out of hell," Amelia said. "Say it."

The temporary pacemaker had no effect on the rapid heartbeats that were converging into one sound.

"Forgive my sins and keep me out of hell. Please, Jesus, please."

"I'm yours, Jesus," Amelia coached him, feeling like a caricature of the sleaziest

336

television preachers she'd seen.

"I'm yours, Jesus," William Carruthers said. "Oh, Jesus, I'm yours."

Carruthers had been clutching at Amelia's white jacket, almost pulling her off balance. Suddenly, his grip loosened.

But he wasn't dead. The heart monitor had gone back to regular, healthy beats.

His convulsions had ended. His eyes were wide open. "The demons are gone," he breathed. He closed his eyes. Peace relaxed the strained muscles of his face. "I hear singing. Glorious singing. Thank you, Jesus. Thank you."

The heart monitor pinged a reassuring rhythm.

"He's back," Amelia told Rachel. "Let's get this cleaned up."

✳ ✳ ✳

That was Amelia's story. She told it in a straightforward way, without apology for how it might have sounded to an astronomer grounded in the scientific need for proof.

"What do you think about it?" she asked when she finished.

"You mean do I think you're telling the truth? My answer is yes. If you're asking if the guy really was in hell or just thought he was . . ."

"I've read everything I can on near-death experiences, and I can tell you all the medical theories. But really, none gives a good explanation. Blood test studies on oxygen deprivation for cardiac arrest patients show no difference between those who experienced an NDE and those who didn't, so we know it wasn't a hallucination caused by lack of oxygen in the blood cells. Other studies on trauma-induced polypeptide proteins —"

"Hang on," I said. "Polypeptide proteins?"

"They attach to endomorphin receptors to relieve pain. But even at high levels of pain, they don't produce NDEs. Only those who clinically die and return are the ones who bring back the stories. Electrical stimulation of various parts of the brain don't reproduce the experiences. Then there's all the visual details of the emergency room event that trauma victims can recall even though they were unconscious. A blind person able to tell doctors what clothes and jewelry they wore."

"Most people see an angel of light," I said. Amelia raised an eyebrow, and I answered her unspoken question. "I've read about NDEs too."

"You're right, though. William Carruthers

saw an angel of death. Most people report an angel of light. Even those who weren't believers are greeted by the sight of an angel of light. But what if there really is a hell?"

She looked directly at me with such intensity all of a sudden that it felt like we touched. I held her look, saw sad desperation, and did not flinch.

"What if on the doorstep of eternity, the ultimate evil spirit provides the ultimate deception? The devil. Lucifer. Latin for 'angel of light.' What if those who have yielded their souls to God in this life reach out to the true light when they pass through the curtain? What if those who haven't are reaching out to embrace hell, the angel of light who is only a deception? What if that's what's waiting for my father?"

The only reply I could think of was that he deserved it. So I said nothing.

"Since William Carruthers," she said softly, "I began to wonder about it all. A lot. There a person is. Putting out the trash. Getting stuck in traffic. Hard to think of a soul and infinity and existence without a body when all the mundane daily things get in the way. Life and death sometimes seem so unrelated, it is unreal. But doctors and nurses are in a different position than most. We see death frequently. And there was no way to get away from the question he brought me: Are we eternal?"

She answered the question herself. "I believe we are. And that's why I'm afraid for my father. There was no way to convince him to wonder about heaven or hell. Now he's dead."

I had long pinched off my soul too tightly to want to think about God.

"Nick, I made a point of visiting William Carruthers the next day. I had questions. He told me something I'll never forget.

"He said it would have been okay if he died, once I'd helped him through the prayer. Then he told me about when he first died. He said it was like he was floating in an absolutely pitch-black place until it began to glow and a beautiful bright light pulled him closer and closer. But when he got to the light, suddenly he felt intense heat and he saw the outline of a woman. She came closer, calling his name. He heard groaning behind her. There were other black outlines of people. No eyes. No mouths. Feeling more and more dread weighing him down, he said it seemed like he was on the edge of that huge black void, with a fire in front pulling him in. He knew if he fell, he would fall forever. That he would be alone forever, lost and burning.

"Just as abruptly he was back in the hospital room. He told me whenever I would stop pumping his chest, he would be back there, on the edge, ready to fall. And when he prayed for Jesus' help, he was removed and his terror subsided. He didn't go back to hell, but his wife appeared beside him. Smiling, actually beaming. She told him he could go home with her. They walked away from the edge and she pointed at someone ahead. Carruthers told me he knew it was Jesus. That Jesus called his name and reached for him. And that was when it would have been okay for him to die."

She had been talking in a hurry, trying to spill out the story, and she paused for breath. "Nick, God gives some of us many different ways to first think about him. I'm in medicine so that's how he nudged me to begin looking more for him. It was amazing. With the tiniest bit of faith, I began to recognize miracles for what they were. Even the birth of a child is so amazing when you think about it. You're an astronomer, perhaps you . . ."

She waited for me to contribute something. I didn't.

"That's when I started my own search,"

Amelia said, to fill the silence. "It's not about church or following the rules. It's about trying to understand death. Because once you understand death, you understand life.

"Nick, God is there waiting. If you understand that, you'll have peace and meaning and hope that nothing in this life will ever take away from you, no matter how bad it gets. I'd like to talk about it with you. If you want to listen."

I tried for an ironic smile. "The last woman who tried to lead me to Jesus was my mother. And she ran away on me when I was ten."

"You're right," she said. "What you believe is none of my business."

"No . . . no . . . ," I protested.

But the damage had been done.

Her face tightened slightly. I had glanced over earlier, when she sat on the rocker with her eyes closed. Her face then had had the innocence and softness of a child's in sleep. Instantly, with my touch of cynicism, I'd thrust her again into the adult world, where sincere thoughts must be guarded. I saw it in her face.

"We share the one night of our childhood that changed both our lives," she said. "And we are both trying to understand exactly what happened that night. There's a difference, though. I'll freely admit I'm hurt. I'll freely admit I need to try to get past that. I'm not afraid to look upward and ask for help. Especially now, with my father dead. But you . . ."

Anger began to swell her voice. "You think you've brought yourself to the point where you're beyond the damage that was done to you. You believe you're above it all, beyond needing anyone. But look at yourself. Not married. No children. A career of indifference at a small college. You haven't allowed yourself to care about a single thing. Who are you really spiting, Nick? Who are you really punishing? Yourself."

Delicate red circles began to flush her cheeks. "You think you're here to find out the truth about your mother. But I wonder if that's it. I see it in your questions, in your eyes, in the rigidness of your body. I think you're here to destroy what you can't have. You're a damaged person, Nick. And you won't heal until you admit you need healing."

"I thought you were a medical doctor. Not a psychiatrist."

"I don't need to be one to see any of this about you."

Amelia stood.

Always the perfect southern gentleman, I stood too. I watched her walk down the cobblestone path. Away from me.

I felt an unsure emptiness. I'd lost something just now but couldn't understand what.

CHAPTER 36

Unlike earlier, I did not enter Pendleton's office with a sense of triumph. There was no attractive blonde-haired, plastic-enhanced secretary to stop me at the front desk of the outer office.

They must have expected any visitor to knock, because when I pushed open the door to Pendleton's inner office, she was coyly perched on the edge of his desk, one leg crossed over the other, her skirt barely managing to maintain public decency.

My entrance stopped her in mid-giggle.

She, at least, had the grace to blush as she quickly stood.

Pendleton did not. Blush. Or stand. "Whatever it is," he said, remaining behind his desk, "I'm not interested. Go away."

"Sure," I said. "After we talk about our father."

I had expected a lot of different reactions. Puzzlement. Anger. Curiosity.

Instead, he allowed a small frown to crinkle his perpetually composed face. "Denise, have that condo contract finished in a half hour. I'll be ready to take it down to the bank by then. And please close the door behind you."

It was not a subtle command. She stepped past me, the swish of her nylons seeming loud in the quiet of his office.

With the door shut, Pendleton regarded me, then, surprisingly, smiled. "I was wondering if ever we would have this conversation."

He rose from behind his chair. His expensively tailored suit dropped to hang perfectly as he straightened. He stepped toward me. In the sunlight that filled his office, I saw the touch of makeup across the top of his forehead, where traces of powder clung to the roots of his hair.

I wondered if he was going to swing at me.

"Lift your arms," he said pleasantly.

When I did not, he maintained his pleasant voice. "Do you want us to talk freely? Or with attorneys on both sides of us?"

Slowly, I lifted my arms.

He reached for me. I flinched.

"Relax," he said. He patted the sides of my ribs, patted my stomach, my back. I winced at the touch of his fingers against the scabbed wounds from the dog attack. He squatted and quickly slid his hands up and down the insides of my legs.

By then, I realized what he was doing.

"Interesting life you've had, Pendleton."

He stood again and pressed his hand hard against my lower back. "Imagine my surprise," he said, patting my upper body one more time. "The out-of-town Realtor I took for dinner turned out to be IRS on a fishing expedition. And wired for sound. Who would have thought anyone that attractive worked for the Feds? Basically, it turned out to be a two-million-dollar date, and while the resulting hangover nearly killed me, I didn't get so much as a kiss."

He walked around to a black leather chair in the corner of his large office and pointed to its match, opposite a low coffee table.

"Sit. Let's talk then. About our father."

I sat, reminding myself that his easy charm was something he could use as a magical cloak whenever necessary.

"You know then," he said. "How?"

"Not relevant."

"Nicholas, we're brothers. You finally know it. We truly can speak freely. I mean, this is almost like a homecoming, discovering each is the other's only remaining family."

"Then you tell me," I said. "How did you know? When?"

He crossed his legs and leaned back,

hands behind his head. "I was fourteen or fifteen. I overheard my parents arguing. Their marriage was finished long before you came on the scene, but I think having you there every day as a reminder of Father's extramarital habits made it even more hellish on her. Which in turn made it hellish on him. You understand, of course, why they both hated you. But they couldn't get rid of you. Helen made sure of that. In fact, that's what they were arguing about that day. Helen and how my father could at least have the decency to stop taking her to restaurants in the city and perhaps limit his philandering to out of town and on weekends. Great role models my parents were."

"Helen," I said, "made sure I stayed with you?"

"She protected you more than you might know. She had something over my father. But I don't know what. Mother and Father moved their argument into the garden, and I couldn't follow them out there without being seen."

Pendleton dropped his arms from behind his head and leaned forward. "So what now?" he asked. "Now that you've finally discovered he was your father too?"

I wasn't the poker player that Pendleton

348

was. He laughed as he watched the conflicting emotions on my face. I couldn't understand his friendliness.

"Nicholas, we're talking money here. There is nothing personal about money. I totally understand why you're going to try to take it from me. Just as you should totally understand why I did my best to make sure you couldn't get it. It simply means we can get past any antagonism and be very practical about this."

"You did your best to make sure I couldn't get it?"

"Naivete is refreshing, Nicholas. I rather enjoy it. I think it will be a pleasure partnering with you."

"You did your best to make sure I couldn't get it?" I repeated, understanding what he meant but unable to actually believe it.

"I almost decided to smother you that night behind the steering wheel. Pinch your nostrils shut and cover your mouth, but even I couldn't stomach cold-blooded murder. I wasn't, however, going to be much upset if natural events took you away from my world. If the ambulance had arrived a half hour later, Nick, you wouldn't have been a problem for me ever again."

It was not easy to remain seated as I

watched that easy, charming smile.

"There," he said. "We've got all of it out in the open now. Or at least I have. It's your turn. What do you intend to do?"

I didn't answer. I was trying to absorb all he'd said.

"Since your return, I've thought it through from your point of view," he continued. "Thanks to DNA testing, I have no doubt you could prove the paternity. If I decided to fight, you'd face a long legal battle, however, just to get Father's remains exhumed. How I wish Mother had cremated him, as I begged at the time."

Pendleton paused to take a small silver case out of the inside pocket of his jacket. He snapped it open, revealing a row of cigarillos. He offered me one, which I declined. He shrugged, took one out, and lit it. He held it in an elegant pose as he watched me through curls of smoke.

"It may surprise you to find out that I may not even contest it. My current situation with the IRS, of course, is the main factor. As it stands, I won't have much to keep, one way or the other. You, though, can choose to make it simple or difficult. Trust me, I've given this considerable thought."

Trust and *Pendleton* were two mutually

exclusive words. I told him as much.

"Nicholas, you are now one of the heirs apparent of Charleston. Our standards are different. Things that apply to ordinary people don't apply to us. It's not about trust. Learn not to take these things personally, Nicholas. You'll see how easy it is to fit in."

He blew several smoke rings, appearing very comfortable in his role as my new mentor. "Here it is, Nicholas. And now you'll understand why I made sure you weren't wired. I'll do everything I can to help you rightfully claim as much as possible from the Barrett fortune — under one simple condition. I want some of it back. Without the IRS knowing. There's a couple deals on the way that I can leverage into a surprisingly large nest egg, if I have the necessary equity on the front end. I'll even help you get in on the investments, if you like."

"Just so I understand, Brother, you'll help me if I kick some of it back to you. Or you'll fight me if I don't."

"You do learn fast. The first way, we pull as much away from the IRS as possible. Or the second way, I spite you because I'm losing most of it anyway."

"Interesting," I said. "And you'll trust

me to kick some back?"

"Sure, Nicholas."

"You were willing to let me die in that accident. I know it now. A lot of what happened when we were growing up *was* personal. Why should you trust me not to take my revenge?"

"That's just it. It's money. For money, you can forget everything. I mean, what can that other stuff matter?"

"What if I think otherwise?"

"You'll learn differently."

"You sound sure about it."

He smiled. "Nick, I trust you'll help me because when you do, you'll finally be one of us and that's what you've always wanted, needed."

I stood. There are some truths a man never wants to face.

"Where are you going?" he asked.

Until this moment, I hadn't even been sure if I wanted to lay claim to my inheritance. Now I did.

"See you in court." I paused in the doorway. "And please, consider it a personal matter."

CHAPTER 37

An hour later by telephone, Gillon reached me at the bed-and-breakfast. He requested that I join him for a private meeting.

I was not interested.

His promise, to entice me to the meeting, was offering the truth behind my mother's disappearance from Charleston.

Where? I asked.

I'll find out, he said.

For my convenience, he dryly informed me, he would send his limousine.

It arrived late in the afternoon.

❋ ❋ ❋

From the car, Gillon's chauffeur pushed Gillon in his wheelchair across the parking lot of the Carolina Yacht Club. Gillon held an umbrella and shielded himself from the rain.

I held an umbrella for myself. The rain slashed at me almost sideways, and I fought to keep my balance against the wind. The walk to the senator's yacht was mercifully quick. I did not stand on the dock and admire all seventy feet of the sleek lines — I was already soaked from the waist down — but followed the chauffeur as he guided the senator in his wheelchair across the swaying gangplank.

The yacht was equipped with a motorized wheelchair ramp to give the senator easy access to the lower level of the interior, into a saloon the size of a small apartment. Once I was inside, it hardly seemed different than stepping into the luxury suite of a hotel.

The walls were burnished mahogany, decorated with framed oil paintings. The floor was hardwood, well cushioned by Oriental throw rugs that would have been appropriate in any of Charleston's mansions. The furniture was dark leather — couch arranged in front of a large-screen television, three side chairs in a square around it. The bar filled the back wall of the suite, with a hallway leading to bedrooms at the stern of the yacht.

Admiral Robertson stood at the bar in the back, filling a glass with ice.

I said nothing as I watched him pour a drink, gesture at me.

I refused his offer.

He shrugged.

I resisted an urge to speak. What I wanted to do, of course, was demand explanations. For the admiral's presence. For the purpose of this meeting. And most of all, explanations about my mother's disappearance from my life.

It felt, however, that my impatience would too easily be seen as a weakness. I forced myself to wait until Gillon was settled.

The chauffeur departed, and Admiral Robertson took a chair.

I did not want to sit; that would be acknowledging I was part of this tiny circle. I did not want to stand; I knew my leg would begin to hurt. I compromised and sat on the armrest of the couch.

I let Gillon speak first.

"We all know each other," he said. "Let us not waste time."

There seemed to be strength in being silent, so I remained that way.

"The questions you have persisted in asking are about to do some spectacular damage," Gillon told me. "Damage, I might add, totally unjustified to those of us who remain to remember the answers. My hope is that this conversation will bring all of it to a resolution."

I snorted. "As compared to resolving it by encouraging a dog to rip my throat apart?"

Gillon nodded in the admiral's direction. "McLean here will apologize for that to you, as he already has to me. It was short-sighted stupidity on his part. A result of premature panic. Am I correct, Admiral?"

"You are correct." The admiral remained stone-faced.

Gillon spoke to me. "It has already been a long day. I have spoken with Amelia Layton and discovered from her that both of you know of her father's secrets. I encouraged her to destroy the collection in such a way that I could attest to others that it is safely gone. My word to that effect, circulated among those who matter, will be the protection both of you need. Otherwise, there may be others, who, like the admiral, panic unnecessarily and in unseemly ways."

"Pardon my cynicism," I interrupted. "But what in that collection worries you, Senator?"

"Frankly, everything. Edgar Layton accumulated evidence of some of the vilest vices of an entire generation of the wealthiest and most powerful Charlestonians. It will do no good to unleash these old, irrelevant sins on the innocent wives and sons and daughters of that generation."

"I should have remembered I am speaking to an attorney," I said. "Let me rephrase. Pardon my cynicism, Senator, but what in that collection pertains to you?"

Gillon sipped his drink before answering my last question.

"I have been guilty of many things in my life, but not of being stupid enough to let my client Edgar Layton add me to his collection." Gillon smiled sadly and savored another sip of his numbing beverage. "Nothing in that collection pertains to me but the Colt .45 with the admiral's fingerprints. For that was the weapon that fired a small piece of lead, which crippled me for life on the night your mother disappeared from Charleston."

"Not," I said, "a bullet from a random thief as you told me earlier."

"That was a lie. Are you ready for the truth?"

"More importantly," I said, "are you capable of the truth?"

Gillon ignored the insult. He reached into his vest pocket and pulled out a silver object. He tossed it to me. Not until I had it in my hands did I recognize it. A cigarette lighter. With the initials C.B. engraved on the bottom.

"Yes," Gillon said. "Your mother's. She left it in my office that final afternoon. Still works perfectly."

I tucked it into my pocket. I could remember it because of how my mother frequently complained that she wanted to quit smoking. Then, of course, cigarette smoking did not have the stigma it does now.

"That afternoon your mother came to me in my law office," Gillon said. "She wanted the trust fund money that had been set aside for you until the age of eighteen. You, of course, were only ten years old, and it was an unexpected request. I did not find out until that night that she wanted it to begin a new life with Admiral Robertson's assistant, Jonathan Britt, with whom she had begun a tempestuous affair." Gillon raised an eyebrow. "Admiral?"

Admiral Robertson spoke with his hand around the bowl of his pipe. Gillon's question had caught him halfway through lighting it. "I had had my suspicions about Jonathan Britt for some time. I believed he was the person behind misappropriation of pension funds, but I could not prove it. Not until I overheard him speaking to your mother on the telephone that afternoon. I had gone golfing, thinking my clubs were in my trunk, only to find out I had left them behind. When I returned to get them, he was speaking freely in the adjacent office, believing I would not be back for hours. He was arranging the time and place he would pick up your mother to flee town, promising to have the money. I said nothing and quietly left, intending to give him enough rope to hang himself by confronting him at the prearranged place with the pension funds in his possession. I was at the park on the outskirts of town then, hidden and waiting for her arrival."

"The admiral was not alone at the park that night," Gillon added. "That afternoon, he had contacted me to use as a witness."

"I didn't want to use a naval lawyer," Admiral Robertson said. "Simply because the only proof I had was an overheard conversation. I was afraid of being wrong and unnecessarily dragging the navy into it until I was certain. Hence, my request that Gillon be an impartial witness."

"Which I was," Gillon said. "At the park, your mother showed up as arranged by Jonathan Britt. It was as they were leaving that the admiral and I confronted them. The admiral was armed with his Colt .45."

"Every day since, I have hated myself for that." Admiral Robertson tilted his head back and drained his glass. "The chain of events . . ."

He stared at the floor.

Gillon continued for him. "It was confusing in the dark. We stepped out from behind some bushes. The admiral was not clear in identifying himself. All we can assume is that his assistant thought it was armed robbery. He dove for the admiral's gun. A shot was fired. It was the bullet that struck me in the back."

Gillon gave another sad smile. "A bullet that changed the rest of my life. For obvious reasons, I'm not clear on the rest of what happened in the next seconds after that. I do know the consequences."

Gillon paused. The admiral did not pick up the story. "Admiral?" Gillon said.

Admiral Robertson drew hard several times on his pipe. "My natural reaction was to fight to keep possession of the pistol. I fired it again, and that bullet . . ."

The admiral sighed. "That bullet tore through the throat of Jonathan Britt."

The admiral set his pipe down. He moved back to the bar. He poured more from the decanter, took two big gulps from his tumbler, and spoke in a monotone. "The bullet did not stop there. It also killed the woman with him. With a single shot, I had killed them both." His voice was beginning to slur conspicuously.

Gillon spoke softly. "Nick, your mother died that night. I wish I did not have to tell you this. But I hope you can take some blessing from that. She did not run away from you."

"Twenty years is a long time to wait to deliver such wonderful news." I stared at Gillon until the senator was forced to blink and look away.

Gillon coughed. "We couldn't let you know. You were a boy."

"A boy without a mother," I said. "The admiral shot in self-defense. Trying to stop a criminal. There was nothing to cover up. How could you let a boy believe his mother abandoned him?"

"That's where you are wrong," Gillon said. "Jonathan wasn't a criminal. At least not that anyone could prove. The money was gone from the pension fund. But he did not have it with him. To the world, it would look like the admiral had shot an innocent man and an innocent woman."

Gillon pointed his nearly empty glass at the admiral, who sat leaning forward, elbows on his knees, head down. "Panic, Nick. He reacted without thinking, like the attack with the dog. He knew Edgar Layton would help, and he called Layton without thinking through the consequences."

"There I was," the admiral said, "with

two dead and a third dying. When Layton arrived, he told me there was no sense in throwing away my career. It wouldn't change what had happened. I hadn't meant any wrong. It was just bad circumstances . . . bad circumst— Anyway, I was only too happy to agree."

I was numb to such objective discussion about the death of my mother. Which surprised me. Was it because I was trying to fit this in with what Amelia had told me? Had she been confused as an eight-year-old? Or were these two men lying to me? And how could I ever determine which?

"Edgar took care of everything," Gillon said, filling in the silence. "Found a way to hide their bodies, arranged a cover-up that would make it look like they had taken the money and fled, filed false reports that had them one step ahead of the law until they safely got out of the country. The admiral paid a steep price for it. Edgar retained the gun with the admiral's fingerprints and knew where the bodies were buried with bullets that came from the gun."

I pondered that, again trying to fit this in with the story Amelia had given me. Where were my emotions? Was my soul so callused now that my mother's disappearance was merely a puzzle that needed solving?

The admiral rose for still another drink, speaking as he moved back to the bar. "Edgar Layton bled me dry over the years. Blackmailed me. Not only did I have to face my conscience every night . . ."

Gillon spoke to me in a soothing voice. "The price has been paid, Nick. By the admiral. By you. Now that Edgar is gone from this world, so is the knowledge of the location of their bodies. Even with the gun that shot them in your possession, even with the admiral's fingerprints on the gun, there is nothing you can prove, not anymore. Not without a body. Or Edgar's testimony. Had he not died, we would not be having this conversation now."

Gillon finished quietly, like a trial lawyer protecting a widowed defendant who deserved the jury's full sympathy. "So let me ask. Is the truth enough? Can you now let it rest?"

"If you can explain to me," I said, "why Amelia has a different story."

"Amelia?"

"She was in her father's car that night. Hidden in the backseat. Last night she told me her father picked up a woman and later brought her to the train station."

Gillon and the admiral exchanged glances. My question hung. The seconds ticked past, clearly echoing from a clock on the bookshelf.

Gillon adjusted his tie. He was delaying his answer far too long.

"Obviously," I said, "you did not tell me the truth."

"No," Gillon said, "not all of it. There was a woman involved. Layton did pick her up that night. It was a woman who agreed to pretend she was your mother, so that the story about her leaving town by train would seem more believable."

"Who?" I asked.

"It was —"

Gillon cut the admiral short. "No. We swore not to reveal her name."

"Strange time for ethics," I said. "Especially in light of how you have presented the rest of the cover-up. Perhaps instead you're afraid she won't corroborate your story?"

"Not at all," Gillon said. "She died of natural causes a few years ago. It wouldn't be right to involve her family in this."

There it was. A story with enough truth to serve me. With too little truth to believe. Either way, these men were completely protected.

"Will you let it rest?" Gillon asked again.

Before I could answer, movement at the

stairs behind us drew our attention.

"I was the woman," came a voice. "It was me at the train station."

She wore a full-length black dress, shadows thrown across her face from a wide-brimmed black hat, tiny black purse hanging on thin black straps from her arm. Helen deMarionne.

Helen moved downward, holding the stairway railing to keep her balance. She stepped into the room, the purse swaying like a pendulum.

Gillon turned his wheelchair to face her. "Helen, I didn't expect you."

Her face remained in shadow. "I know Gillon. It's been years since you looked forward to my presence."

"No need to be snappish. It's just that I didn't realize you wanted to be part of this tonight."

"Why not? After all, most of it was my idea." She spoke to the admiral. "McLean. How are you this evening? Tense? Worried?"

"Relaxed. Why should I be anything but?"

"Of course." Her tone suggested the opposite.

As Helen moved across the room to take the chair opposite the admiral, she staggered slightly to keep her balance. She sat to the left of me and settled herself in the chair, with the admiral now seated to our right. Gillon in his wheelchair in front of the television, between Helen and the admiral, completed the square.

"Did I do a good enough job of easing us out of the slip and into the harbor?" she asked. "Any of you notice the boat in motion? Soon we'll be out of the harbor and the chop of the waves will pick up; then it won't feel like we are rocking in the moored position. In fact, the autopilot has us headed directly east on a course that would take us to Portugal."

"You?" Gillon was openly astounded. "Autopilot? What about —"

"Your boy Friday?" Helen finished for him. "Your chauffeur slash yacht pilot slash nurse? He's back at the yacht club, probably pacing the dock, getting wetter every second, wondering where we've gone. I sent him away to get us some more bourbon."

To me, she said, "There are some advantages to belonging to the moneyed set, being seen at the same parties. Not only do you pick up boating expertise over the years, but a familiar face is not questioned. Especially one as easy to remember as mine."

She removed her hat, letting light fall onto her face. The left side of her mouth sagged, her cheek fallen and distorted. Her left eye gleamed brightly, almost freakishly, from skin tightened across her upper face.

"I do not apologize for my pride," she said. "I did not want you to see me like this until it was entirely inescapable."

"I'm sorry for you," I said.

"Stroke," she said matter-of-factly. In the light, it was obvious by the movement of her lips how much effort she put into enunciating her words. "A year ago. Lost all the nerves to the lower left-hand side of my face. Followed by a botched job by a plastic surgeon, who failed miserably in his attempts to tighten the skin and muscle damage. Until then, I had done remarkably well, holding my beauty. Well enough that until then Lorimar Barrett still looked upon me with quite some favor. Until my stroke. I thought it was love. I was wrong. When his little Barbie doll lost her perfection, it was time to throw the doll away. Then he died of a stroke himself six months ago, an irony I would have found amusing, except that I, unfortunately, loved him."

A wave rocked the yacht. She was forced to cling to the arms of her chair for balance.

"Enough bitterness." Helen's smile was macabre. Turned up on the right side. Turned down on the left side. "I've got center stage, and I should not digress. After all, there was a reason that I helped Gillon plan this melodramatic little get-together."

Helen fumbled in her purse and pulled out a derringer. "Very appropriate for a southern belle, wouldn't you agree? Not that I intend to use it, but I do want a captive audience. Because I finally want to tell you the truth about your mother, Nicholas."

CHAPTER 38

The prow of the yacht banged hard into another wave. Muted thunder reached us in the depths of the saloon. As the yacht settled low in the water again, Helen continued.

"Nick, Gillon called me this morning after you spoke to the admiral about the pistol in Amelia's possession. I must admit, the admiral has done an excellent job over the years, hiding his lack of intelligence behind a military bearing of great distinction. The admiral, of course, was still sulking that he'd lost a perfectly fine guard dog and, short of trying to kill you again, had no clue how to proceed next. Thus his call to Gillon and Gillon's call to me. I suggested that Gillon avoid doing anything as clumsy as resorting to the heavy-handedness of killing. Not that he's squeamish, but to kill someone properly requires too much effort, too much to cover up. As they both well know. After all, it's been more than two decades since Carolyn's death, and look where they are now."

The admiral braced his hands on the arm of his chair to push himself into a standing position. Helen lifted the derringer and pointed it at his chest.

"I merely want to refresh my glass."

"And get the pistol that's hidden behind the bar," Helen said. "Stay where you are. Don't think I'm bluffing. I don't have anything to lose by shooting you."

The admiral let himself fall back into his chair. Slowly, he raised his tumbler to his face, eyes still on Helen, tilted ice from the tumbler into his mouth, and began to crunch on cubes.

Helen spoke to me. "Their plan, at my suggestion, was to get you out at sea, then try to convince you to leave all of this matter alone. I must admit, they did weave a compelling story, with enough of the truth in it that finding flaws would have been difficult. And the acting was superb."

She looked to Gillon. "Did you practice it a few times? It was all I could do not to applaud from where I was standing hidden halfway down the stairs."

Gillon frowned at her. "It *is* the truth."

"Please," Helen said, "I'm here to testify otherwise."

Helen resumed speaking to me. "If you did believe them and agree to their requests, they were to return you, none the wiser of how close you had come to your death. But if they failed to convince you to drop it, of course, then they intended to throw you overboard to drown. Crude. But effective. With the two of them to testify that you fell overboard — and both such respected men — they would have convincingly presented it to the authorities as a tragic accident. Especially with their political connections to help them."

Gillon smiled, the first sign that his cockiness had not been entirely destroyed by Helen's appearance. "It's not too late, Helen. I mean, you have your own part to protect. And with three of us to testify that this poor man fell overboard . . ."

I hid a shiver. His casual tone spoke utter conviction. This man was discussing my murder. In front of me.

"You are so tiresomely predictable," Helen said. To me, she said, "The yacht was my suggestion because I wanted to know where they would take you tonight. I also wanted to be here so that they would not kill you. And lastly, I wanted all of us together."

Helen casually lifted her derringer again and cocked it, a click of metal against metal terrifying in its simplicity. The admiral, who was inching out of his chair to leap forward at her, froze.

"Be a dear," she told the admiral. "Sit on your hands. If you're fortunate, we'll hit a large unexpected wave and I'll be knocked from my chair, and you can try one of your ludicrous commando techniques to stop me. Otherwise, don't be tedious. I won't take long to finish my little talk."

She extended her derringer with an unwavering hand and centered its aim on the admiral's nose. "Sit on your hands, Mac!"

He drew a breath of resignation and did as he was told.

"Nick," she said, "you have heard some truth, but not all of it. Remember I told you that your mother visited Gillon on her final Thursday afternoon in Charleston? Remember you asked what leverage she had?"

I nodded.

"Tell him, Gillon. Tell him about her visit. The truth."

It was one day after I had broken Pendleton's nose, the Friday afternoon that my mother paid a visit to the office of a man who would later become senator on his reputation for law and justice.

I can picture my mother, Carolyn, stepping into Gillon's office. For such an occasion, she would have worn a blue dress, hem cut well below her knees, summer hat to match, holding a pair of white gloves, small leather purse hanging from a strap on her arm. I can picture her sitting elegantly in that blue dress, drawing from a cigarette, for back then, it was an act of rebellion for a woman to smoke.

"I'm leaving town," she said.

Gillon moved out from behind his desk. He was proud of the size of his office. He liked to walk over to the window that surveyed the nearly abandoned harbor and some of the rusting ships at the wharves. He believed it added to his mystique that he had chosen a seedy part of Charleston to establish his working quarters. Although he was as young as Carolyn, mystique was important to him; he saw his political future clearly and it was unfolding as it should.

Gillon ran his fingers through his thick dark hair as he turned to face her. It was a gesture like walking to the window to admire the view. Or like snapping his suspenders against his strong chest. A way to draw attention to something that gave him pride.

"You cut yourself," he said, leaving his statement open-ended to serve as a question. He pointed to her upper cheekbone, where makeup could not hide a tiny but deep slash that marred her skin.

She ignored that too. "I am here to tell you I am leaving Charleston."

"Where are you going?"

"A ranch in Montana," she said. "A houseboat in San Francisco. Anywhere so far away that I never again hear the Barrett family name."

"I trust then, you want me to forward the monthly checks?" Gillon asked my mother that afternoon when she demanded the money.

"No," she answered. "Nick is almost ten. The trust fund agreement covered him until he was eighteen. Eight years remaining at twelve months per year equals ninety-six payments. I want a lump-sum check from the family trust fund for all of it. After I leave, you won't know where I am. Nor will you hear from me again. That is a promise I will be very, very happy to keep."

"If that's the way you want it," he said. "It is Nick's money. This may not be the most convenient time for a check that large. Monthly payments were much easier to . . ."

"To conceal?" There was scorn in her question. She found a cigarette from her purse and lit it with an elegant silver lighter.

"If you want to phrase it that bluntly,

yes," he said. He deliberately drawled his words as if that would soften the truth.

"You are the Barretts' family lawyer. You can do what it takes to get me that check. If you don't, what was once concealed will no longer be concealed. I'm sure you want to protect your client from that."

Gillon smiled to show Carolyn he was not afraid. "It's not much of a threat. No one will believe you after all this time. Especially with all the rumors buzzing about you and that navy boy."

"Scandal has hung over my head since I married into the Barrett family," she said. She inhaled from her cigarette, waited a beat, then exhaled. "It doesn't hurt me at all. But we both know what the truth will do to the rest of the family. And if that isn't enough, there's last week's naval base announcement."

Gillon's smile froze. His body shifted. While he remained seated at the edge of his desk, he was no longer relaxed.

Carolyn saw this, and it would be her turn to smile if she chose. She didn't.

"Naval base announcement," he said, repeating her words slowly, as if unsure he heard correctly. "I have no idea what you mean."

"Liar."

Without realizing she was doing it, Carolyn lightly rubbed the cut on her cheekbone. She clearly wanted to be away from Gillon and Charleston and the Barrett family as soon as possible.

"Last Christmas, the society ball," she said. "A young ensign, the admiral's assistant that you included on the list. Eyes wide, impressed at himself for being included in such exclusive company. Remember? The navy boy you mentioned? A rented tuxedo that fit him like a cardboard box. You made a point of sitting him beside me, as if you were promising him the only single woman there. Like you wanted him to believe that all of that wonderful world could belong to someone as sophisticated as he."

Gillon reached across his desk for a pack of cigarettes on top of a pile of legal folders. He tapped a cigarette loose. Hung it from his lower lip. The lighter he pulled from his trouser pocket was gold plated. He lit the cigarette with apparent unconcern. But the shiny gold lighter he set on the desk was greasy with sweat from his fingerprints.

"You should be warned," she continued. "Your young pigeon needs to learn to handle his whiskey. He got drunk enough that first night to beg me to marry him. Told me he would be very rich within the year and that someone of society like me would be a perfect wife at all of the events. I believe he assumed because I have the Barrett name that I already knew what was happening. He wanted me to understand clearly that he was the one ready to deliver the information that would make swampland worth millions, if all of us treated him right."

Now Carolyn smiled as she let her words hang there. Then she continued. "It made me wonder. Enough that I allowed him to escort me to other functions. Now you know why. I wanted to learn more from him. I wanted the biggest hammer I could get to hold over your head because I wanted to be ready for the day I arrived in this office to demand the money I would need to leave this city."

She smiled more, staring down Gillon so he knew she was serious. "This is the day. I am ready. You see, I also went to the courthouse and checked the land records. Last January, less than two weeks after that Christmas party, you purchased land on behalf of anonymous clients. Swampland, on the edge of the Cooper River, a few miles north of Charleston, at next-to-nothing per acre. Here we are, six months later, and it is announced that the government has chosen that land as the location for its new navy base annexation."

"Coincidence."

"That's not for me to determine," she said. "But after a few well-placed letters, the attorney general may decide the coincidence worth investigating. Even if nothing is proved, won't that hurt your own political chances?"

Gillon ground his cigarette into a clean, clear glass ashtray. "I'll need a couple of days to get the check ready," he said, exhaling a final lungful of smoke as he said it.

"No," she said. "Have the check ready by four o'clock this afternoon. You'll find a way to get it. Even if you have to take it out of the navy money you earned by using that young ensign."

"I have no doubt I can get it. Just not that soon."

She emphasized her words. "Four o'clock this afternoon. I have two tickets for the train that leaves tonight. I intend to be on it. With the money. And with my son."

When she left, Gillon picked up the phone and dialed a number.

"Layton," he said, when the phone on the other end was answered, "we have a problem."

*** *** ***

"Just so I'm sure I understand," I said. "My mother threatened to expose some fraudulent land deal unless you made it easy for her to leave town with me and my trust fund money."

"Yes," Helen said. "It was that simple. They should have let the two of you go. But Gillon and Layton had other ideas."

"Helen!" Gillon said.

"I am beginning to believe that the human body does contain a soul," Helen continued, as if Gillon had not interrupted. "A most unfortunate notion. For years, I had scoffed at it. But it truly hurt me when Lorimar Barrett ended our affair. I began to wonder why. Strictly speaking, if we were mere animals, there should be no reason for love or hate. Not a single gland in our bodies to program it that way. Lust, certainly, is gland driven. Anger, fear — adrenaline driven. But the hollowness that comes with lost love?"

She sighed. "And then there is remorse, regret. I had slowly begun to hate myself for keeping secret what I knew about your mother, Nick. I had to ask myself why I

379

hated myself. What happened to her wasn't my fault. I would have done anything to help her. Yet my conscience has troubled me all these years and only gets worse with time. Where and how would such an idiotic, self-destructive impulse fit in the human body if not forced upon us by a soul?"

Another sigh. "A youthful body, of course, has plenty of distractions that make it easy to deny the soul. The best of those distractions were mine, for longer than most, but —"

Gillon snapped. "Helen, is this maudlin exhibition necessary?"

"For me, yes. Don't worry, dear; soon I shall turn the attention where you crave it most. On you."

Helen spoke to me. "When you were a boy, this was my life. Young, beautiful, rich. I did not care much for my husband, but it didn't matter. He was old and would be gone soon. Immediately after becoming a widow, I had Lorimar, the toast of the town. We reveled in our affair, not caring who it might hurt."

The yacht pitched sideways, then straightened.

"Where was I?" Helen asked. "Yes. Young, beautiful, rich. All of this gives one the ability to satisfy one's immediate desires by any way possible — but only for as long as you can remain convinced that all you will ever have is this life and the body you inhabit. But when your skin becomes pitted and begins to erode, you begin to realize the same has happened to your soul. Especially when the youth and beauty and wealth is gone, and everything you once thought important seems meaningless."

Gillon snapped again. "Helen, for the love of —"

"God?" She smiled through her distorted face. "Give me long enough, I speculate on that subject too."

To me, she said, "In the last six months, I've discovered three things that have brought me to this point, here at the yacht. The first was, in another irony, cancer will take me as it did Edgar Layton. The second was that Pendleton, Lorimar's son, had found a way to bleed my estate so that it was nearly penniless. The third, far worse, happened as I helped Claire and Pendleton sort through Lorimar's private papers after his death. Claire had gone down to the kitchen. She screamed at seeing a mouse, which took Pendleton down there to see what had happened. So I was alone in the library as I found a carbon copy of an old police report that allowed me to understand the truth behind the car accident that had killed my only son. One that I immediately hid before Claire or Pendleton could return."

"You knew all along," I said. "You sent me the letter and the plane tickets and paid for my stay here in Charleston."

"Yes."

"And you sent me to Gillon one day, then to the admiral the next. You wanted them scared. You wanted them to panic at what I might discover."

"I wanted them alone, here, with you, at sea. It took me six months to think through this plan. Simple, wouldn't you agree? You were the baying hound that spooked them from the underbrush."

"Why?" Gillon asked Helen. "You're as guilty as we are."

"In a way," Helen said. She stood, derringer still in hand. "And in another way, not. This is your moment, Gillon."

"My moment?"

"You get to be the center of attention. Nick will lead the way up the stairs to the deck. The admiral will remain with you and your wheelchair, with me following. If the admiral lifts either hand from the wheelchair, I will shoot him in the back. Am I clear?"

Gillon said, "Helen, this does not make the slightest bit of sense."

"Probably not, Gillon. I hope you find it ironic that one other impulse with no glandular origin has pointed me toward the complexities of the human soul."

She smiled. "And that impulse would be revenge."

CHAPTER 39

A spotlight threw a harsh glare across the back deck of the yacht. The rain had slowed as the storm moved inland, but the lines and railing and canvases were soaked and drops of water glittered. The yacht pitched with the waves, and Helen was careful to keep her distance from the three of us in front of her.

"All of you," she shouted. "Into the lifeboat."

It sat at the very rear of the yacht, sideways, from bow to stern as long as the yacht was wide. Slowly, with a backward glance over his shoulder, the admiral pushed the wheelchair forward.

"You too, Nick," she said. "Into the lifeboat."

Helen watched carefully as the admiral and I pulled the canvas back off the top of the lifeboat. It hung in a cradle from steel arms that extended over the water.

"Lift Gillon," Helen told the admiral and me. "Both of you. Lift Gillon into the boat."

"There is no dignity in this," Gillon said. "You are a perverse woman."

"No," she said. "Just angry."

The rain stopped completely. A temporary calm fell over the yacht. The only sounds were the slap of waves against the hull and its powerful engines driving it forward to the open ocean. Eight or nine miles behind us, the lights of Charleston glowed off the bottom of the cloud bank heavy above it.

Gillon clutched at the side of the lifeboat to keep his balance.

"Now you two," Helen told me and the admiral. "Both of you inside the boat. I will shoot if you try anything differently."

Once we were inside the lifeboat, Helen moved closer and inspected the interior. The spotlight behind her made it impossible for me to read her face.

"Throw the life jackets out," she said. "And the flares."

"Just put a bullet in us," Gillon said. "If you want to kill us, save all the work."

"I don't want to kill you," she said. "But if you would prefer the bullet over an opportunity at freedom . . ."

The admiral threw the life jackets into the dark water. They bobbed in the phosphorous wake of the yacht, then were lost immediately from sight as the yacht continued to power forward. Next, he tossed out the flares.

"Thank you," Helen said. "Nick. You come out now."

"What?"

"Out of the boat. I needed you in there so you wouldn't try to stop me from setting Gillon and Robertson loose. But come out slowly. I don't want to have to shoot you if you try to stop me."

Helen kept her distance from me as I clambered out of the bow of the lifeboat.

"Good," she said. She pulled a lever, and electric motors began to whine, lifting the lifeboat away from the yacht. She let the motors run for thirty seconds, pulling the lever to stop position when the lifeboat had completely cleared the yacht and hung above the water.

"Good-bye," she called out to Gillon and the admiral, her hand still on the lever.

"Helen," Gillon said, "this is insanity. You are stealing my yacht. Piracy at sea."

"You think that matters?" she said. "If you survive, I'm sure you won't press charges. I know too much. As does the admiral. Remember how Layton played us each against the other. We all knew too much for any of us to come forward with our story. Tonight will be no different."

Helen lowered the lifeboat until it was almost touching the water. She kept her derringer trained on me, making sure I wouldn't try to stop her.

"Edgar Layton is dead," she told the two men in the lifeboat, raising her voice to be heard above the yacht engines. "The doctors give me four weeks, five weeks at the most. That means when I am gone, there will only be the two of you."

The breeze whipped at her black dress as she leaned forward. "Think about it. If one of you is dead, the other is totally free. With Edgar gone, and me gone, and one of you gone, there will be nobody to testify against the final survivor. Nothing that Nick or Amelia do can prove you had anything to do with the murder of Carolyn Barrett."

She lowered the lifeboat another two feet, so that the water pushed against it, hungry to carry it away.

"Don't waste your energy trying to start the motor. No spark plug. You are only seven miles offshore. If you work together, you can make it back safely. On the other hand, if one of you goes overboard and drowns, I'm sure the survivor can come up with a good story when the Coast Guard finds the lifeboat in the morning."

"Helen —"

"You understand, don't you?" Helen interrupted Gillon's plea. "This is what I planned, what I wanted. Not justice of the courts. I could have gone to the police myself for that. But I wanted Nick to bring you here so that I could send the two of you into the night. For a different kind of justice. Call it survival of the fittest. My bet is only one of you makes it back. May the best man win."

The yacht rose and fell again. A wave hit the lifeboat, throwing water on Gillon and McLean. Already each was eyeing the other, edging apart as she spoke.

"By the way," she shouted, "if you're wondering why I wanted this revenge so badly, it's simple. She was my sister."

Helen hit the lever a final time.

Released from its cradle, the lifeboat dropped into the water.

The yacht surged forward, leaving the two men to disappear into the night, alone together, in a tiny boat on the big cold waters of the Atlantic.

"After we return, you can tell the authorities what you like," Helen said. "I really don't care what happens now."

We stood on the back deck of the yacht, the lifeboat now out of sight. With the storm completely inland and the clouds starting to break, pinpricks of stars began to show. Helen tossed her derringer into the water.

"Revenge," I said. "You told them you wanted revenge. For what? What do you know about my mother?"

"She didn't abandon you, Nick."

Helen was tired. Her words slurred slightly. She couldn't make the effort to keep her lips tight as she spoke.

"Finally, Nick, I can tell you."

CHAPTER 40

This is the story of my mother's final night.

On that night, with Amelia alone and afraid in her father's police cruiser, Edgar Layton took my mother farther into the darkness. He had handcuffed her wrists in front of her belly, and he pushed her along with one heavy hand, and with the other hand shone a flashlight on the ground before them. The beam was powerful; it was a flashlight that held eight batteries, almost as long as a billy club, something he had used it for before.

The beam showed long woven grass of a rarely used path. Insects fluttered toward the beam. Bushes on each side of the path plucked at my mother's legs.

Their walk took five minutes. Except for the rasp of Layton's breathing — like a bull plodding across a pasture — each walked in silence. My mother did not give in to her fear and ask questions about her fate or beg for release.

They reached an old shack. The flashlight beam showed a buckled doorway — no door — bent hinges with a couple of screws remaining where the door was once attached.

"It's me," Layton said.

A young man stepped through the doorway. He warded off the beam of the flashlight with upturned palms, squinting against the harsh light.

My mother would have recognized him immediately. Jonathan Britt, the admiral's young assistant, dapper in a leather bomber jacket, smiling nervously.

Layton took the flashlight beam off the young man and turned it to my mother. The admiral's assistant gasped at the sight of her handcuffed hands.

Layton unholstered his pistol and placed the end of the barrel against my mother's head. This, too, was obvious in the flashlight beam.

Layton cocked the hammer. A click of iron against iron.

"Jonathan," Layton said to the admiral's assistant, turning his flashlight back again into the young man's eyes, "have you told anyone about our little land deal?"

"No," he said. The flashlight beam hit his eyes directly. He squinted, bewildered. "I could have told you that before you dragged me out here."

"Listen carefully," Layton said. "You know this woman."

Jonathan nodded. His hair was shaved

short, navy style. Tiny white crescents of scalp showed where the razor had gouged too deep.

"This woman knows about it," Layton said. "This is not good."

"You can't kill her. We've gone on a few dates. That's it."

"I'm going to shoot her if you don't tell the truth. Was it you who told her about the naval base deal?"

Jonathan gulped a few times. He was trying to weigh his options. "Some, all right? I mean, she's one of you. Don't kill her for what I did wrong."

Layton dropped his hand, taking the gun away from my mother's temple.

"Have you told anyone else?" Layton asked Jonathan. "Think carefully. You see how serious I am about this. If I find out later that you told someone — and I will find out — then I'll shoot you."

"No. No. I swear. I've told no one else."

The flashlight was unwavering on Jonathan's face. Because the light was squarely in his eyes, he didn't see Layton lift the gun again. He didn't see Layton pull the trigger.

My mother saw. All of it. The bullet caught Jonathan high and left in his leather jacket. It made a neat hole. His face puck-

392

ered in surprise. He sagged to his knees, deflating like a balloon.

❀ ❀ ❀

At the gunshot, four others stepped from the shack where they had been hidden spectators to Edgar Layton's brutal dispatch of the naval assistant.

Geoffrey Alexander Gillon, casual slacks and a sweater.

The admiral himself, the creases of his uniform crisply ironed.

There was also her sister, Helen deMarionne, who wouldn't meet my mother's eyes. And Lorimar Barrett, father of Pendleton and my mother's brother-in-law. He was built like an Ivy League football player, now with a rounded belly and the beginning of a stoop to his back. Once he was handsome like David, his dead war-hero brother. Now Lorimar Barrett was a man content with middle age — round spectacles, balding. My mother loathed him. Knew that he was having an affair with Helen deMarionne.

"Are you crazy?" It was Gillon, screaming.

Cordite was heavy in the air. My mother must have known by then that she would die. They would not let her witness murder and walk away.

"I shall miss him," the admiral said. "Few could handle paperwork like he did."

"Are you crazy?" Gillon screamed again.

Lorimar Barrett placed a hand on Gillon's arm. "We are not playing for marbles," Lorimar said. "He was the weakest link. And now he is gone."

"But this . . . is . . . murder . . ."

"Shut up," Layton told Gillon. "Or we'll bury you with him."

Gillon shut up. In the light given by the edges of the powerful flashlight beam, he could not help but stare at the body near his feet where Jonathan had fallen face forward. Although the entry of the bullet was like a neat punch drill, the exit through his back tore apart the leather like shrapnel.

"Now," Layton said to my mother, "does anyone else know what you told Gillon this afternoon?"

"No. I only mentioned it to Gillon because I wanted the settlement for Nick."

"I will kill Nick myself if you have lied."

Her wrists were still handcuffed in front of her. She brought up her hands in prayer. Nothing had broken her in the past ten years. She had grown strong and tough. But this broke her. She begged for me and my life.

"Please. Believe me. I know you are

going to kill me. But don't kill Nick. I haven't told a soul."

The flashlight was now shining squarely in her eyes. She tensed, waiting for the impact of the bullet.

✳ ✳ ✳

"Don't kill her," Lorimar said. "Killing her was not part of this."

"You can't kill her," Helen said. "I will not allow it."

The body of Jonathan Britt lay between them as they argued.

"Shut up," Layton said. "There is no other choice."

"There is a choice," Lorimar answered. "She knows we will kill her boy if she doesn't keep this a secret. You can let her live."

Layton laughed at Lorimar. "You've called her a problem for years. Why wouldn't you want it ended?"

Blinded by the flashlight in Layton's left hand, my mother made a guess about where Layton's right hand was, the hand with the pistol. She dove for the gun. Her hands bounced off Layton's forearm. She clutched for his wrist, clutched for the gun.

But another explosion ripped through the blanket of insect noise. Followed by a gurgle of disbelief.

Layton threw my mother off his arm as casually as if discarding a piece of clothing. He threw her to the ground. He stepped on her neck to hold her in place. He pointed the flashlight beam at the source of the agonized gurgling.

It showed Geoffrey Alexander Gillon. On his back, holding the lower part of his belly. Blood crawled over the tops of his fingers.

There was another click of iron against iron. Layton kneeled and pushed the barrel into Gillon's temple, as dispassionately as if about to put down a horse with a broken leg.

But Gillon was a smart man. He was thinking, even as he fought the spasms of pain that came after a bullet had torn out a piece of his lower spine and the nerves that connected his brain to his legs. He knew what the click of iron against iron signified.

"Don't shoot me," he gasped. "If I die, a sealed package gets opened in Washington."

With that simple statement, Gillon saved his own life. Layton decided against the kill and eased the hammer back into place without shooting.

"We need to get him to a hospital," Lorimar Barrett said. "We can't let him die."

"What about the woman?" the admiral asked.

Layton reached down and pulled up his pants leg. He had a smaller pistol in an ankle holster. He tossed the pistol to the admiral.

"No!" Helen screamed.

Helen tried to take the gun away, but Layton held her off with one hand.

"You shoot her or I shoot you," Layton told the admiral. He had his own pistol trained on the admiral's head. "You shoot her. I keep the gun with your fingerprints. That's our insurance."

My mother saw it clearly. The admiral nodded.

And that was my mother's death sentence.

CHAPTER 41

Helen turned to me, keeping the good side of her face in profile.

"I was part of the group in on the land deal, through Lorimar. I had no idea until later that your mother had made the threat she did. Lorimar took me out into the country that night. It was Edgar Layton's plan to involve all of us, so that none of us would ever dare reveal what had happened."

Helen's voice became dull, as if keeping herself from feeling her story would lessen its impact. "I believe I lost my soul that night. Going to Lorimar after having an affair with the man who did what he did with my sister, who was there that night — was a way, I know now, to punish myself. And, in a way, to punish him. He was bound to me by the evil we shared, and I never let him forget it. You cannot imagine how much I loathed who I became over the years. It no longer mattered how much I debased myself in pursuit of distractions to rid myself of that pain. And you . . . you were always a reminder of my sin. I hated you because of that, even as my guilt forced me to try to protect you by forcing the Barretts to look after you." If possible, Helen's voice became even duller. "All I can say in my defense is that by the time I figured out what Layton meant to do, it was too late. I watched as the admiral shot her. I didn't have a chance of stopping them. When she was dead, there was nothing I could do. Layton drove me back to the train station, left Lorimar to take his own car. I never knew what Edgar did with the bodies."

"Layton drove *you* back to the train station. Not my mother?"

Amelia had heard *two* women get in and out of the car that night. Not one. My mother first. Helen second.

"We wanted someone of her build and size. That way, Layton could find witnesses to testify that she had boarded the train with the tickets she had purchased earlier."

When Amelia had heard her father in the car, he had been speaking to Helen, not to my mother. *"Listen, you tramp. I know where you came from. I think I even know who killed your father. White trash."*

"Layton left me at the train station, then went to bury your mother. I am so, so sorry, Nick. Sorry for everything. There is no way I could expect your forgiveness. I can't even find a way to forgive myself."

I thought of all the implications as a full minute passed in which Helen did not speak. How could the memory of that night ever leave Helen? Watching her sister die. For all these years, helpless even to mourn her in public. For all her scheming and selfishness, I found pity for her.

When Helen found her voice again, she said, "Carolyn spoke directly to me just before the admiral pulled the trigger. The others there didn't know she was speaking to me because they didn't know we were sisters. I've always wanted to tell you about this. Now I can. Your life was more important to her than her own life. She didn't beg me to try to save her. She saw him lift the gun and said these simple words. To me. 'Please tell Nick I love him.' She spoke with such urgency, I almost did. But I couldn't. Not without letting you know how she had died."

Another full minute passed. Helen did not know how much it hurt me to think of my mother's final words and to think of the reason for my mother's urgency. She knew, my mother, how badly I would need to hear those words.

"What I can't figure out," Helen said, her voice exhausted, "is why Carolyn did what she did. There was no reason for her to leave Charleston. She'd moved away from the rich set. Lived in a town house with a maid who was her best friend. She worked for the museum, lived a simple life, and loved you fiercely. She was so at peace with her life that I envied her.

"But on that afternoon, she threw away everything she had by demanding what she did from Gillon and Barrett and Layton, the three most ruthless men she could have ever faced. Something had driven her to want to leave Charleston in the fastest way possible. What?"

I thought of the tiny deep cut on my mother's face. I turned away from Helen and kept my silence.

❋ ❋ ❋

"I am tired," Helen said. "When we get back to Charleston, you will find me in one of the bedrooms below. Don't disturb me until then."

"I don't know how to handle a yacht."

"It's not on autopilot. Go to the wheelhouse. You'll see what I mean."

Helen left me on the back deck of the yacht and took the stairs down to the saloon.

I wanted to be alone. Desperately. I wanted to be alone and to think of nothing. I wanted to be away from Charleston and away from my memories. I wanted to be away from myself.

But I could not remain here, watching the dark waters pass by and listening to the hiss of it against the hull.

Two men were out in this vast ocean. Much as I might hope for their deaths, it would not be right to let them die as Helen intended. I could pretend I had some noble moral sense that their two murders would not make the other murders right. I want to believe that is partly true. But I also knew I did not want Helen's carefully laid plans to succeed. She had brought me in, certain my curiosity would serve her purposes. She had played Gillon and McLean expertly, rousing their fears and then setting up this meeting on the yacht. Six months, she'd said, planning this night on the ocean for them. In truth? Helen's schemes had destroyed so much of my life already that I knew I would find satisfaction in ending this one for her.

So, much as I would have preferred to stare at the water as the yacht plowed farther and farther out into the Atlantic, farther and farther away from Charleston, I forced myself to go to the wheelhouse.

Where I found Claire at the wheel.

"Mayday, Mayday."

I had the radio microphone in my hand. I spoke on the emergency frequency, trying to raise the Coast Guard.

"Mayday, Mayday." I had never been part of the yachting set. This phrase was all I knew.

The radio speakers crackled in response. "Report your position and situation."

I gave them our position, ignoring Claire as I tried to make sense of the electronic readings given by the global positioning unit. I'd already ignored her for the previous minute since stepping into the wheelhouse.

"We have two men at sea in a lifeboat without power. We are circling now to look for them, but we need help."

I confirmed our position one more time.

Then I told Claire to turn the yacht around so we could join in the search.

❄ ❄ ❄

"May we talk?" Claire asked.

"I'm listening," I said. I suppose there was little encouragement in my voice. My eyes were focused on the wide circle of white cast by the yacht's spotlight. The waves were a couple of feet high, capped with froth.

Claire moved directly beside me. She'd been holding a folded piece of paper. She gave it to me.

"Read it out loud to me."

In the dim light of the wheelhouse, I glanced at the first few words. "No. I know what it says."

"Read it aloud. The day Pendleton told me you would never come back to me, he gave me that piece of paper. He'd gotten it from Helen. Both of them wanted me to marry Pendleton. They used this piece of paper to force me away from you. Read it."

"You know what it says too."

"Read it."

" 'I, Nicholas Thomas Barrett, declare in my own handwriting and by my own free will, that I was the driver of the 1965 Plymouth Valiant that crashed on Oxbury Road the night of . . .' "

I refolded the paper. "I don't want to read this."

"Read it. Please."

I unfolded it again. My voice faltered as I continued. " 'I am aware that I may be charged with manslaughter in the event of the death of Philip deMarionne, a passenger injured in the car at the time of the accident. I understand that by signing this

404

confession, this police investigation will be considered complete and that charges will not be pressed if I follow these conditions. One, I sign a certificate declaring my marriage to Claire deMarionne null and void. Two, I leave Charleston and South Carolina indefinitely. Three, in lieu of a divorce settlement, I will receive from Helen deMarionne a monthly stipend of —' "

I stopped. Handed the paper back to Claire. "No more," I said.

I looked out at the dark waters. How difficult would it be to find the lifeboat?

"Can't you say it out loud? To me? That you agreed if you returned to Charleston, or made any attempts to communicate with me, you would forfeit your right to the monthly deMarionne handout and that the police investigation would be re-opened, with manslaughter charges immediately pressed."

"There is nothing left to say about it. That's my handwriting. I signed it. I left Charleston."

"But you weren't the driver," Claire said. "Two nights ago, I thought you were the man who had taken money to leave our marriage. Two nights ago, I thought this confession was truth. This afternoon, Helen told me this wasn't true. She told me to come here and ask you about it. Is it true, Nick? You were not driving?"

"No. I was not."

"Why sign it? Why leave? Then why appear now? And why keep the truth from me once you returned?"

❋ ❋ ❋

Claire badly wanted her little brother to join us at the beach house we had rented for our short honeymoon. She wanted a little wedding party to celebrate. Her younger brother was too young to drive. The only one able to bring her brother by car was Pendleton. She called Pendleton by telephone with her request and swore him to secrecy.

Pendleton arrived with her brother and with champagne and bourbon.

For that celebration, he and I set aside our hatred — he was, after all, a good friend of Claire's. And I, after all, could afford to be magnanimous in victory, for I had finally won her hand.

I drank too much. I was not accustomed to alcohol. I was giddy with joy anyway, filled with the memories of three days alone with Claire and with what we had learned about each other.

So, much of the last hour of celebration was blurred to me. I do remember with distinctive horror, however, one significant detail.

When all of us piled into the car to return to Charleston, it was Claire behind the steering wheel.

❁ ❁ ❁

"I signed it because I didn't know Pendleton had been the driver."

"Him?" Her voice was a long gasp of slow comprehension. "Him? Pendleton?"

"He crashed the car. He dragged me from the passenger side and sat me behind the steering wheel. Then he sat on the passenger side and finished the bottle so that when the police finally arrived he would be merely a drunk passenger. Layton got there first, took photographs. The blood on the floor of the passenger side was mine, from my leg. Pendleton didn't have a scratch on him. There was no damage on the driver's side that would have crushed my leg. Layton knew immediately what had happened. He knew it would be worth something to him to protect Pendleton. And Pendleton paid him over the years for that."

Claire still spoke with disbelief. "All these years, I thought you had killed my brother. Instead, I married the man who did it. I was sleeping with the man who let you take the blame, the man who used that blame against me."

"You'll understand my anger," I said. "If Pendleton had gone for help, I might not have lost my leg. If your brother had reached the hospital earlier, he might have survived. Instead, Pendleton sat on the passenger side and drank himself into oblivion."

Claire clutched my arm. "I don't understand." She looked upward at me. "If you knew you hadn't been driving, why take the blame? Why leave me? Why leave our marriage?"

"I thought it was the only way to save you."

"I don't understand."

"Remember when we left to drive home to Charleston that night, you were driving because I'd had too much to drink? I was asleep on the passenger side. You were behind the wheel, Claire."

"Only for the first half hour," she said. "Until I became too sleepy. You were passed out on the passenger side. I stopped the car. Pendleton switched from the backseat and took the steering wheel. I went to sleep in the back where he'd been. The car crash must've knocked me out. When I awoke with the car in the marsh, I saw you behind the wheel. Pendleton must've moved you while I was unconscious. All these years I thought you had started driving again while I was still sleeping, before the wreck occurred."

Claire began to cry. She lifted my hands to her face so that I could feel the tears. "You thought . . ."

"Until I received the police report two weeks ago," I said, "I thought you had driven the car into the bridge."

CHAPTER 42

The yacht's spotlight showed nothing but waves. I had no idea if we were close to where Helen had first set the lifeboat adrift. Nor could I guess at the currents. I hoped the Coast Guard would arrive soon to search for it in a proper grid.

"I'll divorce Pendleton," Claire said quietly. "You and I have always belonged together."

My eyes strained as I tried to peer beyond the spotlight.

"Nick?"

I could not look at her. This was the moment I'd always dreamed might happened. Yet I could not look at her.

"You know who my father was," I said. "Helen must have told you when she told you about the accident."

Claire hesitated for too long. That in itself told me she knew.

"Yes," she finally said.

"So you know I can now make a claim of inheritance. The money Pendleton can't touch, I can. You know that, don't you? Helen explained it to you, didn't she? That now I'm a rich man and Pendleton is not."

Longer hesitation. I didn't give her a

chance to lie to me, to tell me this was about love.

"I think," I said, "I want to be outside."

❀ ❀ ❀

Although the storm had passed, the waves had not calmed.

The yacht lifted and fell.

I stood at the railing near the prow. The beam of the spotlight seemed to reach out from below my feet, widening in the circle empty of any sign of the lifeboat. Occasional spray from the hull banging into the ocean licked at my face and shoulders.

Although my eyes strained to see beyond the light, my mind was elsewhere.

All I needed to do was walk the few short steps back into the wheelhouse. The revenge I wanted from Pendleton would be complete. I would have taken from him everything that was important. His money. His status. And Claire. I would have a chance to begin again with Claire.

Why then did I remain here at the railing of the yacht? In the cold of the night air. Alone.

It struck me that I had long been martyred to the memory of Claire. Not for Claire herself, for she was no longer the woman I had left behind. Time and circumstances had changed her, as they had changed me.

Why had I clung so stubbornly to that memory, using it to push aside any chance at any other relationship? Was it because I didn't feel I deserved love? After driving my mother away, did a part buried deep within me recoil from the chance at fully committing my soul to vulnerability once again?

Since my leaving Charleston, Claire had always been unattainable, making it simple for me to fool myself into believing if I could not be reunited with her, then I wanted no one.

And now.

I had that excuse no longer. She was attainable. I was reluctant.

Perhaps, however, all of my self-analysis was merely psychobabble. Maybe I could not reconcile myself to begin again with a woman who found it more convenient to be with me now that I was in a position to inherit. Yesterday, when she didn't know, she hadn't offered to divorce Pendleton.

Did I love Claire? Or did I love a memory?

❋ ❋ ❋

I remembered a brief conversation I'd had once with an English instructor at the community college in Santa Fe. He'd been very drunk during this conversation; it took place in a bar where students and profs often went in the evenings. This English instructor had left his wife of fifteen years for a young coed. He'd even moved in with the coed, and as he told me in drunken tears, regretted it immensely.

"I can tell you what love isn't," he'd told me, clutching the edge of the table with one hand and his seventh gin and tonic with the other. "It isn't that big beautiful spark. Sure, that starts it. But it's the finish that matters."

He'd gulped back his entire drink, determined to hurt himself badly with the poison.

"Say there ever comes a day you want out," he slurred. "Like the way I had wanted out. You start seeing someone else. She's younger than you. Always had a couple hours to primp and get ready before you go on your dates. All you do is go to upscale restaurants before you sneak away to high-priced hotels with twenty-four-hour room service. Well, let me tell you something. That's not love. Don't let it fool you."

He'd tried waving for the barmaid's attention, but I pulled his hand down. He hardly seemed to notice.

"I'll tell you what love is," he said. "It's when you hug her while she's crying and her face is splotchy and red. It's when you drive a twenty-hour trip together to the in-laws and fight all the way. When you hold her hand while she's throwing up with morning sickness. When you stay with her during the agony of giving birth. When you become the one person in this world she depends on as a best friend through everything good and bad."

He'd stood. A lanky man with a goatee. Immaculately dressed. Always well spoken. And now falling-over drunk.

"I miss my wife," he'd said. "I miss her so badly. And I can't go back."

I heard later he'd tried to hang himself that night in the coed's apartment. He'd been too drunk to succeed. Shortly after, when the relationship with the college student tore apart, she'd lodged a sexual harassment complaint and he'd lost his job.

Where he moved after that, no one really cared.

❊ ❊ ❊

I had to ask myself if this was what it was with Claire. If I'd been able to keep her memory idealized because I hadn't grown with her, held her while she cried, fought

414

with her on long drives, gone through a birth with her.

Perhaps the first love lost truly was a perfume as subtle and unpredictable as a dancing breeze. But perfume has no substance. And a first love lost will never have the chance to grow beyond the idealized, untarnished, undecayed memories.

Or was it even worse? Had I wanted her so that I would be an accepted part of the Charleston life?

I'd come a long way to ask myself those questions.

While I was still tempted to turn around to go into the wheelhouse and take Claire in my arms, I knew in my heart that I could not do it and still keep my soul.

This realization was like stepping out of a prison.

I pondered this sensation of freedom.

And found myself thinking of Amelia. Remembering the current we'd shared when our eyes met. Regretting how and why she'd walked away from me earlier in the day.

I made a decision. To risk rejection. To call Amelia as soon as I returned to Charleston. There was something there, and I wasn't going to let it slip away because of fear.

Almost in the same moment as I made this decision, Claire appeared beside me at the railing.

Wordlessly, she knelt at my feet and clutched my legs. For a moment, I thought she was going to beg.

But I was wrong.

It wouldn't have taken her much strength. Her position gave her good leverage, and I was totally unprepared, already leaning over the railing as I strained to see ahead of the yacht.

Claire lifted, and before I could comprehend why, she flipped me forward.

Away from the railing. Toward the black of the ocean.

CHAPTER 43

The impact and coldness of the water was such a shock that any shout or scream was sucked from my lungs. I fought for the surface, churning my arms and legs. When I reached air again, the wake of the yacht tumbled me sideways, and I had to fight again to get my head above the water.

The yacht's lights receded from me.

Waves threw me from one side to the other, and I kicked frantically to stay on the surface. I paddled with my arms, fighting the weight of my wet clothing.

And still the yacht's lights receded.

Had I any thoughts that Claire's actions were somehow an accident or that she felt sudden remorse, those thoughts ended when the lights finally disappeared.

I was alone in the cold, dark ocean.

My greatest danger was not in drowning. Farther south, in the gulf currents, I might have the hope of staying afloat long enough to drift to shore.

Not here. The Atlantic this time of year, this far offshore, could not be any warmer than midfifties Fahrenheit. The heat of my body would be sucked away without mercy. I guessed I had fifteen minutes, twenty at the most.

Yet I would not go quietly.

I kicked off my shoes as I paddled.

With difficulty and much gasping of the salt water, I pulled off my jacket and dropped it too. I kept my sweater, not really sure if it helped retain any body heat.

Wave after wave spun over my head.

Already I was tiring.

I thought of my pants. Long, long ago, during the swimming lessons that all of us children were required to take, the instructors had shown us a trick. Tie the end of each pants leg in a knot; grasp the waistband on each side and raise it high and pull down quickly, trapping air inside the legs so that it might serve as a temporary life jacket.

I wondered if I would have the dexterity to do that. Already, my hands were becoming terrifyingly numb.

Then I remembered.

The cigarette lighter in my pocket.

One of my legs, of course, was heavier in the water than the other. My prosthesis, made of plastic, bobbed somewhat.

I knew what I needed to do; I did not know if I would be able to do it, or even if it would work.

With difficulty, I dug the lighter out of my pocket. I put it in my mouth and bit hard. It was the only way I could hold it and peel off my pants.

Paddling with one arm, I reached down with my other and undid my belt and pants. I leaned over and pulled my pants off, using both hands. With only a leg and a half to kick myself afloat, I began to sink.

I let go and thrashed to the surface again. I took the lighter from my mouth, sucked in the biggest lungful of air that I could, and once again attempted to remove my pants.

The extra air in my lungs helped keep me higher in the water. With agonizing slowness — and still sinking — I peeled my pants down and off my legs.

Again, I fought for the surface. I paddled for a few moments, trying to get energy back. I felt numbness creep into my arms and legs.

I was tired. Oh, so tired.

I thought of Claire pushing me off the yacht. Did she believe that my death would prevent me from contesting her husband's inheritance? Had she made a choice that if I would not marry her, she was better served remaining with Pendleton?

I let anger warm me. It was an illusion,

of course. No anger could defeat the cold of the Atlantic. But it was enough to force me to fight.

Again, I filled my lungs with air, and again I leaned forward, using my arms, not to paddle but to remove my prosthesis. And again, I slowly sank.

When I finally had it loose, I kicked toward the surface, lopsided because a whole leg had so much more propulsion than half a leg.

How many minutes had passed? How many minutes before my life slowly ebbed from my body?

I could not tell.

I could only concentrate on my final hope, one I doubted would work.

Paddling my arms, prosthesis in my left hand, and buoyed now by the air in my pants, I took the lighter from my mouth with my other hand.

I kicked with my legs as hard as I could, trying to keep my shoulders and head clear of the water as I lifted both arms into the night.

Water slapped at my face, stinging my eyes.

I flicked the lighter.

As Gillon had so casually mentioned, it worked.

A sure, bright flame appeared in my right hand.

I attached it to the toes of my prosthesis.

This was my hope. That the rubberized plastic would take the flame and begin to burn.

I kicked hard, but it wasn't enough. My shoulders sank beneath the surface. Then my chin. My nose. My eyes and the top of my head.

I kept my arms aloft, blindly trying to hold the flame of the lighter against the prosthesis.

When I could hold my breath no longer, I brought my right hand down and paddled with it. That was enough to bring me to the surface again.

I blinked against the salt water.

The foot of my prosthesis was embroiled in flame, so bright it almost hurt my eyes.

Paddling with my right hand and kicking with my good leg and my other thigh, I fought the waves as long as I could.

Would it be enough?

Would spotters in the Coast Guard chopper sent out to search for Gillon and McLean ever see this light among the swells of the waves?

I didn't allow myself the luxury of guessing.

I paddled — one-armed and one-legged — until exhaustion forced me to drop the beacon that was my burning prosthesis. I dropped it with a sour thought. If I died, at least I was rid of it.

I concentrated on staying afloat.

I had another sour thought. They called it the dead man's float, the instructors during those long-ago lessons.

"Lie on your back in the water, tilting your head so that your face is skyward; fill your lungs and hold. Those few quarts of air in the lungs will help the body float. Release the air slowly, draw in again. Use your arms to maintain balance in the water."

I felt more and more of my body going numb. As I felt, too, my willpower draining away with the heat of my body.

And, with my mother's final words echoing in my mind, I had a peace of sorts.

She had not abandoned me.

Nor had God.

※ ※ ※

I was about to die. I knew it. One minute, maybe two. No matter how much willpower I summoned, my brain would shut down as all heat drained from my body.

I was about to die with a final memory,

422

knowing how much I had hurt the woman who paid such a price to be my mother.

"Oh, God," I croaked.

It hurt so badly, thinking about my mother. I desperately wanted to be able to cry, to find tears for the first time since I had been orphaned. Even now, I could not.

"Oh, God. Oh, God."

I felt warmth on my face.

Tears.

"Please, God. Forgive me. Please, God."

I was becoming confused and disoriented. I couldn't get my mind to move past those words. I couldn't put any thoughts together to complete my prayer to the God I'd spurned all my life.

It seemed I was struggling to find something important.

My lips were numb.

What was it?

What was it I wanted so badly to remember?

My arms and legs were deadweights. I could hardly command my body to maintain the rhythm of the deep breaths that were allowing me to float nearly submerged.

Deep from my memory it came. A slow gradual recollection of Amelia and how she had coached the man she brought back to life.

"Jesus," I cried. The terror of death filled me completely. I was not so much afraid of death itself, but of dying with such emptiness and futility. My life had meant nothing because I had chosen to do nothing with it.

"Jesus," I cried again. Did I cry it aloud, or was this plea only in my mind? "Jesus, Jesus. Oh, Jesus. Please forgive me."

It was my last conscious thought before sinking beneath the surface of the water.

With that final cry, the light of heaven washed over me.

I did not die, of course.

The pitiful flare I had improvised from the synthetic materials of my false half leg did draw that same Coast Guard chopper in my direction.

The light of heaven was not the light of heaven. But in another way, it was.

I do not have a near-death experience to relate. I am no William Carruthers, brought to religion and faith by the voice of Jesus sparing me from the flames of hell.

In a media-driven age where only the near-hysteria of fanatical religion is able to gain any prominence, I cannot relate, as some do, the touch of a higher power.

Yet.

The edge of death profoundly changed me.

✳ ✳ ✳

In calling out the name of Jesus, peace filled me. The cynical will maintain that my brain manufactured a natural opium. I will not defend myself against the scorn of cynics. They will never understand because they will never allow themselves to understand.

The peace is certain.

Because it finally let me believe that in this life my soul is like a fledgling, held to a nest constructed of gravity and time and the spatial existence of my body. That the God of love who created me and this universe around me stands outside of it in a way I will not comprehend until the day that my soul is released from my body. That through his love, he waits for my first flight beyond the nest, a flight into eternity that I will not and cannot fully understand during the minute span of years I spend on this tiny planet lost in the mysteries of the universe.

All I need to do to learn to fly is believe.

✳ ✳ ✳

The light flooding me as I began to slip under the water was the light of the chopper's searchlight.

I was told later that my life hung on a difference of thirty seconds. It was so close that the Coast Guard rescuers didn't wait to lower a line. Instead, the chopper dipped low, and my rescuer jumped directly into the water as my body began to sink. I was caught just under the surface and held there as the line was lowered.

When I woke, the roar of the chopper confused me. Until I was able to focus my eyes, I truly wondered if the light of heaven had been a deception to take me into a rattling, shaking hell.

Then I realized I was wrapped in a blanket, propped and held in an upright sitting position as the chopper swept back toward Charleston and the same hospital where Edgar Layton had breathed his last.

I was alert enough in the chopper to see the lights of the city approach as we crossed above the dark outline of Fort Sumter.

I knew the first call I would make upon reaching shore was to Amelia. Perhaps the one night that caused our lives to intertwine as children could lead us to exploring more of life together as adults.

Ahead, the lights of the mansions of East Battery were a distant necklace of glittering diamonds.

Diamonds I never wanted to possess.

CHAPTER 44

The door to the Barrett mansion was open a few inches. I pushed it open the rest of the way and stepped inside.

It had been years since I'd walked across the gleaming hardwood of the wide entrance hallway, years since seeing the curved stairway that led to a landing that overlooked the entrance.

I was not trespassing; this house was mine, if I wanted to claim it.

"Claire?" I called out. "Claire?"

I had not seen her since the night before. At the railing of the yacht. Less than twelve hours had passed. I'd been sent to emergency, then released. Her phone call on this morning had woken me at the bed-and-breakfast.

"Claire?"

"Here." Her voice echoed in the mansion. "In the sitting room."

❋ ❋ ❋

In odd contrast to the centuries-old oil paintings on the wall, the sitting room held a large-screen television and home-theater system and was almost filled by a large sectional sofa. It smelled faintly of stale beer, and broken potato chips littered the floor at the edges of the sofa.

"You weren't afraid I called you over to try again?"

Claire asked it almost sweetly. She wore a red dress, matching her shade of lipstick. Her hair was tied back in a short ponytail that looked oddly elegant. She sat on the far end of the sectional sofa, her legs and feet curled beneath her, her hands tucked beneath her body, as if she were a cat in repose. Her face was so eerily calm that I felt a stab of fear.

I looked closer. What I'd thought was lipstick were traces of blood. Her lip had puffed. I saw shiny tears in her eyes.

"No," I said, hiding my fear. "Last night, it was simple for you. Man overboard is an easy story to defend. Here and now, you'd have much more difficulty."

"Killing you? Helen did have a gun, you remember."

"No. Hiding the fact that you killed me." I tried to make light of it. The calmness in her face was almost unworldly. Either that or insane. "I weigh too much for you to throw me over your shoulders and hide in the trunk of your car. Plus there's the bad publicity. Might ruin your run for mayor."

"I thought the first thing you'd do after last night was —"

"Bring the police into it?" I shook my head. "So that it would be the word of a respected soon-to-be-mayor against mine? Not likely. Besides, I'm too tired of all of this. I just want to go. To be away."

"I wish I had known that." An attempt at a smile. She licked at the blood trickling from the corner of her mouth. Smiled at the taste. "I heard the news this morning. About your rescue. Here I thought if I was going to get hung for one, I might as well get hung for another."

I leaned against the opposite armrest of the sofa, keeping distance between us. "Well," I said, "there's lots of things I wish I had known."

"Helen's dead. Did you know that?" It was the conversational tone of her voice that kept me off balance. That and the blank calm of her face.

"I did not know," I said. Carefully. I began to realize Claire's calmness was that of someone on the verge of shattering.

"Oh yes. When I docked the yacht last night, I went below to get her. But she wouldn't wake up. The doctors believe it was sleeping pills. She'd touched up her makeup and laid back on the bed. No fuss for anyone. No mess when she was found. Some might have used a gun. I mean, it was in her purse. But then, she *was* a lady of the South."

"Of course." I said this carefully too.

Claire locked her gaze on mine, and it took effort not to look away from the growing madness in her eyes.

"You called me here this morning," I said.

"Yes. Yes, I did." As if she'd forgotten until I reminded her. "I wanted to show you something. I thought it would make you happy. I owed you that after last night."

"Pendleton knows you're here?"

Her smile, this time, remained on her face. "Yes. He's in the kitchen. You can say good-bye to him if you want."

"I will," I said.

"You're not angry with me for last night?"

I drew a deep breath. "No. I feel sad for you. I even feel sad for Pendleton. What you've both chosen to make important, that's enough punishment. I doubt either of you would tell me that you're sorry for all that happened, but that doesn't matter. I wish the best for both of you. Really."

I meant it. Holding on to my anger and bitterness simply let them control me. It had taken too much for me to learn that truth. I'd always thought forgiveness was a gift to the wrongdoer. But it also gave blessed freedom to the wronged.

"You have no idea how hysterically funny this is." Her monotone voice contradicted her words. "I should have spoken with you first."

"Spoken with me before . . ."

"Pendleton's in the kitchen. Say goodbye to him, Nick. Before it's too late."

❋ ❋ ❋

I saw blood.

Pools of it. Beneath Pendleton's crumpled body. He'd fallen beside the kitchen island. Smears of blood on the side of the island showed where he had tried to pull himself up, only to slide down again.

I reached him in two steps.

He breathed in shallow gasps, with a wheezing particular to a punctured lung. The knife was on the floor beside him.

I yanked open drawers, scrambling to find what I needed.

Plastic food wrap.

Cellophane tape.

I knelt beside Pendleton and pulled open his suit jacket. His white shirt was soaked red.

I put him flat on his back. I took off my sweater and folded it to make a pillow. I rested his head on the sweater. His eyes fluttered open a few times. I don't know if he recognized me.

The wound entry was difficult to find in the gore. I stood again, grabbed a towel. I wiped him clean and found the wound oozing blood like a hidden spring. Another wipe. I slapped a patch of food wrap over it, and his next breath sucked it flat against his skin. I taped it as well as I could, knowing it would slide off as more blood leaked.

I'd been kneeling with my back toward the kitchen entrance, but when I stood and turned to get to the telephone, Claire was watching from the door frame, leaning against it with the pose of a pinup calendar girl.

"What are you doing?" she asked. Same weird calmness.

"Call the paramedics," I said. "I'll hold the wrap in place."

"I already made my phone call. To you. I thought this would make you happy."

The phone hung on the wall beside the entrance. I saw blood on it too, evidence of the truth in her statement.

"Make another call," I told her.

"No."

"Then I will."

"No," she repeated. "Let him die. He'll never hurt me again."

"Listen to me, Claire. It's not too late. For you. Or for him. This is your chance to turn it around. What you did was in self-defense. Any jury will buy that. Don't let his life be on your hands. Move on from it."

I took a step toward the phone.

She lifted the gun higher, training it on my chest. We were only three paces apart. "You can let him die, Nick. No one would blame you."

"Claire, you're going to have to shoot me to stop me from making the phone call."

"All right then," she said. "I will."

Her hands shook. Then wavered. Then dropped.

"I'm all messed up," she said. She sagged to the floor and buried her head in her arms.

CHAPTER 45

Another few days passed after the paramedics saved Pendleton's life before once again, I sat on a pew in the coolness of the Mount Carmel African Methodist Episcopal Church.

On this morning, I was not alone with Pastor Samuel, who stood gravely near the organ as Etta sat behind it and with a puckered face concentrated on long, sad notes that filled the church and my heart. Glennifer and Elaine had joined us, their black dresses appropriate for the occasion. Nor was it just the five of us. At the front, beneath the pulpit, with the backdrop of the cross on the wall behind it, was the mahogany coffin that held the remains of my mother.

I wished there was one other here. I had not been able to reach her, but I had left a message. I guessed, however, it was too much to hope that she would join us.

We were all here to say good-bye to Mama. Quietly. Away from the media barrage that had overwhelmed me in the hours after finding her. I had given the reporters nothing beyond the clichéd — that I was glad to finally discover she had not run away from me.

The rest of it I had not divulged, except to Glennifer and Elaine as fulfillment of my bargain with them. Nothing about Claire and her attempt to kill me — it would be my word against hers. Nothing about my inheritance — that battle I intended to begin away from Charleston, hidden behind the lawyers who would happily protect me for their percentage of the Barrett fortune. Nothing about who had murdered my mother — I wanted time to absorb and understand all of what I had learned. In that regard, the story would safely remain secret, with no one else to tell it but me. Edgar Layton and Helen deMarionne were gone. So were Geoffrey Alexander Gillon and Admiral MacLean Robertson. Their lifeboat had been found at dawn, drifting empty as testimony that they had chosen to fight each other rather than join together for survival.

Etta finished her prelude to the funeral and, with a swish of her dress, pushed away from the organ to join Glennifer and Elaine and me at the pew second from the front.

In those seconds of silence between the end of the organ music and before Pastor Samuel began to speak, the door at the back of the sanctuary opened.

Glennifer and Elaine turned their heads first to see the visitor, then gave each other knowing smiles before looking at me. I finally turned, too, and watched Amelia walk up the aisle with hesitant steps.

I stood and met her halfway. We each stopped.

"I'm glad you left a message," she said softly. "I wanted to see you again."

I put a hand on her shoulder and escorted her to the front.

Pastor Samuel waited until we were seated.

He cleared his throat and began to read from the Bible open in his hands.

The Lord is my shepherd; I shall not want. He maketh me to lie down in green pastures.

After my release from the hospital the morning after surviving my time in the ocean, I had walked past the Barrett mansion for the final time and remembered Amelia's description of what had happened on the night of her eighth birthday. It had occurred to me that perhaps she had misheard her father's dying words.

Sister. The dry sister.

I'd heard of a lawyer who had purchased

a house on Lamboll Street. As part of his renovations, he had converted his cistern into a wine cellar. It was perfect, he had explained once, deep enough and wide enough that he could stand upright in there and line it with shelves. What he had told me was that Charleston's land base was barely above sea level. Wells could not be dug for fresh water. Instead, each mansion funneled rainwater from the roof through a series of gutters into a cistern below the house. The cisterns were centered beneath the kitchen, the water raised into the sinks by a hand pump. As Charleston modernized and ran a grid of sewage and water lines, the cisterns became obsolete tanks of emptiness. This lawyer had been proud of his ingenuity; most people, he'd bragged, sealed their cisterns with a concrete plug and found no use for them.

Most people except for Edgar Layton.

What Amelia must have seen with her glimpse out of the car on the night of her eighth birthday was his flashlight beam as he entered the crawl space beneath the Barrett place. Amelia had described to me what Edgar had told the man who must have been Lorimar Barrett: *Remember the cuff links you lent me for the last charity ball?*

She's got them in her pocket. And she'll be staying at your house. Anyone finds her, they find your cuff links. Trust me. It's a very safe place.

The cistern was a very safe place.

Not *sister*. Not *try the sister*.

But *cistern*. The dry cistern.

And so, finally, I had found my mother.

He leadeth me beside the still waters. He restoreth my soul.

I knew what I would soon tell Amelia. That she was right. That God does reach many of us in many different ways.

As an astronomer, I know it is impossible to understand or explain all of the workings of the universe. People who prejudge any event as impossible by saying that rational or scientific explanations are the only reality deny the mystery of love or other human passions and deny the inspirations that reflect those passions in music, art, poetry, or novels. Reality is not fixed and closed but is wonderfully open and filled with the mysterious possibilities of a universe created with an equally awesome and incomprehensible God behind it.

We are handicapped because we view this world only with the five senses of a human body, and we too easily believe there is nothing beyond what those senses can comprehend. But in our body, we are only fledglings, waiting for eternal flight beyond.

Faith is letting go and trusting that God is there and waiting, trusting that God sent us a way to reach him through Jesus and his message, trusting that Jesus proved this love by allowing Pontius Pilate to send him to the cross, trusting that Jesus reappeared on earth after his death by some means I will not understand until my own soul leaves my body.

Surely goodness and mercy shall follow me all the days of my life.

We all are lives in shattered pieces, our disappointments and betrayals strewn as debris across the paths of each of our histories, with God longing for us to allow him to reassemble these brittle shards and fragments into what he always intended us to be, yearning for us to allow him to heal the damage we inflict not only on our souls but upon the souls of those close to us in love or hate.

A fortunate few understand this in one compelling moment, dramatically transformed from the grips of personal hell of addiction or depression into the embrace of peace with the suddenness of one who steps from a prison into freedom and full sunlight.

For many, it is a slow, gradual comprehension. Prosperity, or the search for prosperity, numbs them to the erosion of their souls until they can no longer ignore the abscess that comes from life without meaning; and as they wake from the edge of this dark night, the sun edges above the horizons to spill its rays across the land and warm their cold aching bones.

Yet for others, like me, the courtship between God and the human soul is a complicated dance, filled with our own clumsy human mistakes, making the result uncertain until the music ends.

We are the ones who most resist his call. We know in his light there is something we need, yet we are wild animals, injured and skittish and determined to nurse our wounds unseen in the depths of the valleys. We do not want to risk coming out of the shadows, preferring to remain in the darkness of lives of quiet desperation, afraid of all that is unknown about God and holding on to our only certainty, even if this certainty is the pain we know and understand.

For us, the stubborn ones, when faith finally gives our soul the vision to see God, this new light is not the sudden sun of stepping out of a prison or the slow dawning of a new day. Our journey to the light is a life of enduring a storm. For us, the ones who chose to hide, patches of dark clouds sweep across the sky, with his presence hinted at occasionally by glimpses of the sun, until finally the storm passes.

With those final steps out of the shadows and into the light, we finally understand what was always there and waiting.

And in so doing, we are given the gift that allows us to endure the deepest valleys of all that we might face during our lives on earth.

We are given peace.

※ ※ ※

My final moments with my mother, before she began the chain of events that would lead to her death, took place upstairs at the Barrett beach house on the Wednesday evening after I had punched Pendleton. So, in a way, it was that punch that began it all.

"Where would you like to be?" she had asked when I refused to tell her why I had punched him, putting her hands on my shoulders.

"Away." I pushed her hands off my shoulders. "Just away."

A long, long silence held us, until my continued rejection forced her to speak.

"Away from me?" she asked softly.

"Yes. Away from you."

In the dying sunlight, my mother saw two halves of a torn photograph on the dust of the windowsill. She reached past me and pieced them together. It was the wallet-sized snapshot of David Barrett, handsome in his navy uniform. The precious photo that she'd seen me pull out of my wallet endless times, asking her for stories about the father I'd never met.

"Nick?"

I believe this was when the first brush of dread touched her soul, the exploratory tentacles of a monster stirring as it finally woke from a long hibernation.

I turned my head toward her. "Babies take nine months, don't they?"

My mother slowly shifted her gaze from the torn photograph to the defiance on my face. "Yes."

How she must have prayed that this, the inevitable, would never arrive.

"When was the last time you were with him?" I asked. "The last time before I was born? Less than nine months? Or more?"

"Nick," she said, "I've always wanted to talk to you about this. But I never knew when you might be ready. And I never was ready either."

I jutted my chin in defiance as I stared at her. "Who is my father?"

Now she flinched.

Her silence confirmed all the suspicions and doubts I had faced alone during the eternity of that afternoon waiting for her. The order and stability and foundation of my life were gone. As if I had been standing on a sheet of wood across an elevator shaft, and my own mother had pulled it out from under my feet, with the drop of doom into the darkness of the waiting shaft.

"Go away," I said.

"Nick . . ."

I slapped away her hands. I would not reach up to her as I began my lonely fall into the darkness of that horrible shaft.

"I hate you," I said.

I needed her and loved her, but it was my only defense.

"I love you," she answered. "You are my world."

"Go away. I want to stay here. I'll apologize to Pendleton. Just go away."

She stood. The beauty in her trim figure,

something that had once given me such innocent pride, suddenly disgusted me. Unbidden, Pendleton's words leaped into my thoughts: *A sleazebag. A tramp. Does bad things with men.*

She moved reluctantly to the door, probably hoping that I would not see her cry.

She stopped in the doorway. I did not allow the hardness in my face to dissolve at the pain I saw in her eyes.

I desperately wanted to call her back. This was the moment. One word and she would have rushed back to me and held me. The very fact that I needed and loved her so much tormented me in the face of her colossal betrayal. I was so alone, and she was my only answer. I hated her for it.

A sleazebag. A tramp. Does bad things with men.

"Sleazebag," I said, blurting my angry thoughts aloud and repeating Pendleton's accusations. "Tramp. You do bad things with men."

When she bowed her head and covered her face with her hands, I knew with finality that Pendleton had not lied.

"You do bad things with men!" I screamed. "Don't you! That's why you can't tell me who my daddy is!"

She did not lift her head.

"Don't you! Bad things! Don't you!" I screamed louder, hoping against hope she would deny it.

When she took her hands away from her face and looked at me, it was with such sadness that again I wanted to rush to her and cling to her. Yet I also wanted to rush to her and flail my fists against her. *Tramp. Does bad things with men.*

"Nicky . . . ," she pleaded.

She only called me Nicky in special moments. When our love had no other way to release itself except in the intimacy of the name I allowed no other person but her to call me. Nicky.

Our eyes met. I should have heeded the depths of pain and love that reached to pull me in and share that pain. But I rebelled. How could she now call me Nicky after she had lied to me for so long?

"Sleazebag," I said. Quietly. Almost a whisper. I now knew what the word meant.

"Nicky . . ." Her voice broke.

"Tramp. Go away, you sleazebag tramp. I hate you."

I hurled the silver cross at her. It spun through the air, end over end, chain and cross whirling. The cross hit her beneath the eye and landed at her feet.

She picked it up, blinking away her pain,

her determination to hold back her tears shattered by the impact of the silver cross. The edge of the cross had torn deeply into the skin of her left cheekbone. Drops of blood mixed with her tears.

"Sleazebag," I repeated. "Tramp. Go away."

Slowly, she turned, cross in her hand, chain draped from her fingers.

Even then, I knew I could call her back and all would be forgiven.

I did not.

I turned my face toward the window. Not until the door closed did I allow myself to sob.

I will dwell in the house of the Lord for ever.

With those words, Pastor Samuel closed the Bible.

Amelia touched the tears on my face and smiled. "You all right?" she whispered.

Helen could have given me no greater gift than passing on my mother's final words to me.

Please tell Nick I love him.

I'd been forgiven. Even as she faced the death I had brought upon her, she'd forgiven me. As my mother died, she could only hope her forgiveness would reach me.

Because of those final words, her love will wash over me always. The silver cross she once gave me as a gift hangs from my neck again.

"Yes," I answered. "I'm all right."

Amelia put her hand in mine.

ABOUT THE AUTHOR

Sigmund Brouwer's writing began to receive widespread acclaim when his first hardback novel, the suspenseful *Double Helix* hit the stands in 1995. This best-seller is a riveting tale of top-secret genetic experiments, a novel that anticipated the ethical issues of cloning by several years.

Now, with over a million books sold in a half dozen languages, his work has been lauded in such publications as *Library Journal*, *Booklist*, and many others.

As a novelist also committed to helping children read, Sigmund cofounded The Young Writer's Institute with home education expert and author Debra Bell. To motivate and encourage reluctant readers, he also speaks to thousands of children a year at schools across North America. (His Web site is coolreading.com.)

He and his wife, recording artist Cindy Morgan, and their daughter split their time between Red Deer, Alberta, Canada, and Nashville, Tennessee.

For more information on *Out of the Shadows*, please visit www.tyndale.com